HER ROYAL HIGHNESS

ALSO BY RACHEL HAWKINS

Prince Charming
(previously titled *Royals*)

Rebel Belle

Miss Mayhem

Lady Renegades

HER
ROYAL
HIGHNESS

NEW YORK TIMES BESTSELLING AUTHOR

Rachel Hawkins

PENGUIN BOOKS

For Jules

PENGUIN BOOKS
An imprint of Penguin Random House LLC, New York

First published in the United States of America by G. P. Putnam's Sons, 2019
Published by Penguin Books, an imprint of Penguin Random House LLC, 2020

Visit us online at penguinrandomhouse.com

THE LIBRARY OF CONGRESS HAS CATALOGED THE G. P. PUTNAM'S SONS EDITION AS FOLLOWS:
Names: Hawkins, Rachel, 1979– author.
Title: Her royal highness / Rachel Hawkins.
Description: New York, NY: G. P. Putnam's Sons, [2019] | Companion to: *Prince Charming*, previously titled *Royals*. |
Summary: An American girl goes to an exclusive Scottish boarding school where
she becomes the roommate, best friend, and girlfriend of a royal princess.
Identifiers: LCCN 2018035750 | ISBN 9781524738266 (hardback)
Subjects: | CYAC: Boarding schools—Fiction. | Schools—Fiction. | Foreign study—Fiction. |
Friendship—Fiction. | Love—Fiction. | Princesses—Fiction. | Lesbians—Fiction. | Scotland—Fiction.
Classification: PZ7.H313525 He 2019 | DDC [Fic]—dc23
LC record available at https://lccn.loc.gov/2018035750

Penguin Books ISBN 9781524738280

Printed in the United States of America

Design by Suki Boynton
Text set in Fournier MT Pro

1 3 5 7 9 10 8 6 4 2

When it comes to boarding schools in Scotland, none can beat #4 on our list, Gregorstoun. The forbidding fortress up in the Highlands of Scotland has been the chosen spot for matriculating Scottish royalty and nobility since the early 1900s, but it's never had the same gloss as some of the other schools on our lists, possibly because of its remote location. It could also be the school's reputation for strictness and austerity keeping some notable names away. In any case, the school sits on 200 acres and was once the showplace estate of the McGregor family, hence the name. Students at Gregorstoun may have to face early wake-up calls, bracing exercise in the frigid Highland winters, and a particularly grueling Outward Bound–esque competition known as "the Challenge," but they can do so among some of the most stunning scenery in Scotland and among the country's most famous residents—Prince Alexander graduated from the school in 2009, and his brother Sebastian currently attends. Next year, the school becomes co-ed, welcoming its first female class in the school's hundred-year history.

("Best Boarding Schools for Landing a Royal," from *Prattle*)

CHAPTER 1

"THERE'S A UNICORN ON THIS."

Grinning, I take the letter out of Jude's hands, leaning back on the nest of sleeping bags and pillows we've built inside the little orange tent I've set up in the backyard. The sun set about an hour ago, and the only light left comes from my Coleman lantern, which is affixed to a little hook on the ceiling of the tent. We haven't done a backyard campout since we were in fifth grade, but it's summer, and we were bored, and setting up the tent seemed like a fun thing to do.

"Now you see why I wanted to go to school there," I say, stuffing the letter back into its envelope. "Anyplace that uses unicorns in its official correspondence is a good place for me."

"Obviously," Jude echoes, leaning back, too. Her long blond hair is dyed turquoise at the ends, and as she gets situated on the sleeping bags, those bright blue strands brush against my arm, setting my pulse racing and a whole fleet of butterflies loose in my stomach.

Propping herself up on her elbow, Jude looks at me, the

freckles over the bridge of her nose bold in the lantern light. "And you got in!"

Nodding, I look back at the envelope from Gregorstoun, a fancy boarding school in the Highlands of Scotland, fighting the urge to pull the letter out and reread the heading.

Dear Miss Amelia Quint:

    We are pleased to offer you a place at Gregorstoun . . .

The letter has been sitting in my bag for over a month now. I haven't even told my dad about it. And I hadn't planned on talking to Jude about it, either, but she saw it while she was looking for lip balm.

"So *why* aren't you going?" she asks, and I shrug, taking the letter and tucking it back in the front pocket of the beat-up canvas satchel I bring everywhere with me. A light breeze rattles the nylon of the tent, carrying the smell of summer night in Texas—freshly cut grass and the smoky scent of someone grilling.

"Millie, you've been talking about this school for, like, a year now," Jude presses, reaching out to push me with her free hand. "And now you got in, and you're not gonna go?"

Another shrug as I sigh and fiddle with my bangs. "It's super expensive," I tell her, which is true. "So I'd need to apply for financial aid. And it's pretty far away." Also true, not that that stopped me from dreaming about it all last year. Gregorstoun is up in the Highlands of Scotland, surrounded by mountains and lakes—sorry, lochs—plus all the cool rock samples a geology freak like me could want.

But last year, things were different with Jude.

We've been friends since we were nine, and I've had a crush on her since I was thirteen and realized that I felt the same way about Jude as I did about Lance McHenry from Boys of Summer (look, everyone liked Boys of Summer back then, it wasn't as embarrassing as it sounds now).

And my crush on Jude had just as much a chance of being requited as the flame I'd carried for a floppy-haired boy bander.

Or so I'd thought.

Now she scoots closer to me on top of the sleeping bag printed with daisies she's had since that first fifth-grade campout. Unlike me, Jude isn't much for camping.

She trails her fingers over my arm, nails lightly scratching my skin, and my breath comes out all shaky as I break out in goose bumps. Each fingernail is painted a different shade of purple, her thumb a pale lavender, her pinky a violet so deep it almost looks black. There in the tent with the summer night all around us, it feels like we could be the only two people in the world right now.

"You're not turning it down because of me, are you?" she asks, and my heart does a neat little flip in my chest. This . . . thing between me and Jude has been going on since the beginning of the summer, but I'm not used to it yet. Being with her still makes me feel like I'm on some amusement park ride, heart pounding, stomach dropping.

"What?" I ask, trying to huff out a laugh, but I'm the worst liar in the world, and the word basically comes out a squawk.

Jude is really close to me now, so close our knees bump on top of our sleeping bags.

"It's okay if you want to admit you can't stand being away from me," she teases, and I go to shove at her, but she catches my wrist, tugging me closer so she can kiss me.

Her lips taste like my cherry-vanilla lip balm, and in that moment, there's only Jude and her mouth and the way she tucks my hair behind my ears as she kisses me.

When we pull apart, she's smiling at me, cheeks pink, our legs tangled on the sleeping bags. "I'm not going because it's too expensive," I tell her. "Like I said."

"They'd give you a scholarship," she counters. "You're, like, the smartest person in our school."

"That's not saying much."

My high school isn't terrible or anything, but it's massive, and sometimes my classes feel more like an exercise in crowd control than anything else. That's part of why I started looking at fancy schools far away.

That and my dad taking me to see the movie *Brave* when I was ten. And the fact that geology, my favorite subject, was practically invented in Scotland. And the way I felt when I'd looked up pictures of all those massive, rocky hills surrounded by green, like something out of a fairy tale. There was this one place called Applecross that I—

Okay, no. No more thinking about that. I've made up my mind to stay because even though I got in, running off to Scotland is insane, right? And not a thing people do. I'll be perfectly happy finishing out my senior year at Pecos with Jude and our other besties, Darcy and Lee. There are tons of good colleges here in Texas that I can get into, and some fancy

Scottish boarding school won't count for more than my killer ACT scores and awesome GPA. It'll be fine.

But Jude is still watching me with a funny look on her face, three little wrinkles popping up over her nose.

"I'm serious, though, Millie," she says. "If this is about me or us . . ."

She sighs, her breath warm on my face and smelling like that lemon-mint gum she always has on her.

"It's not," I tell her again, pulling a thread from my plaid sleeping bag. "And we're not really an us, anyway. I mean, we are in that I'm a person, and you're a person, and together, that makes two people, which means the common grammatical definition of 'us' technically fits, but—"

Her hand clamps over my mouth, and she laughs. "No nervous-talky Millie," she says, and I nod behind her palm with a muffled, "Sorry." There's this fun thing that happens sometimes when I get nervous where words just come out, but not in the right order, exactly, and half the time, not the words I want to be saying, but there they are anyway, a flood of words between me and Jude, yet again.

But when she drops her hand, those wrinkles are back. "We *are* an us," she says, reaching out to twine her fingers with mine. "Maybe nobody knows we are, but to me, I feel . . . us-ish."

Cheeks hot, I squeeze her fingers back. "The us-iest."

Jude reaches over to fiddle with the ends of my hair again. "The most us I've ever felt with anyone," she says.

"More us-y than with Mason?"

The words are out before I even have time to think about

them, really, and I immediately wish I could call them back. Mason is Jude's ex, the boy she'd dated since freshman year, and they broke up last spring. Right before it all started with me and Jude. Since that first kiss, sitting on the floor of her room last month, we haven't mentioned Mason. It's been easy, since he's away at soccer camp or something for part of the summer, but sometimes I wonder how it'll be when he comes back. I've always liked Mason even if I *am* head over heels for his girl-friend, but there's no doubt things have been easier with me and Jude without him here.

Jude flops onto her back, studying the ceiling of the tent. "Weren't we kind of an us even when Mason was around?"

She rolls back onto her side to face me, and I feel my cheeks go hot again, because yeah, we were. There wasn't any of this kissing or other fun stuff, but she was definitely my favorite person to be around.

"Maybe," I acknowledge, and she grins before draping an arm over my waist.

Jude kisses me again, and thoughts about Mason, Scotland, and fancy schools with unicorn crests vanish in the warm summer air.

CHAPTER 2

"MASON IS BACK."

I'm sitting in Darcy's game room at her house, slouched on the floor with my back against the couch, an Xbox controller in my hands.

On the giant TV in front of me, I watch a dragon grab my avatar, Lady Lucinda, by the head, shaking her so hard that the body goes flying offscreen.

Great.

Sighing, I rest the controller on my stomach as the screen goes white. "That was my last life," I mutter, reaching for the can of Sprite Zero beside me. Darcy nudges my foot with hers, her toenails a bright purple.

"Millie, did you hear me?"

On my other side, Lee sits up, taking the controller from me and restarting the game. "She heard you, Darce. She doesn't care."

"I do care," I insist, "because I like Mason, and it's nice that he's back. I just don't think it has anything to do with me."

Crossing her legs, Darcy sits up straighter as she looks at me over the tops of her glasses. They're new, the acid-green frames bright around her dark eyes. "Millie," she says, and I roll my shoulders, uncomfortable.

"They're done," I remind her as I sit up, too. "Over. And me and Jude are—"

"A summer fling that will break your heart," Darcy fills in, and I scowl at her.

This is the drum Darcy has been beating ever since I told her about me and Jude—that Jude is flighty, that she changes her mind more often than she changes hair colors, that I know what Jude is like.

I know she's saying it because she cares about me, but it's still not exactly my favorite stuff to hear, and besides, she's wrong. And maybe a little jealous. Jude and Darce were really close a few years back, but as Jude and I got tighter, Darcy sort of ended up on the outside a bit. Our Foursome Friend Group is constantly shifting.

Me and Jude now being a thing has obviously shifted things even more.

"Jude is kind of flaky," Lee acknowledges as his fingers fly on the controller's buttons. He glances at me, auburn hair flopping over one eye. "Sorry, Mill, but you know it's true. It's one of the things we love about her, but I can see it making her a bad girlfriend."

"You're not exactly an expert in girlfriends, Lee," I say, and he gasps with faux outrage, his eyes still glued to the game.

"How *dare* you, Amelia Quint?" Then his face breaks out in a grin. "Also, yes, fair. But I am an expert in *you*, and I don't want to see you get your heart smashed. Darcy is being kind of bitchy, but Darcy is not necessarily wrong, which is usually the case with Darcy, let's all be very real here."

"Why do I even invite you over?" Darcy mutters, picking up her can of soda and taking a long sip.

"Because you love me, and you want to support my video game habit," Lee says, then gives a triumphant whoop as the dragon on the screen flops down dead.

Tossing the controller to the thick carpet, he leans over me to grab the bag of cheese puffs that have ended up stuffed under the sofa. "This setup is so wasted on you, Darce," he tells her. "You don't even play."

Darcy shrugs, and I take a cheese puff from Lee, careful not to get any crumbs on the carpet. Not that Darce or her parents would care. But their house is so nice that I feel like *I* should care.

Darcy's dad works for some oil company in Houston, which means her family has a lot more money than mine or Lee's does. It's never been an issue, but I'm still really aware of the pretty flooring, the giant TVs, how Darce has her own bathroom attached to her bedroom.

Now she looks at me, eyes narrowed a little. "Jude said you got into that fancy school in Scotland."

"What?" Bright orange flecks fly from Lee's lips as he brings a hand up to his mouth, and I look back and forth between the two of them, my stomach dropping.

"She told you that?" I ask, and Darcy grabs the bag of cheese puffs from Lee.

"Yes," Darce tells me. "Are you not going because of her?"

I pick up my soda again, more for something to do than because I'm actually thirsty. "No," I finally say. "I'm not going because it's expensive."

Lee snorts at that. "Right, because a scholarship is totally beyond you, O Lady Smartypants."

"Exactly," Darcy agrees, and I just shrug. It bugs me that Jude said anything to Darcy, especially since I hadn't told anyone else myself.

But I just say, "It's probably too late to get financial aid. And it was a stupid idea to apply in the first place. I just . . . wanted to see if I could get in. I didn't really want to *go*."

"Calling major BS on that, Mill," Lee says, wiggling his toes at me. "You were talking about Scotland all last year."

"We watched *Brave* at least three times over winter break," Darcy adds, and I give both of them what I hope is a stern glare.

"A girl is allowed to change her mind," I say, and then watch as they exchange glances.

"All I'm saying," Darcy finally says before taking the controller from the floor and shutting off the Xbox, "is that you shouldn't give up a great opportunity for Jude."

"I'm not doing it for her," I reply, but there's that look between Lee and Darce again, and scowling at the two of them, I take the controller back, powering on the system again. I've still got two hours before I need to be home, and dammit, I'm going to kill a dragon.

"This isn't about Jude, and even if it were, who cares? Mason coming back isn't changing anything."

CHAPTER 3

"I WOULD GIVE UP FLUSHING TOILETS FOR THAT man."

I look up from my phone toward the TV my aunt Vi is gesturing at or, more specifically, the very hot guy in a kilt she's referencing.

It's my third day over at Aunt Vi's apartment, eating Snackwell's and watching a show called *The Seas of Time*, about this lady who travels back in time and falls in love with a hot Highlander. I got addicted to it last year in the midst of my Scotland Fever, and brought over the DVDs for moral support. Aunt Vi's latest breakup (Kyle the Bartender) has hit her hard, hence the sexy time-travel show and cookies.

I frown, studying the guy on the screen. "I like Callum a lot," I say at last. "Especially his hair. But I feel like I enjoy flushing toilets more? Maybe?"

From her spot on the sofa, Aunt Vi sighs. She's showered today, which is something, at least, and her dark hair is pulled back in a messy bun. "You have no sense of romance, Amelia," she says, and I once again fight the urge to look at my phone.

It's been two weeks since I've seen Jude, two weeks since we were kissing in the tent in my backyard, and she was supposed to get back from visiting her nana three days ago. I've been waiting on a text, but so far, no dice.

It's hard not to make a connection between the return of Jude's ex-boyfriend and her sudden radio silence, but trust me, those are dots I'm really *trying* not to connect, no matter what Darcy said.

I know what me and Jude have, and it's not just "a distraction" or whatever. It's real. It's an us, like Jude said . . .

There's a buzz from the table, and I lean over, snatching the phone up only to deflate back into Aunt Vi's uncomfortable-but-extremely-stylish white leather chair.

It's a text, but it's from Lee, asking me if Jude texted yet.

No, I type back, bagpipes and heavy breathing in the background. *But she's still hanging out with Nana?*

Another buzz, and there's a series of ☹ ☹ ☹

Thanks for the positive vibes, I text back, frowning.

The phone buzzes again, but I ignore it this time, focusing on the show, where Callum and Helena are now lying down, thankfully covered up.

"Everything okay, kiddo?" Aunt Vi asks, and I nod, forcing myself to smile at her.

"Yeah, just . . . you know, worried about Callum and Helena. Soon this British guy, Lord Harley, shows up, and he's bad news."

Aunt Vi gives me a look, tucking a stray curl behind her

ear. She's my dad's younger sister, and was born when he was in high school, so she's sometimes more like a big sister to me than an aunt. But every once in a while, she also tries the Mom Thing on for size, and I can tell that's what's about to happen now.

"You don't seem okay," she says, turning on the couch to face me. "Is it school?"

"It's summer break, Aunt Vi," I remind her. "But yes, in general, school is fine. School is always fine for me, you know that."

She screws up her face, looking an awful lot like me as she does. "I don't know where you got your nerd gene from," she says, "but it is strong with you."

I shrug. "From Mom, maybe?" And Aunt Vi's face immediately crumples into a sympathetic frown.

"Of course," she says. "Your mom was super smart. Way too smart to have married my brother, I thought, but there's no accounting for taste."

I smile back at her, not wanting her to feel weird, which is a thing that can happen when you bring up a dead parent, I've learned. Even with other family members. So I lighten my tone, crossing my legs as I say, "And being good at school equals scholarships, which equals money, and you know I love the hustle."

Aunt Vi laughs. "That you do."

Picking up one of the roughly five thousand throw pillows on her couch, this one in a slightly different shade of white— Aunt Vi is all about the monochrome look—she squeezes it to her chest. "So not school. Boy?"

I nearly glance at my phone again, but just manage to avoid it. "No boy," I say, which is true to the letter of Aunt Vi's question if not the spirit.

I can tell she's about to press further, but then, thank god, Helena and Callum start making out again and her attention is diverted.

"I miss Kyle," she says on a sigh, and okay, yeah, that's about enough of that.

Rising to my feet, I put my phone in my pocket and point to the empty cookie box on the coffee table. "Oh, look at that. We're out of cookies. I'll run and get some more."

Her focus now back on the television, she gives a faint nod, waving a hand toward the kitchen. "There's a twenty in that Himalayan salt dish by the front door."

I walk toward the bowl she mentioned, fishing out the twenty-dollar bill from a sea of change and ponytail holders. Once it's in the pocket of my shorts, I look again at the bowl, holding it up briefly, then, after a second, tentatively touching my tongue to it.

"This isn't actually salt," I call to her. "It's probably just a pink quartz."

"Nerd!" she calls back, but I smile as I put the bowl back down and head out the door.

It's warm outside—hot, really—and the sky is almost painfully blue overhead. Aunt Vi's apartment complex is in this new little community they've built that's supposed to re-create the experience of small town living, so just down a redbrick sidewalk, there's a little square with a drugstore, some restaurants, and a handful of boutiques.

I make my way past the fountain, letting my hand trail along the wrought-iron fence, my rings making a satisfying clinking sound as I do. I think my dad feels bad that we haven't gone anywhere this summer, but my stepmom had to work, and my little brother isn't even one yet, so this didn't seem like a great year for a Quint Family Vacation. I don't really regret it, though. It's given me a chance to do extra studying for the AP Environmental Science exam next year, plus I've gotten to hang out with Aunt Vi, who clearly needs me.

And then there's Jude.

As I step on the mat activating the automatic doors to the drugstore (just a chain store, but with a redbrick entrance and striped awning to make it look nicer than it is), my phone buzzes again in my pocket, and my hands fumble to pull it out.

Still not Jude, and my heart sinks a little.

Can you get tampons while you're there? Aunt Vi asks, and I text her back that I will.

Inside the drugstore, the air-conditioning is going full blast, raising goose bumps on my arms and legs, and I hurriedly get the cookies and the tampons, stepping back into the sunshine with a relieved sigh, the bag dangling at my side.

I turn to head back, and as I glance up, I see two people standing by the fountain.

The girl isn't facing me, but I'd know that hair anywhere.

Jude.

Like all my angsting over her text conjured her up or something.

Except I'm pretty sure that if I'd magically made Jude appear, I *wouldn't* have also brought forth Mason Coleman.

And they for sure would not be kissing.

My heart is pounding so hard in my chest that it almost hurts, a dull roar in my ears.

They're kissing. Jude and Mason. Kissing. By the fountain because yay, cliché, I guess, and also kissing, kissing, Jude is kissing someone, and it's not me, and I am such an idiot.

My face hot and my throat tight, I duck my head and try to move past them as quickly as I can, tears blurring my eyes.

And maybe that's why I don't see the oh-so-charming old-fashioned sandwich board in front of Y Tu Taco También until I crash into it, sending it clattering to the ground.

"No," I whisper, possibly at the universe itself.

But the universe is clearly not on my side today because I hear Mason call my name.

Closing my eyes and taking a deep breath, I count to three before turning to see him and Jude walking over to me, their fingers interlocked as Mason pulls her along behind him.

Of course Mason has no idea that this is weird. As far as he knows, we're all friends. Have been since middle school. There shouldn't be anything weird about me seeing him and Jude together, and also *together*.

But Jude had said we were an us.

The us-iest.

And now she seems to be us-ing pretty hard with Mason. Again.

"Hi!" I say, way too loud, waggling my fingers at them. Unfortunately, when I lift my hand, I've still got the drugstore bag dangling from it, and the flimsy plastic strap chooses that second to slide off my wrist, sending two boxes of Teddy Grahams and one package of Tampax onto Mason's feet.

I hate . . . literally everything about my life right now.

Mason, to his credit, doesn't get weird about picking up cookies and feminine hygiene products. Honestly, that just makes it worse. If he were the kind of jackass who seemed afraid of tampons, I could at least feel superior to him.

I smile, taking my stuff and shoving it back in the plastic sack. "Thanks. Those aren't mine. The cookies or the . . . I mean, I eat cookies, and I use tampons, because duh, but I was just . . . my aunt . . ."

"No worries," Mason says cheerfully. "I have sisters."

"Right," I reply, but I'm still looking past him at Jude.

She's smiling at Mason, but I see the tightness of her shoulders, how she keeps playing with his fingers nervously.

I cannot cry here in this fake town square, holding tampons and cookies in front of a taqueria, so I nod, then jerk my thumb toward the next block.

"Well, hope y'all are having a good summer. I'm just gonna . . . head back. See you later!"

I've salvaged about as much dignity as a girl who just basically flung tampons at the girl she likes and the boy the girl picked over her possibly can.

I'm at the corner when my phone buzzes, and this time, finally, it's the text I was waiting for.

But all Jude says is *I'm sorry.*

I don't bother replying, making my way back to Aunt Vi's as quickly as my legs will carry me.

Unlocking her door, I toss the bag down by the not-Himalayan-salt bowl and go into the living room, flopping myself back into the uncomfortable chair, my face still flaming, my eyes burning.

On-screen, Callum and Helena are, for once, not doing it or being threatened by evil Brits. Instead, they're on horses, galloping over rocky terrain, craggy hills rising around them and disappearing into the mist.

Something lurches in my chest looking at them, and I think of the letter in my purse again. The school that I'd been turning down for Jude.

The phone in my pocket buzzes again.

I ignore it.

"I'd give up flushing toilets for *that*," I say to Aunt Vi, pointing at the screen. "You can keep the hot dude."

Aunt Vi looks over and blinks like she's just realized I've come back, then she laughs a little, shaking her head.

"Oh, right, you and the Scotland thing. Didn't you apply to a school there?"

I nod. We're in full montage mode now, Callum and Helena passing through valley and vale, and there are more of those green, stony hills, more shifting sunlight behind clouds, more glimmers of a gray ocean in the background. If I were there, wandering the Highlands in 1780-whatever, I definitely wouldn't bump into Jude and Mason. I wouldn't accidentally throw tampons at anyone. I'd be . . . a whole new Millie, probably.

"Well, there you go," Aunt Vi says, getting up and heading for the cookies. "You don't have to time-travel to get to Scotland."

She gets the box and comes back into the living room, frowning slightly as she sees I bought Actual Cookies, not those fat-free ones she usually buys. But then she shrugs and tears into the box anyway. "Literally just a plane ride away," she says through a mouthful of cinnamon bears. "You could be there tomorrow if you had a passport and enough money."

I stare at her for a second, then look back at the screen. She's right. Scotland is a real place. A place that's relatively easy to get to. A place with a school that already let me in.

"Yeah," I say to Aunt Vi, but I'm still looking at the screen, my heart thumping hard in my chest.

Getting away from here. Not having to deal with seeing Mason and Jude kiss against lockers. Not hearing Darcy's I Told You So, or seeing Lee's sympathetic looks.

I could just go somewhere else.

Start over.

Me.

Scotland.

CHAPTER **4**

"WE'RE BACK ON SCOTLAND?"

My dad stands by the stove, a frown creasing his brow, spatula in one hand—yay, Pancake Wednesday—and I wave a handful of papers at him.

"Not just Scotland, but Scotland *school*," I say. "You're a teacher, Dad. Anna's a guidance counselor. We live and breathe school."

Before he can respond to that, I sift through the printouts. In the past few days since the Jude Incident and my epiphany at Aunt Vi's, I've been a one-woman Financial Aid Research Machine.

Finding the paper I want, I pull it from the stack, brandishing it. "Gregorstoun offers all kinds of scholarships. And it's one of the best schools in the world, Dad. Gregorstoun 'has educated kings and princes and prime ministers,' and this is the first year they're admitting women. I'd be part of the first female class ever allowed, which means *technically* I'd be part of history. My picture would probably be in history books."

"Scottish history books," Dad counters, and I nod.

"Even better. Have you ever read up on Scottish history? It's wild. Gonna be me and Braveheart, side by side."

That makes Dad smile, as I'd suspected it would, but when he turns back to the stove, he's shaking his head. "I guess I just thought this was off the table, kid. You seemed so set on *not* going just a couple of weeks ago."

Dad only busts out the "kid" thing when he's feeling out of his parenting depth. Which isn't very often. Although sometimes I wonder what kind of dad he would've been if Mom were still around. But that feels unfair to him or disloyal or something. Like I don't think he's enough.

Putting the papers on the table, I go stand behind him, my hands on his shoulders. "I just . . . changed my mind," I tell him. "The more I thought about it, the more it felt like I'd turned it down too fast. I got freaked out by the idea of how far away it was, but I can't let being scared keep me from doing something awesome."

Leaning closer, I add, "And again, it's *school*, Dad. It's not like I'm asking to go follow some band around Europe for the next year."

He scoffs at that, twisting a little to look back at me. "I feel like I'd know how to handle that better than this, if I'm being honest. That I can understand."

Smiling, I give him a firm pat with both hands before stepping back. "Maybe this is my way of rebelling. Tragically uncool daughter of very cool parents."

"I think you're *very* cool," Dad counters loyally, flipping a pancake. "So cool, in fact, that I was thinking we might go camping this weekend? Just me and you, like we used to. I also saw an ad for a gem and mineral show in Houston next week that might be fun. Haven't gone to one of those in a while."

I give him a look. "Dad, are you trying to bribe me with science?"

"A little bit," he acknowledges, then nods at Gus, my baby brother, who sits in his high chair, happily smacking his plastic spoon against the tray.

"I mean, if you leave, who can I camp with? This one is terrible at setting up tents. And you should have seen the mess the last time I asked him to gather firewood."

Gus shouts a word that kind of sounds like "TENT!" and I chuck him under his chin. "The family honor of keeping up with tent stakes and the camping stove falls to you, my brother."

Gus gives me a gummy grin, tilting his head to try to put my fingers in his mouth, and from behind me, Dad sighs.

"You don't . . . If this is about Anna, or Gus, or you thinking—"

I cut Dad off with one raised hand. "No," I say. "No tragic backstory at play here."

Dad married Anna three years ago, and they had Gus last year. It was definitely a change, going from being an only child with a single parent to having a stepmom and a baby in the house, but it's also been a good change. I walk over to the kitchen table, picking up a can of cereal puffs and dumping out a handful for Gus, and I'm rewarded with another smile. My whole heart melts as I smooth a hand over his reddish hair. Gus looks way more like my stepmother than my dad or me—both of us have fairly boring brown hair and eyes.

He's also just about the best thing in my life, so my desire to try out school in another country has nothing to do with feeling out of place or unwelcome.

"Scarecrow, I think I'll miss you most of all," I coo to Gus now, who babbles back, shoving a handful of the puffs into his mouth, and I sigh. "I don't think he gets my pop culture references yet."

"Give the Padawan time," Dad replies, and I grin at him.

He's a good dad. A great one, even, and the idea of leaving him, even temporarily, is the only black cloud hovering over my perfect plan. Well, leaving him and Gus and Anna. Spending my senior year abroad would be a lot easier if I didn't like my family, I guess.

"This isn't about anyone but me," I say to Dad now, and that's almost totally true. I mean, there are parts of it that are also about Jude, but I still haven't decided to get into that with Dad. It's not that he wouldn't be okay with me liking girls—it's just that things have felt complicated and messy, and I don't really want to talk to him until I've sorted it all out in my own mind.

Jude has texted me a few more times since I saw her and Mason by Aunt Vi's apartment. I haven't known how to reply, so I convinced myself that I am too busy to answer her anyway, and that I need to focus on Gregorstoun.

Which isn't a total lie. I mean, I'll be leaving home and everything familiar. Yes, it might be scary. Yes, there is a part of me that is maaaaaybe, possibly running away. But there's also a part of me that gets more and more excited every time I look at the school's brochure.

Sitting back at the table, I move a place mat out of the way to spread out my Scotland School File again, tapping my fingers over the different pictures. St. Edmund's in Edinburgh would be cool. Living in a city that's in the shadow of an ancient volcano? Definitely something different.

Then there's St. Leonard's, a big sprawling redbrick building on the greenest grass I've ever seen. It's not far from St. Andrew's, which is also beautiful, and wow, they're really big on saints in Scotland, I realize.

Gregorstoun is a former manor house, this gorgeous brick building rising out of the hills, with ivy-covered walls and a very Hogwarts vibe. I fell in love with it the first time I saw it, idly searching schools in Scotland over a year ago.

I pull the paper closer to me, then realize it's gotten quiet in the kitchen.

When I glance up, Dad is looking at me, a funny expression on his face.

"You're not about to tell me I look like Mom, are you?" I ask, and he smiles a little, shaking his head.

"No, you actually look like Vi—which, remembering her teenage years, gives me heartburn."

Then he points his spatula at my papers.

"Go ahead and apply," Dad says. "If you get the aid, we'll deal with the rest of it."

"When I get it," I correct, picking up my pen and pointing it at Gus, who crows at me before tossing his spoon to the floor.

"*When.*"

CHAPTER 5

FOR THE NEXT TWO WEEKS, THERE'S ALWAYS A little bit of my head in Scotland, waiting and wondering. I sent in the financial aid papers the day after my talk with Dad, complete with an essay on why I am the perfect Gregorstoun Girl (it mostly consisted of "Look at my GPA and PSAT scores"). I rewatched *The Seas of Time*, I read guidebooks, and I started imagining myself wearing a lot more plaid.

But other than that constant low-level buzz of "Scotland Scotland Scotland" in my head, the summer unfolds as usual. Friends, babysitting Gus, working at the library three days a week.

Avoiding Jude.

That's been easy enough to do, since she and Mason are Very Much Back On, so she isn't spending nearly as much time with Lee and Darce as she usually would.

Well, not as much time with Lee, at least. I've seen a few pictures of her with Darcy on Instagram, and my last text to Darce has been on "Read" for two days with no answer.

So mostly I just wait and hope. Gregorstoun is supposed to send a letter letting me know how much of my tuition they're prepared to pay for—so old-school of them—which means I stalk the mailbox every day, wishing I hadn't waited until so late to apply for financial aid, wishing I hadn't let my relationship with Jude dictate such a massive life decision. I check the mailbox again as I head out for the library on a hot morning in late July, but it's too early for the mail to have come.

The library is only a few blocks from my house, hence a lot of its appeal as a job, and I park my car in the employee lot. It's technically Anna's car, but I get to use it on the weekends, which is nice.

As I get out of the car, one of the librarians, Mrs. Ramirez, is just unlocking the front door, and she waves at me.

"Any news?" she asks, shifting her bag from one shoulder to the other. With her cool haircut and hot pink glasses, Mrs. Ramirez is total #goals, and I wish I had good news for her.

"Nothing yet," I tell her. "But there's still time."

Her face creases into a grimace of sympathy as she reaches out to pat my shoulder. "Any school that doesn't shower you with scholarships isn't worth going to," she says. I smile at her, but it wobbles a little.

"Definitely my thought," I reply before moving into the library.

I'm on reshelving duty today, so once I've signed in, I make my way to the back room, grabbing the metal cart full of returns, which I start pushing through the stacks.

After an hour or so, I'm in the back of the library, my favorite place to be, where the smell of old books is the strongest.

It's quiet here, which is always a plus, and it's one of the coolest spots in the whole building.

I mean that literally. The air-conditioning seems to blow harder here than anywhere else in the library.

I'm supposed to be reshelving some old reference books, but really, I'm checking my email every five seconds. Maybe I won't get an acceptance letter through snail mail. Maybe there will be an email after all. Even old-fashioned boarding schools in the Scottish Highlands have to be part of the twenty-first century, right?

But other than a text from Lee asking if I want to get fro-yo later (I do, obviously), my phone is silent.

I've just shelved the last book on my cart when I hear footsteps.

It's probably someone wanting to use one of the study rooms, but it could also be people looking for a private spot to do . . . whatever (trust me, I've seen it all), so I steel myself for either/or.

But it's not a studious college kid or horny high schoolers.

It's my dad.

And there's a letter in his hand.

"Is it . . . ?" I ask, but I know that it is. Dad would not have come all the way out here to give me junk mail.

And when he turns the envelope to face me, I see the Gregorstoun unicorn up there in the corner.

"Omigod," I say softly, and Dad nods.

"Oh my god, indeed."

I take a few steps forward, my hand outstretched, and Dad gives me a little grin.

"Millie, you know this is just a school, right? This isn't your Hogwarts letter."

"And you're not an owl," I remind him, "but this is absolutely the closest thing I'm ever going to get to a Hogwarts letter, so hand it over."

Dad does, but his grin slips just a little bit. "Millipede, if they're not offering you anything, we can still find a way to make it work. Or we can try to."

I make myself smile back, even though it's hard. I *have* to have gotten a scholarship. Gregorstoun was calling to me for some reason, I know it, and places don't call just to reject you, right?

But my hands still shake as I open the envelope, my chest tight as my eyes scan the letter, landing on *Pleased to offer you a full scholarship for the upcoming*—

The scream I let out probably causes at least three heart attacks in the reading room, and I hear one of the old guys in the soft chairs give a startled "Hoozit?"

Clapping my hand over my mouth, I look at Dad, but he's laughing silently, his shoulders shaking as he wipes at his eyes with one hand.

"I'm guessing you got it, then?" he asks when he's done cracking up, and I look back at the paper, rereading carefully, hoping I didn't misread it because I wanted it so badly. But nope, there it is in black and white.

Full ride, room and board, everything covered.

I'm going to Scotland.

Oh.

I'm going to Scotland.

OOOOOOH Y'AAAAALLLLL!!

I have some INTERESTING NEWS TO REPORT! Okay, so you know how Prince Seb went to that Fancy But Totally Terrifying Boarding School in the Highlands? One of those places where your roommate is probably a sheep and you have to get up at 4 a.m. every day? WELL.

It looks like Seb is DONE WITH THAT. St. Edmund's Academy in Edinburgh just announced that Seb is doing his last year of school with them, and APPARENTLY the tea is that Queen Clara wants Seb muuuuuuch closer to home, what with the Big Wedding Kicking Off in December. You angels remember what happened last summer, right? With Boring Prince Alex becoming UNBORING for a hot minute, and knocking Seb into the dirt? Appears THAT little drama got Seb sentenced to Life Under Mum's Nose.

So sorry, all you Highland Lassies who get to go to Gregorstoun this year and were hoping to lay eyes on Seb the Dreamboat/Hot Mess! At least you'll have pretty views to look at? And sheep? Honestly, a sheep would probably make a better boyfriend than that dude, let's be real.

("Dreams! Crushed!!" from *Crown Town*)

CHAPTER 6

"WILL YOU HAVE TO WEAR PLAID ALL THE TIME?"

Lee sits on the end of my bed, hands clasped between his knees as he watches me pull things out of my closet. It's mid-August, which means it's very hard to imagine a time when I'll need heavy coats, but the weather app on my phone tells me that if I were in Scotland right now, I'd want to be wrapped in wool. Besides, I won't be back home until December, so my heaviest winter coat gets tossed on the bed with the rest of the things I'm packing.

"The uniforms are plaid," I tell Lee. "But a dark plaid, so it's not so bad."

Lee attempts a smile, but his eyes keep returning to my suitcase.

Walking over, I put a hand on his shoulder. "The internet exists," I remind him. "Email, FaceTime, Facebook, probably some other face-based technology they'll invent while I'm over there . . ."

That gets a genuine smile out of him at least, and he runs a hand over his hair. "Face Plate," he suggests. "Faces showing up in your plates so you can eat dinner together."

Giggling, I throw another pair of socks in my bag. "Gross. I don't want to eat off your face."

Lee smirks. "Then I guess you don't even want me to get into Toilet Time, because that's where technology will really take off."

"Why am I friends with a boy?" I muse to my poster of Finnigan Sparks, tapping my fingers against his space helmet.

"Because you love me," Lee replies, and I heave a sigh.

"Sadly, I do."

Lee is not doing great with the whole Me in Scotland Thing, but he's definitely trying at least, hence the moral support while I pack. Gregorstoun's first day is later than Pecos High's, so he's already back in school, while I have a week before I'll start my senior year.

It's a weird thought, graduating somewhere else. Don't get me wrong, I'm excited about finishing my high school experience in another country, but it still felt bizarre, looking at everyone's First Day of School pics on social media last week.

"Have you talked to Darcy?" he asks, and I turn away, shrugging.

"A little."

That wasn't really true. She'd finally responded to my text with a *HEY GIRL! Sorry, been CRAZY BUSY!* but that was about it. True, she and I have never been as close as me and Lee (or me and Jude, or *Darcy* and Jude), but it still stung, and

I can't escape the feeling that she might be a little happy to have been right. I've seen more pics of her and Jude hanging out on Instagram and Snapchat over the past two weeks than I have in over a year.

Now that Jude and I aren't friends—or More Than Friends— anymore, it seems like Darcy has taken back Her Rightful Place.

"And have you talked to Jude?" Lee asks, pulling me from my thoughts, and I point at him.

"You know all Jude talk is still forbidden."

Usually, my Pointy Finger of Justice is enough to dissuade Lee, but now he just grabs it, pushing my finger out of his face. "We've had a two-week Jude-Free Zone," he says. "I think the statute of limitations is up. Have you talked to her?"

Sighing, I pull my finger out of his grip and flop into the chair at my desk. "No. But why should I? Did you miss the part where she broke my heart?"

"A, that rhymes," Lee replies, "and B, no, I didn't. I am very Team You in this, trust me, I just . . . don't want you to leave feeling unresolved. You deserve your big country-song moment where you tell her how much she sucks and then commit felony vandalism on her property."

I laugh at that, shaking my head. "Right, because me and confrontation are BFFs."

"You could stand to be a liiiiittttle bit more confrontational, it's true," Lee says, holding his thumb and forefinger apart. "How you can be so competitive, but still hate arguing—"

"I'm not that competitive," I interrupt, and Lee makes a rude noise.

"Okay, tell that to my neck. You know that game of Red

32

Rover in fifth grade is why I can't turn my head all the way to the left, right?"

"It's been nearly seven years, Lee, let it go," I joke, tossing a pair of socks at him. "And why are you so worried about me dealing with Jude anyway? Don't you have your own romantic life to fret over?"

Lee throws the socks back at me with a snort. "My dating life is fret-free at the moment. I have a date with Noah this Friday, *thankyouverymuch*."

"Chicken Finger Place Guy?"

Lee wrinkles his nose. "Y'all have got to stop calling him that."

Laughing, I turn back to my packing. "Sorry, you called him that first, and now it's stuck. I look forward to you one day becoming Mr. Chicken Finger Place Guy."

With a groan, Lee flops onto his stomach on my bed, sending a few pillows thudding to the floor. "Miiillllllllllliiiiie," he whines. "Why do you have to leave me? What's Scotland got that Texas doesn't? Other than discernible seasons, I guess."

"All kinds of things," I tell him. "Kilts."

"I can wear a kilt."

"Bagpipes."

"I'll learn those."

"Cool geology."

"Texas has so many damn rocks, Mill."

Grinning, I put another sweater in my suitcase. "It's different," I say. "And I'm ready to be somewhere different for a little while."

"Just promise me you're doing this because you really want

to go have fun, exciting new experiences," Lee says, picking at my comforter. "Not because you're running away."

"I am only mildly running away," I tell Lee, holding up my thumb and forefinger close together like he did earlier. "The teensiest bit of running. Every girl is allowed that."

I can tell Lee wants to argue with me over that, but in the end, he just sighs and says, "Fine. Then at least use your time wisely by hunting the Loch Ness monster."

"That," I say, giving him finger guns, "I can definitely do."

There's a knock at the door, and my stepmom pokes her head in. "Everything going okay in here?" she asks. Her red hair is pulled back from her face, and she's got Gus balanced on one hip.

Seeing me, he gives a happy shriek and reaches his arms out, so I cross the room to the two of them, taking one of those chubby hands and pressing a smacking kiss to the back. "Going great," I tell Anna. "I've almost finished making a Gus-sized cubby in my luggage."

She smiles, bouncing Gus a little as he continues to babble. "I'm sure he'd love that," she says. "And then I'd get to raise a kid with a Scottish accent, which could be fun."

I laugh and cross back over to the closet, pulling out a sweater. "You promise to smack me if I come back all 'aye' this and 'bonny' that, right?"

Anna nods, shifting Gus to her other side. "Stepmother's honor. Now, do y'all want pizza or Chinese for dinner?"

"Pizza," Lee and I say in unison, and Anna gives us a thumbs-up, which Gus mimics before they head back out into the hallway.

Lee gestures to my laptop. "Show me this school again at least," he says. "Let me form a clear picture of the place you're ditching me for."

"Easy enough."

I've got the Gregorstoun website bookmarked, and I bring it up now, feeling that same flutter in my stomach at the sight of those gorgeous brick walls, the breathtaking scenery around it.

Clicking through the pictures, Lee pauses on one of a bunch of boys dressed in off-white tank tops and long shorts that look like they're made out of canvas. They're all grimacing slightly at the camera, their pale skin red with cold.

"Who are these jokers?" he asks, and I look down at the caption.

" 'Class of 2009, participants of the annual Challenge.' "

Lee looks over at me. "What the heck is the 'annual Challenge'?"

I grin, practically wiggling on the bed. "Omigod, it's the coolest. They basically send you off into the Highlands in teams, and you have to camp out there, then find your way back to the school."

The Challenge was actually one of the reasons I'd picked Gregorstoun over other schools in Scotland. The idea of getting to be out on my own—well, kind of on my own—in the Highlands, wind whipping through my hair, camping out underneath Scottish stars? Yes, please.

Lee snorts. "A camping challenge does indeed sound very up your alley. Hope those guys aren't attached to having functional limbs."

Pretending to buff my nails on my shirt, I lift my chin in the air. "Gonna kill it, obviously."

Turning back to the laptop, Lee taps the screen. "Okay, but what if they're not telling the whole truth? What if the Challenge involves being thrown into a Sarlacc Pit to be eaten, hmm? Have you thought about that?"

"It's clearly not, because this fellow *here*," I say, pointing to one of the taller guys in the back, "is Prince Alexander of Scotland, and last time I checked, he was very uneaten. And marrying an American."

"Ohhhh, yeah," Lee says slowly. "My mom is obsessed with that. Getting up early for the wedding and everything."

I've seen Prince Alexander and his fiancée on the covers of a few magazines here and there, and there was some kind of scandal earlier in the summer with the fiancée's sister, but I didn't pay much attention. Royal gossip has never been my thing, and it's not like it's going to affect me anyway. Prince Alexander is long gone from Gregorstoun, and his brother, Sebastian, isn't going back.

"Millie Quint, going to school where royalty went," Lee muses, still looking at the pictures, and I shake my head.

"Millie Quint, going to a great school," I correct him.

"Besides," I add, closing out the webpage, "the chances of me meeting royalty are, like, nil."

FLORA'S OFF TO SCHOOL!

Seen here at Waverly Station in Edinburgh, Her Royal Highness, Princess Flora of Scotland, boards the train taking her north to Gregorstoun in the Scottish Highlands. Once a males-only institution, this year, Gregorstoun opens its doors to women for the first time in over a century. While Princess Flora's brothers both attended the school, this year, Flora will be the only Baird at Gregorstoun, her twin, Sebastian, having chosen to finish his schooling closer to home in Edinburgh. Rumors that the princess is being sent to the imposing school to curb some of her wilder impulses are, according to the palace, "completely fabricated."

("School's In for the Royals," from *People*)

CHAPTER 7

TO SAY THAT IT'S SURREAL TO FIND MYSELF IN
Scotland only a week after packing my bags with Lee does
not even come close to describing how weird I feel as I lean
forward from the back seat of a Land Rover and watch Scotland—the place I've spent the past year obsessing over—
unfurl in front of me.

Since flying from Houston to London, I've been on a train
to Edinburgh, and after that, to Inverness. There, I was picked
up by a Land Rover driven by a bearded guy who introduced
himself as "Mr. McGregor, groundskeeper." He looks about a
hundred years old, but I am so exhausted that he could drive
like he was in Scotland's version of *The Fast and the Furious*, and
I'd be fine with it. So long as I'm getting closer to Gregorstoun,
I'm good.

There are three other kids in the car with me, two girls and a
boy, and all three seem younger than me. They've stayed close
together, murmuring in low voices. I saw them on the train from
Edinburgh, huddled together.

That was a weird experience, riding the train up, watching the land change from the suburban houses outside the city to the fields, and then stony hills as we got farther north. I was so unsure of what to do that I stayed frozen in my seat the whole time, not even going to look for the bathroom.

All three of them keep shooting me looks, and finally, as the Land Rover crests a hill, I turn back to face all of them with a bright smile.

"So where do you think the sorting hat will put you?" I ask, then lift my hand, twisting two fingers together. "Come onnnn, Ravenclaw!" I say, and all three of them blink.

Mr. McGregor chuckles. Or maybe he's choking, hard to say.

"You're American," one of the girls says. She's truly little, with ashy-blond hair and giant blue eyes. I can just make out the top of a plastic horse sticking out from one of the pockets on her leather satchel.

"I am," I say. "My name's Millie."

The girl blinks at me before offering, "Elisabeth. Lissie, really. And this is Em"—she gestures to the dark-haired girl beside her—"and Olly."

"Elisabeth, Em, Olly," I repeat, nodding at each of them. They all smile politely, and okay, sure, they're all like twelve, but maybe this is a good sign of the kind of people I'll meet at Gregorstoun. Maybe they won't all be Scary Rich People, but just . . . Awkward Kids.

Rich Awkward Kids, but kids all the same.

In any case, the road is leveling out now, and the school is suddenly rising up before us, just like the website only . . . real.

In front of me.

The pictures didn't do it justice. It's all cream-colored stone against the green, rising up four stories, a long gravel drive in front, windows blinking in the sun.

"Oh, wow," I breathe, and Mr. McGregor looks over at me, a twinkle in his eyes if I'm not mistaken.

"Aye," he agrees. "She's a sight." Then he sighs, brows drawing together. "Used to be my family's home, ya ken, but now I just work here, shuttlin' you lot about."

I'm not sure what to say to that, so I just sort of hum in agreement and turn my attention back to the school.

There are a bunch of students milling around on the lawn, some in uniform, some not. I'm still wearing my jeans and T-shirt, since my uniform is supposed to be waiting for me in . . .

Pulling my backpack into my lap, I take out the email I printed out. *Room 327*, I read, my fingers moving over the numbers. My room. The room I'm going to live in for the next year.

With another girl.

That's one of the weirder parts of this whole boarding school experiment—living with someone else. I was an only child up until eighteen months ago, and I've never shared a space with someone else like this.

Still, good practice for college, right?

Mr. McGregor pulls the car up to the front of the school, where there are already kids heading in, dragging huge roller bags. I have a massive suitcase of my own in the back of the Land Rover (gotten on sale at TJ Maxx, thank you very much), and before I know it, I'm standing there in the huge front hall of Gregorstoun, the handle of the bag in my hand.

It's chaos, people weaving in and out, and I look around, trying to take it all in, a mix of nerves and jet lag making me feel more anxious than I'd anticipated.

I'm mostly surprised by how many boys there are. All kinds of boys. Boys who look about twelve, boys who tower over me as they make their way into the house. There must be five boys for every one girl, and I wonder just how many of us applied to be part of Gregorstoun's first female class.

The ground floor still looks like someone's house. There are paintings on the wall, little tables full of bric-a-brac, and soft carpets underfoot.

Ahead of me, a wooden staircase spirals upward, and, swallowing hard, I head toward it, lugging my bag behind me.

There are no elevators—or lifts, I guess they'd call them here—so I definitely get my cardio in hauling everything I own up to the third floor.

It's a little less chaotic up here, and dimmer. There are fewer windows, and the carpet feels almost moldy as I creep along it.

Ew.

But I find room 327 easy enough, and when I open the door, there's no one in there.

Standing on the threshold, I face two twin beds, one dresser, and a desk on either side of the door. In fact, if you open the door all the way, it hits one of the desks, and for some reason, I decide to go ahead and claim that side of the room. That might endear me to my roommate, right? Picking the crappy side?

Pulling my suitcase all the way into the room, I sit on the little bed with its scratchy white sheets and green wool blanket.

I've done it. I've come to Scotland, and I'm here for the next year.

Before the enormity of what I've done can fully sink in, I whip out my phone, pulling up FaceTime to call Dad.

He answers almost immediately, and I grin with relief to see him there in the living room.

"You made it!" he enthuses, dark eyes crinkling at the corners, and I nod, spinning my phone around so he can see my room.

"Living it up in the lap of luxury, obviously," I say, and Anna pops her head in.

"Oh my god, it's so . . . quaint," she says, raising her eyebrows, and I wave at her.

"If quaint means a little creepy and small, then yes!"

She frowns slightly, leaning closer to Dad's phone. "Millie, if this isn't—" she starts to say, but then the door to my room flies open again, thumping hard against my desk.

"No," a voice insists. "This is *not* what was agreed to."

A girl steps into the room followed by a man in a dark suit, and just for a second, my family and my phone are totally forgotten.

It's not cool to stare, I know that, but this is literally the prettiest girl I've ever seen in my life.

She's taller than I am, and her hair is gold. Like. Literally gold, like dark honey. It's held back from her face with a thin headband, and that face . . .

I realize while looking at her that beauty is more than just the way your face is structured, the weird quirks of DNA and societal norms that make us say, "This nose is the best nose," or "This is why I like this mouth," or whatever. This girl has clearly won a genetic lottery, don't get me wrong, but it's not just that—it's that she seems to *glow*. Her skin is so smooth and luminous I want to stroke her face like some kind of weirdo. I'm not sure she would even know what the word "pore" means. Does she follow one of those intense ten-step skin routines? Has she found magical sheet masks made of pearls?

Maybe this is just what being rich does to your face.

Because there's no doubt this girl is also very, very rich. Her clothes are simple—a sweater and jeans tucked into high leather boots—but they practically smell like money. *She* smells like money.

Also, only rich people can curl their lips the way she's currently doing at the guy in the suit who followed her in. Her dad? He looks a little young, plus it's hard to imagine that a guy with heavy jowls and pockmarked skin could possibly be related to this actual angel of a girl, standing there with a Louis Vuitton bag in the crook of her elbow.

"Your mother—" the man starts, and she throws up her hands.

"Call her, then."

"Pardon?" the man asks, his heavy brow wrinkling.

"Call my mother," she repeats, her voice carrying just the softest Scottish burr. Her chin is lifted, and I can actually feel tension vibrating off her.

"We were told—" the man says on a sigh, but she's not giving in.

"Call my mother."

On my phone, Dad scowls. "Everything okay?" he asks, and

I glance back at my new roommate, still imperiously repeating "Call my mother" every time the man tries to speak. And now I realize he's pulled his phone out, I assume to call her mother, and she's *still* saying it, over and over again, like a toddler.

"Call my mother. Call my mother. Call. My. Mother."

Maybe it's jet lag. Maybe it's the weird, weightless feeling in my stomach that started the moment I walked into the school and the massive change I'd made has fully sunk in.

But I turn to look over at her, and before I can think better of it, I hear myself say, "Hey. Veruca Salt."

Her lips part slightly, eyebrows going up as she stares at me. "Pardon?"

I've never wanted to pull words back into my mouth so badly. Lee was right about me not liking confrontation—it's pretty much my least favorite thing, right there underneath mayonnaise and jazz music. But something about how this girl is talking just . . . bugged me.

So maybe this is who I am now? Millie Quint, Confronter of People.

I decide to keep going with it.

"Do you mind being a little quieter?" I waggle my phone at her. "Some of us are trying to talk, and it seems like my dude here is calling your mom, so, like, maybe take it down a thousand notches?"

She keeps staring at me, and the man with her is now looking at me, too, his florid face going even redder.

Whatever. I take a deep breath and turn back to Dad. "Look, I'm here, I'm safe, everything is great . . . ish, and I'll call you back later, okay?"

Rubbing his eyes, Dad nods. "Sounds good, Mils. Love you."

"Love you, too."

He hangs up, and I go back to the suitcase on my bed. I still have a ton of unpacking to do, and it's going to take a lot of work to get this room looking even the littlest bit homey, so I should—

"Did you really call me Veruca Salt?"

I turn around to see my new roommate standing there with her arms folded. The guy who was with her is out in the hall, talking on his cell phone, probably to this girl's mom like she asked.

I take a second to study her now that I'm not blinded by her bone structure and shiny hair. Her sweater is a pale green that would make anyone else look vaguely ill, but just plays up the gold in her eyes, and yeah, my original take of her being the prettiest girl I've ever seen holds up, but the sulky way her mouth is turning down kills a little bit of her glow.

"I did, yeah," I tell her. "It seemed like you were about three seconds from launching into a musical number about wanting things, so it just felt right."

Her lips purse together, curling up into a smile. "Charming," she finally says, then her eyes drop to my jeans—nowhere near as nice as hers—and my long-sleeved T-shirt. It's the one I got working on the yearbook last year. I'd figured there was no sense in dressing up, since we'd get our uniforms as soon as we came, but now, next to this girl, I feel a little . . . grubby.

"I take it you're my roommate," she says, and I cross my own arms, mimicking her posture.

"So it seems."

That smile again. It's a straight-up Disney villain smile, reminding me that no matter how gorgeous this girl is, she's clearly a witch.

"What a delight for us both," she says, and then she turns, flouncing back out of the room.

She's probably running to the headmaster to ask to be moved or something, and frankly, that suits me just fine.

But hey, maybe school is going to keep us both so busy that I'll hardly even have to see her.

It's only after I've heard her stomping footsteps disappear down the hall that I realize I never learned her name.

CHAPTER **8**

ACCORDING TO THE ITINERARY I WAS EMAILED, I have a "tea" at 4 p.m., and since it's 3 now, I change into my new uniform, which was hanging up in the closet, draped with plastic, when I arrived. There's a knee-length plaid skirt, a short-sleeved white shirt, and two different sweaters, one long-sleeved, the other a vest. I choose that one, the Gregorstoun crest stitched on the front. It's warm enough, so I don't have to bother with the dark tights, settling on the kneesocks instead and finally sliding my feet into a pair of very plain black flats.

There's a mirror affixed to the back of the door, and I take a moment to look at myself, this new Millie. A Gregorstoun Girl.

Same boring brown hair curling over my shoulders, same brown eyes. Same dimples, as I see when I give a forced smile.

Same Millie, different place.

Sighing, I open the door and step out into the hall, only to immediately hear someone calling out.

"I'm telling you, Perry, she's on this floor!"

The voice around the corner is clearly coming from a Disney Princess—sweet, melodious, complete with the perfect cut-glass English accent, and I expect the girl I'm about to see will look like a cross between Sleeping Beauty and Cinderella. There might even be woodland creatures trailing in her wake.

The girl who suddenly appears *is* beautiful, and she's also . . . a giant.

Okay, that's not really fair, but she is easily over six feet tall, although when I glance down, I see she's wearing high-heeled boots. And while she might not look like Cinderella or Sleeping Beauty, she *is* stunning, with long dark hair and smooth brown skin.

And when she looks down at me, I see she has lovely brown eyes that crinkle at the corners as she smiles. "Oh, hullo!" she says brightly. "I didn't even see you there!"

That's probably because I'm basically a squirrel while she's a giraffe, and I give an awkward wave. "I tend to blend in."

"Oh, you're American!" she trills, then gestures behind her impatiently. "LOOK, PERRY, I'VE FOUND AN AMERICAN!" she calls, loud enough to make me wince.

No woodland creatures in her wake, but the boy who follows her is a bit . . . rabbity.

That's not nice, probably, but there's a slight overbite situation happening, plus he seems nervous and jumpy, especially compared to the girl he's standing next to.

"I'm Sakshi." She offers her hand for me to shake, and I take it, grateful that someone in this place seemed like a normal human being.

"Millie."

Sakshi grins, showing a crooked tooth, and finally, something slightly imperfect about this perfect girl. I'd been starting to wonder if you had to be a supermodel to get into this place, and I was some kind of charity case. "Millie," she repeats. "Cute. I like it."

I'd never thought of my name as being "cute" before, but Sakshi doesn't seem to be teasing, so I just go with it. "Technically Amelia, but no one ever calls me that."

She jerks a thumb over her shoulder at the guy standing just behind her. "And this is Perry, who is actually a Peregrine."

"Please stop telling people that," he says, leaning forward so that he can shake my hand, too. He's a good six inches shorter than Sakshi, his hair bright orangey red, freckles smattering his milk-white skin everywhere that I can see.

"So you're American," he says as he steps a little closer. He's also wearing the Gregorstoun sweater vest, but it looks a little big on him.

"Yeah," I say, shifting my weight to my other foot. "From Texas."

It occurs to me that that might not mean anything to them, and when Sakshi says, "Perry and I are both from Northampton," I realize that where she's from doesn't mean anything to me, either. This is a weird bit of culture shock I hadn't really anticipated.

But I nod at the two of them and smile, figuring that *fake it till you make it* is about to be my new motto around here.

"Well, come along," Sakshi says, threading an arm through

mine and tugging me back toward the stairs. "I assume you're on your way to the Girls' Tea."

I nod, letting myself be dragged along in her wake with Perry.

"It used to just be the First Years' Tea," he says as we make our way down the stairs. I spot a few portraits of stern-looking men in tartan, as well as some framed black-and-white photographs of uniformed boys standing in front of the school.

"But they're doing a special one just for the girls," he continues, and Sakshi sighs, waving her free hand.

"Yes, yes, Perry, I'm sure Millie here could put together what I meant by a 'Girls' Tea,' for heaven's sake. She's American, not stupid."

"Thanks? I think?" I say as we come to the bottom of the stairs.

There are more girls milling around now, some who are clearly my age, but a lot who seem younger. Sakshi looks at them, the corners of her mouth turning down.

"Poor loves," she says. "There aren't many of us intrepid ladies this year, and I feel it's going to be harder on the younger ones. I've even got one as my roommate, you know. Some little horsey girl."

"Horsey girl?" I ask, and Sakshi waves a hand.

"There's always a handful. Those girls entirely too invested in horses. Anyway, there aren't enough of us ladies to pair us all up with our own age group, so some of us have to room with the little ones, yours truly included."

She takes a deep breath, folding her hands in front of her. "Like I said, poor dears. I only have to survive for a year. They're here for ages."

Okay, "survive" is not how I want to think of my time here in my brand-new, exciting life.

"It's not going to be that bad," I say, shrugging. "I mean, we all chose to be here, right?"

"Saks did," Perry said. "I have *never* chosen to be at Gregorstoun, and I want that noted for the record. And possibly engraved on my headstone."

Rolling her eyes, Saks leans down and says to me, "Perry has been moaning about this place since he was twelve, so I decided I'd come and see what all the fuss was about." Then she flips her long dark hair over one shoulder. "Besides, if it's good enough for a princess, it's certainly good enough for me."

She leans in closer, lowering her voice. "Princess Flora is here," she says in a stage whisper. "As in *the* Princess Flora."

"Right, not the other, off-brand one," I joke. "Do they give her some kind of special tower room or something?"

Sakshi wrinkles her nose. "You haven't seen her? She's supposed to be rooming on your floor."

I shake my head. "I have seen no princesses," I say, and then . . .

No.

My mouth dry, I ask, "Do either of you have a phone? So you can show me her picture?"

Perry shakes his head, but Saks looks around before reaching into the waistband of her skirt and pulling out a rose-gold iPhone.

"Saks, it's supposed to stay in your room—you're going to get in trouble," Perry says, but Sakshi just holds up one finger, clicking on her phone with the other.

"Here she is," she says. "Shopping in New Town, wearing a truly fabulous coat."

Before she even turns the phone to me, I know, but it's still a shock to the system to see the picture and clearly recognize Princess Flora.

My roommate.

When Princess Flora joins Gregorstoun this autumn, she'll be the first female royal to do so in the school's hundred-year history. However, Flora won't be alone in making her mark as part of Gregorstoun's first female class! Let's have a look at some of the other aristocratic ladies who are heading to the Highlands this year.

Lady Elisabeth Graham: Youngest daughter of the Earl of Dumfries, Lady Elisabeth recently celebrated her twelfth birthday by renting out the entire Edinburgh Zoo for the weekend. Like her mother, the Countess of Dumfries, Lady Elisabeth is quite the equestrian, and we hear she's greatly looking forward to honing her skills at Gregorstoun.

The Honourable Caroline McPherson: Miss McPherson is the daughter of the Viscount Dunrobbin, and like Princess Flora, she will be completing her final year of secondary school at Gregorstoun. Another thing Miss McPherson has in common with Princess Flora: She was briefly linked romantically to Prince Sebastian's best friend, Miles Montgomery.

Lady Sakshi Worthington: As the daughter of the Duke of Alcott, Lady Sakshi is second only to the princess herself in terms of rank. Her mother is noted philanthropist and socialite Ishani Virk, whose wedding to the duke was one of the grandest in recent memory. We're told Lady Sakshi has inherited her mother's flair for entertaining, as well as her interest in charity work.

("Ladies of Gregorstoun," from *Prattle*)

CHAPTER 9

"YOU SERIOUSLY DIDN'T KNOW YOU WERE ROOMING with the princess?" Sakshi asks as we sit on an uncomfortable sofa in what's called "the east drawing room." There's a buffet table against the back wall that has a bunch of china teacups and saucers, plus tiers of cakes and cookies, but I'm definitely not hungry right now. I did take the cucumber sandwich Saks offered me from her plate, but I'm mostly just crumbling it into a napkin.

"I seriously didn't," I tell Sakshi now in a low voice. "But honestly, that seems like the kind of thing someone should've told me? I mean, I got about five thousand emails about what kind of socks to buy, but I didn't get a 'hi, you're living with royalty' heads-up?"

I don't add that I'm here on scholarship, and for all I know, insulting the royal family is automatic grounds for getting all that sweet, sweet school cash yanked back.

God, why did I choose this *one time in my entire life* to be snotty to someone?

Perry is perched on a rickety-looking chair he dragged over from the side of the room, and he leans closer, his bony elbows on his knees. "It would make sense for them to do it on purpose," he says. "To pair her up with someone who's not technically a subject." He shrugs his narrow shoulders. "It's a good idea, really. Makes things less awkward."

I remember calling the princess Veruca Salt and rolling my eyes at her.

"I . . . may have already made it a *little* awkward," I confess. "Although she wasn't exactly the picture of princessy refinement, so it's not completely my fault. I think."

Sakshi's and Perry's eyes go wide, and Sakshi grabs my hand. "Okay, tell me everything *immediately*."

We sit there on the sofa while I pick at my sandwich some more, visions of being stripped of my fancy new uniform on the first day circling my brain, and fill them in on my first meeting with Her Royal Pain. When I get to the Veruca Salt bit, Perry actually hoots.

"Oh my lord, I would've given anything to see her face when you said that."

"It's going to be okay, isn't it?" I ask, crumpling up my crumb-filled napkin. "I mean, they're not going to—"

"Throw you in a dungeon?" Sakshi asks, and I shoot her a look.

"No, I'm not that much of an ignorant American. I was thinking more along the lines of getting kicked out or something. I'm here on scholarship, so what if the punishment for insulting a royal classmate is expulsion or . . . I don't know, demerits or something?"

Perry shakes his head before snatching a tea cake from Sakshi's plate. "No worries on that front," he says before demolishing the cake in one bite. "The whole point of sending the royal kids here is so they're forced to live like normal students. No special privileges, no kid gloves. If they wouldn't expel you for calling *me* Veruca Salt, they can't do it because you said it to *her*. That's the deal."

Speak of the devil—at that moment, Flora comes in the room, flanked by two other girls, both of whom have hair just as shiny as hers, but aren't nearly as pretty. They're both in uniforms, too, but Flora's still decked out in that fancy sweater and designer jeans.

Her eyes briefly land on me before flicking away again, and I'm not sure if that's because she's pissed or because I haven't really registered to her yet.

She walks over to another sofa, this one smaller than the one Sakshi and I are sitting on, and already occupied by three younger girls.

Flora doesn't even say anything to them. She just approaches, shoots them a look, and suddenly all three are scattering, practically tripping over themselves to give Her Highness her desired seat.

I snort as Flora situates herself in the best light, flicking her hair over her shoulder.

"I'm not the only person to want to throw 'Veruca Salt' in her general direction, am I?" I ask, and that makes both Perry and Sakshi laugh.

"Oh, darling, *no*," Perry replies. "I'd bet half the country wants to say that to her. In fact, they probably want to say something much, much worse."

Sakshi looks at me, her dark eyes narrowed slightly. "You . . . really don't know anything about her, do you?" she asks, and I shrug.

"Maybe I should've read up more. I knew both her brothers went here, but that's it."

Sighing, Perry glances up at the ceiling. "Not knowing anything about this crowd," he says, wistful. "What a lovely life that would be."

"Easy, drama queen," Sakshi counters. "It's not like your family has exactly suffered from their connection to those weirdos."

Perry grins then, and I'm surprised how much cuter that makes him look. He has a good smile, overbite and all.

"It's true, it's true, we have all sorts of lovely lands and houses because of the Bairds and the Stuarts before them. But still, bit of a hassle, even you have to admit that, Saks."

"I don't have to admit anything," she says with a little sniff, lifting her chin in the air. "Besides, one of these days, I'm going to be a Baird myself."

She says it with such confidence that I don't even question it, but Perry rolls his eyes. "Give it up. He'll never come back here, not now that he's finally gotten free."

"I'm sorry," I say slowly, fiddling with the edge of my sweater vest. "You're going to have to explain things for the American girl. Who are we talking about?"

"Seb the Wanker," Perry says, but Sakshi shoves at his leg, frowning.

"Prince Sebastian of Scotland, my future husband," she informs me. "That's the whole reason I'm here."

"To . . . marry Prince Sebastian?"

"Mm-hmm." Sakshi nods, like it's perfectly normal to set your sights on a royal husband at seventeen, then plan your schooling accordingly.

"Of course, when I applied to be part of Gregorstoun's first female class, it wasn't all about Seb. It was beyond time they let women into this place, and I was determined to be among the first wave. But one should always have a secondary goal, and mine is becoming a princess."

She lifts one shoulder. "I don't think it's a bad goal to have."

"It's barking mad," Perry says, and I get the sense this has been a long-running argument between them.

Something must show on my face because Sakshi waves a hand at Perry and says, "We've known each other for donkey's, haven't we, Perry? Our families have houses next door to each other in Belgravia, but this is the first time we've gone to school together."

"Bully for me," Perry mutters, but I can tell there's no real animosity there. For all that they keep sniping at each other, they do seem like really good friends, and I suddenly miss home more than I'd thought I would. Perry doesn't look anything like Lee, but he makes me miss him all the same. Lee and Darcy, even.

Jude.

Ugh, no, Scotland is a No-Jude-Thoughts Zone. I'm here for school and finally seeing more of the world, something different from the flat plains of home.

"So you want to be a princess?" I ask Sakshi, but to my surprise, she shakes her head.

"It's not that, exactly. I mean, don't get me wrong, the title, the castle, the jewels, that will all be lovely. But the real goal is the opportunity. There's so much I'd like to do for the world, and being a princess opens up those doors. It's the best way to achieve my humanitarian goals." Then she shrugs. "Also, he's hotter than a bakery on the surface of the sun, so there's that."

"Unbelievable," Perry mutters, but before Saks can reply, a woman walks into the room. She's wearing a fairly boring gray suit, but her hair is almost as red as Perry's, and it's pulled back from her face in a flattering updo.

"Ladies!" she says brightly, clapping her hands together. Then her eyes land on Perry, and she frowns.

"Ladies and Mr. Fowler, perhaps I should say."

Mumbling an apology around a mouthful of cake, Perry gets up, dragging his chair back against the wall before slinking out with a quick wave to me and Sakshi.

She sighs as he goes. "Hopeless Perry."

"I hope for his sake that's not an actual nickname," I mutter, and Sakshi laughs, briefly touching my knee.

"It should be."

The lady in the gray suit gestures for us to stand, and we do. Well, most of us do. I glance over and see that Flora takes her time unwinding from her comfy position on the sofa.

I also notice the way the lady in the suit's eyes flick down to take in Flora's lack of uniform, and the slight frown she gives.

But then she smiles at all of us, hands once again clasped in front of her. "Ladies," she begins again. "I am Dr. McKee, your headmistress. Welcome to Gregorstoun. I hope you've all felt very welcome on your first official day."

We all nod and make general murmuring sounds of agreement, and then a voice rings out, clear and posh, lilting and musical.

"I was not made to feel very welcome, Dr. McKee," Flora says, and then she glances over at me, lips curling.

CHAPTER **10**

WE ALL STAND THERE IN THE DRAWING ROOM, focused on Flora, which is probably her idea of heaven. She seems like the type of girl who's very invested in being the center of attention.

And I stand there and wait for the ground to swallow me up, or for guards to rush in and seize me for daring to call the princess a name.

But then, her lips still curled in that cat-that-got-the-canary smile, Flora looks at Dr. McKee and says, "Sebastian told me there were bagpipers on the first day." She lifts one shoulder in an elegant half shrug. "I'm afraid I don't feel welcome anywhere that doesn't provide the appropriate fanfare."

She winks then—actually winks! At a teacher! No, not a teacher, a *headmistress*—and giggles run through the room.

I sigh in relief, only to feel my shoulders tense right back up when Flora once again meets my eyes.

She winks again, but this time it isn't cheeky or cute.

Shaking her head, Dr. McKee clasps her hands behind her back. "We'll try to do better in the future, Miss Baird," she says. "Perhaps someone can play the kazoo for you as you make your way to the showers in the morning."

More giggles, and then she walks across the room to a heavy wooden door, opens it, and waves us inside.

"Miss Baird?" I ask Sakshi in a low voice as we trudge along with the herd of girls. "Not Your Majesty?"

"That would be for the queen," Saks replies over her shoulder at me. "Flora's an HRH."

When I just stare at her, she clarifies, "Her Royal Highness. But in any case, it doesn't matter here. No titles, that's the rule. It's why I'm Miss Worthington instead of Lady Sakshi."

I almost stop in my tracks, which would've probably caused some kind of domino effect of plaid. "You're a lady?" I ask, and Sakshi nods, flicking her heavy bangs out of her eyes.

"My father is the Duke of Alcott, which makes me a lady, but definitely *not* an HRH." Then she grins. "Yet. But anyway, Flora is Miss Baird whenever she's here, yes."

Maybe it's because I spent so much of my time thinking about what Gregorstoun would mean to me without paying that much attention to what the school was like, or maybe it's that Gregorstoun does a good job of downplaying just how fancy it actually is, but I haven't really thought about what it would be like to go to school with someone who has a *title*. The royals are one thing, but even the "normal" people here are fancier than I thought they'd be, and that's . . .

"Weird" doesn't even start to cover it. How much else don't I know?

The room we've been led into is a lot less cozy than the drawing room, and about ten degrees colder. The walls are stone, the windows thicker, and in the center of the floor is a ginormous circular oak table. The chandeliers overhead appear to be made of . . . antlers? Yeah, definitely antlers, and while they use light bulbs instead of candles, the effect is still awfully medieval.

"Is this where we're made into knights?" I ask Saks, and she snorts as we pull up seats next to each other at the table.

Flora sits near the other end with those other two girls, and Saks glances over at her.

"Blimey, she's a piece of work," she murmurs. "I'd forgotten what she was like."

"You knew Flora before?" I ask, and she nods.

"Similar social circles and all that. She wasn't always as bad as she is now, though. In fact, when we were small, I quite liked her, but then when she turned thirteen, it all went a bit bratty, to be honest. Sebastian's always been a mess. He got banned from an *entire city block* in London when he was only twelve. Or so the rumor goes."

"And this is the family you want to marry into?" I say.

"Seb is a fixer-upper, and there is nothing I cannot improve," Sakshi replies.

Weirdly, I totally believe her. Sakshi could probably lead entire armies into battle armed with her confidence alone.

And sitting at this table, battle seems like a feasible thing to plan.

Dr. McKee stands at the opposite side of the room, just next to a large suit of armor and right under one of those thick windows with the wavy glass that barely let sunlight penetrate the room.

"Ladies," she says with a warm and genuine smile, "I cannot tell you what a thrill it is to be welcoming you to Gregorstoun. I've waited six years now to be able to actually address a roomful of students as 'ladies.' "

Saks leans close. "They hired Dr. McKee to bring Gregorstoun out of the Dark Ages," she whispers. "So of course she started campaigning for women to be admitted, but it took years. Because patriarchy."

I nod. That makes sense.

Dr. McKee is still talking, but to tell the truth, jet lag still has me firmly in its grip, so I'm struggling to follow along until I hear her say, "The Challenge."

Then I perk up.

"The Challenge is one of the hallmarks of a Gregorstoun education," Dr. McKee goes on. "In years past, it was used as an opportunity for some sort of outdated show of masculinity, so to fit both our changing times and our new commitments to the sort of school we'd like to be, we've decided that the Challenge will be a bit different this year. For one, you'll be in pairs rather than working in larger teams."

It is so stupid, so totally elementary school of me, but as soon as Dr. McKee says "pairs," my stomach drops a little. Sakshi seems nice, and I wouldn't mind pairing up with her, but maybe she already has a close friend, someone she's known for more than an hour, who she wants to pair up with.

Unless we're going to be paired randomly? That might save

me the humiliation of trying to find a partner, but it still doesn't seem ideal.

And then Dr. McKee smiles and basically ruins my life. "And to make this a more immersive experience, your partner will be your roommate."

I can't help but glance down the table at Flora, who's already looking back at me with a bored and vaguely irritated expression.

Me and Veruca Salt? Out in the wilderness together?

"Of course, the Challenge won't begin for another month," Dr. McKee goes on with a smile. "So you'll have plenty of time to plan out your strategy along with the rest of your schoolwork."

The rest of the meeting is reminders about rules, instructions on how to best balance "academic life with social pursuits." And then we're dismissed back to our rooms to "have some downtime" before school officially starts tomorrow.

I wave good-bye to Saks as I head up the stairs, my limbs heavy and my eyes gritty. All I can think about is flopping onto my bed and sleeping, even though it's barely 5 p.m.

But when I get to my room, Flora is already there, standing by the foot of her bed, looking out the window.

She's also on her phone, even though one of the lectures we just got involved turning our phones over to the main office. We can have them on weekends, but not during the school week, something I remind myself to email Dad about.

But then, I guess rules don't apply to Flora.

"Well, she'll have to get over it," Flora is saying now, one arm crossed over her stomach as she keeps looking out the window. "I told her that was one of the requirements of me going to school here."

There's a pause, and she glances over her shoulder at me, lips pursing briefly. Then she turns back to the window.

"Don't be ridiculous. I'm safe as houses up here, and *you* didn't have to have security detail. Neither did Seb. So why am I the exception? And I warn you, if you say it's because I'm a girl, I'm going to leak it to the papers that you slept with a blankie until you were eleven."

I don't want to eavesdrop, but you kind of can't *not* when you're sharing a room with someone, and curiosity has me edging a little closer to the window to see what she's looking at.

It's the guy from earlier, the red-faced one in the dark suit, and he's putting suitcases in the trunk of a black SUV. He's got a cell phone pressed to his ear, too, and as I watch, he drops a suitcase, flinging his free hand up in the direction of the school, and, I'm guessing, Flora.

Her lips curve in a slow smile as she lifts her hand to wave at him, but he's not looking.

Then, sighing, Flora turns away from the window, flouncing onto her bed. She's got the same boring white sheets and green blanket I do, and I can see she's added some throw pillows. She's also completely taken over the top of the dresser, and I frown as I look at the expensive scented candles, framed photos of Flora and a bunch of similarly gorgeous girls in big hats and gorgeous dresses, and . . . a porcelain hand?

Apparently a ring holder, since all the fingers are decorated with various sparkly pieces.

While Flora keeps chatting on the phone (*To a prince,* a part of my brain whispers, *who will one day be a king, and who is her brother because she is a princess, you are living with an honest-to-god princess*), I unzip my duffel and pull out the big Ziploc bag I brought with my favorite rock samples.

Yes, maybe it's a *wee* bit dorky to have favorite rocks, but whatever. I found some of these on trips with my dad, and others are from gem and mineral shows I've dragged him and Anna to. They're a nice reminder of home.

Moving over to the dresser, I don't look at Flora as I begin moving some of the candles to the side closer to her bed.

"Alex, let me call you back," I hear her say. "I have a turf war to attend to."

Great.

I ignore her, though, keeping my focus on my task as I place my favorite piece of hematite an inch away from her stupid hand statue.

Leaning against the dresser, Flora studies me.

"Are you a witch?" she finally asks. "Into crystals and all that?"

"No," I answer, putting my citrine just to the left of the hematite. "I'm a geologist. Or I'm going to be."

"A witch would be preferable," she says. "Or at least interesting. What's your name, anyway, O roomie of mine?"

"Millie," I say, finally looking up at her. I wonder if I'll ever get used to looking at someone this gorgeous. Because pain in the ass or no—and she seems like a serious pain in the ass—I've never seen eyes like hers, so light brown they're nearly the same honey-gold as her hair.

Those eyes are narrowed at me now. "Millie what?"

Is this some kind of test? "Millie Quint," I reply. "Sorry, that's all there is to it. No esquires or the thirds or anything."

Scoffing, Flora moves back toward her bed. "And American to boot."

"Not just American," I tell her. "Texan."

"Will today's bounties never cease?" she mutters, leaning down to pluck a magazine out of the leather handbag slumped on the floor.

I look at her for a minute, then back to my rock collection. Reaching out to run a finger over my favorite one, a hematite sample I got in Arizona last year, I make myself say, "Look, I'm sorry about the Veruca Salt thing. I was just tired, and you were . . . really loud."

I'm sure princesses don't snort, but it sure sounds like that's what Flora does as she flips through her magazine. "Amazing that you think I'd be offended by someone like you insulting me, Quint."

I clutch the rock harder. "It's Millie."

"Actually," Flora says, tossing the magazine to the bed and looking at me with a poisonous smile, "it's nothing to me, because you're not going to be my roommate long enough for it to matter what I call you. And that's a promise."

CHAPTER **11**

IT'S NOT THAT I OBJECT TO PHYSICAL FITNESS AS A concept. It's a good one, important for health and happiness, all of that. Yay, exercise. But there's a big difference between popping into a yoga class on a Saturday morning and Gregorstoun's idea of exercise.

For one, it starts at the ungodly hour of 6 a.m.

For another, it's running.

We did laps back at Pecos High, usually when our PE teacher couldn't come up with any other activities, and I'd never been crazy about that, but at least it had been inside, around the gym where it was warm in the winter, cool in the summer, and there was much less chance of stepping in sheep poop.

Which is exactly what I've just done.

It's rainy this morning, my fifth at Gregorstoun, and it's also the fifth morning I've found myself doing our daily run in the rain.

Dr. McKee insists this isn't rain, but "mizzle," a combination of drizzle and mist that, okay, sure, may not technically be pelting rain, but still ensures that I'm soaked within about five minutes. It's also made the ground slippery, which is why my foot slid into said sheep poop as I rounded a corner.

"Oh, gross," I mutter, pausing there on the rocky trail, my heart hammering, my skin clammy, my sneaker maybe ruined forever.

Sakshi stops beside me, still jogging in place, her long black ponytail swinging between her shoulder blades. "Problem, Millie?" she asks, and I gesture to my befouled shoe.

Her nose wrinkles, but then she just shrugs. "Occupational hazard, I suppose." With that, she gives a cheery smile and continues her own jog, hair still swaying.

Suddenly I'm not sure if I like Sakshi very much.

Perry clearly shares my feelings, coming to a stop beside me, his thin chest wheezing in and out, one hand pressed to his sternum. "They're trying to murder us," he wheezes. "That's what this place really is, I've tried to tell people. A Murder School."

Looking back over my shoulder at where Gregorstoun sits on the hill, I have to admit it does look a little bit murder-y. It's definitely very Gothic, all cold stone shrouded in mist. A few of the windows are bright against the gloom, which just has the effect of making the place look even spookier.

Shivering a little, I nod at Perry. "I mean, I can see it. They definitely don't show this side of things in the brochure."

Perry snorts at that, or at least tries to. I'm not sure he has enough breath for it. "I did wonder how they show this place off for the foreigners," he says.

"Little more Fairy Tale, little less Death Castle."

He nods. "Fair. Well, shall we?"

Looking ahead at our jogging classmates, I suck in a deep breath, flick my wet bangs out of my eyes, and nod. "Not claiming us, Murder School."

"Two fewer victims for their roster," Perry agrees, and off we go.

It's hard to believe I've been here nearly a week now. Also hard to believe just how quickly it started to feel like home.

Okay, not home exactly. But there's something about being here that's made me feel like I've finally found a place to be my Most Me. The Millie-est Millie. I actually love going to class in rooms that are hundreds of years old. And while I don't love running—*should one run if a bear is not chasing one?*—I have to admit as I look around at the hills rising up into the clouds, this beats the gym at Pecos High by a mile.

Stopping on the path, I place both my hands against my lower back and take a deep breath, my chest aching from both running and how beautiful everything is. From the smell of the rain and the rocks under my feet. From—

"You're not going to start crying, are you?"

I turn around to see Flora trudging up the path behind me, a cigarette in hand. She's wearing the same sweatshirt and sweatpants they gave all of us for our "daily exercise," but hers look a lot better than mine do.

"No," I tell her now, even though I had been feeling just the tiniest bit emotional.

"Singing, then?" she continues, raising an eyebrow. "Definitely not singing, right?"

"No singing, no crying, just going to keep standing here, minding my business," I reply, turning back around to face the vista stretching out before me. I suddenly wish I had my hiking boots on and my jeans, my compass in my hand. I could spend hours out there, roaming the hills. This—this is what I came to Scotland for.

Flora heaves out a sigh from behind me, and gravel crunches, so she's probably stubbing out her cigarette. I don't know because I'm not going to turn around and look because I am pretending she isn't here. This is just me, out here, in Scotland, communing with—

"Seriously, are you sure you're not going to sing?"

Pressing my lips together, I turn to look at Flora, who's sauntered up to my side. "Yes," I bite out. "In fact, I'm really trying to enjoy the quiet."

I make a point of emphasizing that last word, hoping she'll get the hint, but Flora just crosses her arms over her chest and resumes looking bored.

"This isn't even one of the best spots in the Highlands, you know. Glencoe, Skye . . . those are places worth swooning over."

"Well, I'll be sure and try to visit those," I say, barely managing to unclench my teeth, "but this is nice, too."

Flora snorts. "Where did you say you're from again?"

"Texas."

"Ahhhh, that's right, now things make a bit more sense."

"What does that even mean?" I ask, and Flora flicks a piece of lint from her uniform.

"Just that you're probably not used to views like this."

Okay. Well, that's . . . true, but it still sounded suspiciously mean, so I turn away from her.

Maybe if I don't say anything, she'll go away? Surely being ignored is Flora's worst fear.

So I stare and ignore while Flora stands and looks at me, and I can practically hear her mind whirring as she searches for some kind of baiting comment. We've mostly stayed out of each other's way this first week, but there's definitely tension brewing in our room. I still don't know what she meant by that whole "not going to be her roommate much longer" comment, and I haven't bothered to ask.

Finally, Flora just rolls her eyes and starts half-heartedly jogging up the path.

"Can already tell this is going to be a thrilling semester," she calls out, sarcasm practically dripping from her mouth.

Once the torture portion of the morning is over and I'm showered and back in my uniform, I go to my first class of the day, European history with Dr. Flyte. He appears to be about ninety thousand years old, which is maybe why he's so good at history—he's lived it all.

It's taken me the past week to begin to understand Dr. Flyte's accent. He's English, not Scottish, but every word comes out of a clenched jaw, and he's never met a vowel he didn't like to stretch out way past its natural shape. Now, as he stands in front of the class, hands clasped behind his back, his eyebrows about to take flight, I look down at my notebook, scratching out the "????" after "William" to add "the Conqueror."

Dr. Flyte keeps droning, and I keep listening as closely as I can, but it's hard to do when I still want to look around me.

This class is in what I guess used to be a study. The windows face the inner courtyard of the house, so not much light gets through. There are only a couple of lamps on in the room, adding to the whole gloomy feel, and while we sit in fairly regular desks, there's no whiteboard or projector, no flag hanging near the door, no posters reminding us of important historical dates. It's like the only effort they made to make this place a school was to drop some desks in and call it a day.

And I like it.

Class wraps up, and today's notes only have a few of those "?????s" in them, so I'm considering that a win as I head out into the hall, only to suddenly find myself surrounded by Glamazons.

Okay, maybe "surrounded" is unfair when there are just two of them, but they're still extremely tall and extremely shiny of hair, and as I look up at them, I realize they're the two girls I most often see hanging around Flora.

"Hi," I say, pointing between them. "Just need to scooch by—"

But the brunette moves in closer to the blonde, cutting off my escape.

So it's like that.

"Caroline," the blonde one says, "isn't this the sad little American who took Rose's spot?"

"Hmmm," the brunette muses, pretending to think it over. "Do you know what, Ilse? I think it is!"

A handful of people are still moving past us, and I glance up, hoping to see Sakshi or Perry in the mix. Or really anyone who doesn't look like a supermodel determined to Mean Girl me.

But everyone who passes us seems to be very aggressively not looking in our direction, and I realize I'm on my own here.

"I'm pretty sure I didn't take anyone's place," I say, then attempt the scooch maneuver again. "So I'll just scoooooooch—"

"They only offer one full scholarship a year, did you know that?" Caroline asks. Up close, her features are a little too sharp to call her beautiful, but there's something about the way she holds her shoulders back, chin lifted, that makes her seem more impressive than she is.

"I didn't," I say now, still looking for a way around them. Being New Millie Who Confronts People has only gotten me into trouble thus far, so it's back to Millie Who Avoids This Kind of Thing from here on out.

But I couldn't help adding, "I earned that scholarship, but I'm sorry that—"

Scoffing, Ilse steps closer. "*Earned*. Rose's family has sent students to Gregorstoun since its inception. This is the first year there hasn't been a Haddon-Waverly at Gregorstoun."

"Thanks to you," Caroline adds. "She was devastated when she found out they'd decided to give the scholarship to some little upstart from nowhere."

I gape at them. I can't help it. *Upstart?* Are we in Victorian times? Do they think I was selling flowers on a street corner somewhere?

"Why would one of your friends need a scholarship anyway?

Don't you people have tons of money because of . . . peasants? And oppression?"

Caroline's lips thin as she folds her arms over her chest and glares down at me. "You really have no idea how anything works, do you?"

Heaving out a sigh, I shift my satchel of books to my other shoulder. "I don't, believe me. Now can I *please* scooch?"

I press my palms together, gesturing to the sliver of space between them, and Ilse moves closer. "Lord, Flora was not kidding about you."

Great, so we're at the "implying someone said nasty things about you" portion of this whole deal, and I'm about to reply that I don't care what Flora has said, when I suddenly hear Sakshi's voice, ringing out loud and clear.

"Are the two of you finished?"

Caroline and Ilse turn to see all 567 feet of Sakshi standing there, her long dark hair falling over her shoulders and the most perfectly disdainful, bored expression on her face. It's so great that I make a note to immediately start practicing it in the mirror. I have a feeling I'm going to need that look.

To my surprise, it totally works on Caroline and Ilse, too. They throw me a couple of nasty glances, but they slink off without any other snide remarks, and Saks dusts her hands like she's just completed an unpleasant but necessary task.

"Those two," she says, shaking her head; then she steps forward, her expression concerned as she touches my arm. "Are you all right?"

"Fine," I tell her, smiling. "I went to a giant high school in

Texas, so mean girls are nothing new. And honestly their attempt at bullying was almost . . . quaint?"

That makes Saks smile, and she links her arm through mine as we make our way down the hallway. "I can't believe they're still so upset over Rose Haddon-Waverly. It's done, move on, live in the now, my god."

She says all of that with a wave of her hand, and I glance up at her. "So you overheard?"

Sakshi shakes her head. "I just assumed that's what it was about. It was a bit of a to-do in our circles, Rose not getting in." She gives another exaggerated sigh. "Her father lost the family fortune in some sort of horse fiasco a few years back."

I don't even ask what "horse fiasco" might mean here, because I'm not sure I want to know, but I *do* ask, "So there are poor fancy people mixed in with the rich fancy people?"

Saks nods. "More of the former than you'd think. Not me of course, Daddy owns half of Belgravia. And not Caroline or Ilse, either. Or Perry. It's why he'll probably marry a pop star or something despite his entire . . ." Another hand wave, this one I think meant to take in literally everything about Perry.

Then Saks looks down at me and pats my hand. "Don't worry, though. You'll figure it all out eventually!"

She beams at me, and I make myself smile back, even as I think, *Don't hold your breath on that, Saks.* The rest of the day passes like they always do—class, a bizarre tea break at 4 p.m. that still takes some getting used to, but by 6-ish, I'm back in my room, reading *The Mill on the Floss*, and doing my best to ignore the clacking of Flora's computer.

Which is a feat given that she's pushing those buttons so hard it's like she's imagining they're my face.

My own computer is open on my bed because I'm waiting for Lee to call me in Hangouts, and when there's a *bloop* sound, I put down my book, already sitting up with a smile.

But then I see the message in Hangouts.

It's not Lee.

It's Jude.

There's just one word typed there.

Hi?

That question mark makes me frown at the screen, my fingers hovering over the keyboard. Am I going to reply? Why is she messaging now? Does she—

"Knock-knock," a voice calls.

I look up, and hoooooooly moly. The boy standing in our doorway is model-hot, all dark auburn hair and twinkling blue eyes. He's wearing a green sweater with the best pair of jeans ever created, and I blink at him, trying to figure out where someone this gorgeous came from.

Then it hits me.

This must be Flora's boyfriend. They go together too perfectly for him to be anything but hers. Probably a duke's son or a viscount or something.

And sure enough, Flora leaps up from her bed with a squeal, slamming her laptop closed. "Seb!"

I watch her launch herself across the room and into his arms, and both their faces transform into something really . . . sweet.

Like, they're both frighteningly hot, but they're almost goofy as they smile at each other, and I realize that for as sexy as they both are, there's a distinct lack of spark between them. They seem almost like—

"Who's this?" Seb asks, looking over Flora's shoulder at me, and Flora pulls back to give me her trademark dismissive look.

"Roomie. Quint," she says, like using any more words to describe me might cause her physical pain.

Neat.

"Well, Roomie Quint," Seb says, walking toward me with an outstretched hand. "I'm Brother Seb." Then he grins, a dimple flashing in his cheek. "Brother Seb, that makes me sound like a monk."

Snorting, Flora slaps at his arm. "And you'd be a bloody terrible one."

I'm still hung up on "brother." This is Flora's brother? They look about the same age, sure, but they don't look much alike, even if they were both clearly blessed by the Gene Fairy.

And he's not just her brother, I suddenly remember.

"You're twins, right?" I ask, shaking Seb's outstretched hand. His skin is warm and soft, and I'm sure many a girl has shivered at that touch.

"We don't look much alike, I'll admit, but we are indeed twins," he says before smiling at Flora. "She's older by three minutes and has never let me forget it."

Then he looks at us, a slightly dangerous glint in his eyes. "So," he says with a smirk, "you two ready to have some fun?"

CHAPTER 12

"IT'S FRIDAY," I BLURT OUT, AND BOTH FLORA AND Seb turn to look at me.

Seb grins a little, teeth practically flashing as he slides his hand in his back pocket. "So it is," he says, lifting one shoulder. "But it's just a trip down to the pub. I wouldn't keep you out late, Roomie Quint."

Flora's eyes narrow slightly and my cheeks go hot. Suddenly Sakshi's crush on Seb makes a lot of sense to me, but I'm still not about to go gallivanting off . . . wherever with the two of them.

I'm a rule follower by nature. I've never broken curfew, never skipped school, and never been to a bar.

And Jude's message is still there on my screen, waiting.

So now I just lift my book from my bed and wiggle it slightly. "Homework," I say. "But you two have fun."

"Told you," Flora says in a low voice to Seb, and I'm guessing that means she's already filled him in on what a bore I am. Fine by me.

Then she steps a little closer to her brother. "Are they all here?"

Seb shakes his head, which has the effect of loosing the perfect amount of hair to flop over his forehead. "Not all. Spiffy, Dons, and Gilly were free, but Sherbet's busy with school, and Monters is, of course, dead."

I blink at that, but Flora just rolls her eyes. "He's not dead, and Caroline said he's actually back in Scotland now."

"No, he's extremely dead, and it's all very tragic, but I'm moving past it. In any case, Monters wouldn't have been any help here."

Flora thinks that over, tilting her head to one side, before nodding with a "True," and flipping her hair back over her shoulders. "Oh well. Two is better than none, I suppose. Shall we?"

I pretend to read as I watch Flora grab a gray leather jacket off the back of her desk chair, throwing it on over the sweater and jeans she'd changed into earlier. Then she slips her arm through Seb's, and off they go, the door closing behind them.

I heave a sigh of relief and toss the book to the side, turning my attention back to my laptop. Maybe I'll just reply with a "hi," too. Or I could message Lee and ask what he thinks. That's what I'll do.

I open a separate message to text Lee, but there's something niggling in the back of my mind, and, after a sec, I realize it's a Friendship Alarm.

Saks.

She might not even know Seb is here, and if I tell her that not only was he here, but he came to my room and invited me on a night out, she might never forgive me. Plus I owe her after she came to my rescue today.

Ugh.

I only hesitate for a second before closing the laptop.

Rolling my eyes at myself, I groan and step out into the hallway. "Hey!" I call out, and Flora and Seb turn, almost at the exact same time. I wonder if they've practiced that, stunning people with the gorgeousness of their faces.

"I, uh. I think I'll come after all," I say, and then shooting for the ultimate in casual, I prop one hand on my hip. "Is it okay if I invite Sakshi?"

"Saks Worthington?" Seb asks, his face splitting with a lazy grin. "Absolutely."

Flora raises her eyebrows. "Wait, you and Sakshi are actually friends? I just assumed she'd adopted you as one of her charity cases."

Lovely. "Believe it or not, real friends," I reply, not even rising to that bait. "So can I bring her?"

Flora glances at her brother. "Seb—" she starts, but he grabs her shoulders, shaking her slightly.

"The more the merrier, sister of mine!"

Flora's upper lip curls a little, but she glances over at me and, with a shrug, finally mutters, "Whatever."

That's all the permission I need, and I scoot past the royal siblings to jog down to the second floor.

Sakshi opens the door on my second knock, her hair scraped back from her face, a sheet mask on. "Millie!" she exclaims. "What—"

"*Sebishereandwantstogoout,*" I say in a rush, but, thank god, after just a week of friendship, Saks can interpret Nervous Millie.

Holding one finger out in my face, she says, "Twenty. Seconds."

The door slams, and I stand there on the other side, gaping at the wood because there is no *way*—

The door flies open again, and there stands Saks, wearing a perfect pair of jeans, a T-shirt just short enough to expose her toned stomach, and no sheet mask in sight. In fact, she appears to be—

"How did you get a full face of makeup on that fast?" I ask wonderingly, and Sakshi brushes me off.

"Practice. Now where is he?"

"Where is who?"

We turn to see Perry standing in the hall, two pastries in his hand. Honestly, I don't know how Perry is so thin, given that he eats everything in sight, but now he brushes the crumbs off his jumper—I've learned that's what they call sweaters here—and stares at me and Saks.

"Seb," Saks tells him. "Seb is here with Flora, and they're going into the village for drinks."

Looking around him, Perry mutters, "Well, I'm coming, too, then," before stuffing his pastries into a potted plant.

One hand on her hip, Sakshi gives him a look. "If you screw this up for me, Peregrine . . ."

He lifts both hands, palms out. "Who's screwing up? I want to hang with royalty, that's all."

I'm not sure Perry's presence will be as welcome as Sakshi's, but I nod, gesturing at both of them. "Great, great, we're all living how the other half lives tonight. Now can we go?"

Seb and Flora are waiting by the front door, and I have a feeling that if we'd been even ten seconds later, Flora would've pulled him out and left us behind already, but Seb grins at both me and Saks, and even offers his hand to Perry.

"Fowler, isn't it?" he asks, and Perry turns pink, nodding enthusiastically.

"Yeah, yeah. Fowler. That's me!" When Seb turns back to Flora, Perry gapes at me and Sakshi. "He knows my name!"

"You are so sad," Saks replies, following Seb and Flora outside.

There are two cars parked in the drive, a shiny Land Rover and a tiny but very expensive-looking sports car. There are boys in the Land Rover, leaning out the window. One has hair nearly as red as Perry's, and he waves as we approach. "Flo!" he calls out, and I dart a glance over at Flora. Surely she's not okay with people calling her Flo? Flora is such a—

"Gilly!" She waves, smiling broadly, then drops Seb's arm to jog over to the Land Rover, her ponytail swinging.

Okay, so maybe she's a little more laid-back than I thought.

The boy hanging out the window hugs her, while the dark-haired boys in the back cheer, "Flo!"

"Listen, mates," Seb tells them, striding forward, his hands in his pockets. "You go on to the pub, grab that booth I like. I'll drive this lot."

He jerks his thumb at all of us, and I lean forward to ask Saks, "Are we going to get in trouble for this? Leaving school grounds?"

Perry answers me. "As long as we're not skipping class, and we don't go any farther than the village, it's fine for anyone in Year 13. Part of the whole Gregorstoun experience. Learning to make responsible choices."

I'm not sure cramming into the back seat of Seb's tiny sports car counts as "responsible," but that's what I find myself doing, wedged in with Perry and Saks as Flora takes the passenger seat.

I have a vague memory of passing through the village on my way to the school, but to be honest, that day my mind was mostly full of the bee-buzz of panic and nerves, so I'd barely registered it. Driving down now, shoved in the back of Seb's tiny car, I have a little more time to admire it.

The school sits uphill from the rest of Dungregor, the village itself nestled in a valley, which makes all the little shops and buildings lining the main road particularly charming and cozy. Like a little jewel box of a town, tucked away from the rest of the world.

It's late afternoon, and the light is a soft golden color, sliding over the steep hills. There's a little bit of snow just at the top of the highest peaks, and I remember that it won't be too long before I'm in those hills, on the Challenge.

Seb sighs. "Christ, this place is grim," he mutters. "I always forget."

In the passenger seat, Flora twists to look at him. "Missing it already, Sebby?" she asks sweetly, and he snorts.

"The only thing I miss about Gregorstoun is that I wasn't under Mummy's nose when I was up here."

That makes Flora smirk, and she turns to face the road again.

"Well, if you hadn't been such a prat, you wouldn't have been summoned home."

Sakshi is pressed up tight against my left, her knees practically to her ears because this car was not built for Glamazons, and she nudges me with her elbow, giving me a significant look.

But since I have no idea what that look means, its significance is totally lost on me, and Sakshi gives me that vaguely pitying smile I've seen every time I reinforce her idea of me as the Clueless Colonist.

Patting my knee, she mouths, *We'll talk later.*

Really looking forward to that.

I try to go back to looking at the village, but now Perry is piping up from Sakshi's other side. "I went to St. Edmund's for a bit," he offers. "But Mum thought they were too soft on me, so I got sent to Gregorstoun a few years back."

Seb meets his eyes in the rearview mirror, one side of his mouth kicking up in a smile. He and Flora really don't look that much alike, but that smile? That is for sure a Flora smile, one I've seen curl and twist on her face multiple times in the past few weeks.

"Gregorstoun must have been a whole new world for you, then, mate," Seb drawls, and Perry's cheeks flame red as he gives an awkward chuckle.

"Yeah, yeah, sure," he says, Perry's attempt at Laddish Camaraderie, I guess.

Flora turns to her brother to ask him something, and as she does, Perry leans across Sakshi's acres of leg to hiss, "Bloody hell, I'm *straight*, and that's twice he made me blush. He must be a menace to girls."

I roll my lips together to keep from laughing, more at Perry's vaguely scandalized expression than the idea of Seb as a menace, but Sakshi just looks confused.

"Wait, you're straight?" she asks, and Perry sits up, his eyes darting to the front seat.

Flora and Seb are still talking, surrounded in that bubble I've seen Flora create before where she can pretend we lesser mortals don't exist.

"Yeah," Perry says in a low voice. "Wait, you didn't think I was? Saks, we've known each other since we were *five*. How could you not know that?"

Sakshi gives an elegant shrug. "It's hard to tell with you lot, to be honest."

"My lot?" Perry repeats, aghast, and Sakshi waves her hand.

"You know. Pale weedy aristocrats."

"Weedy?" Perry is about to literally choke on his outrage now, but the car is mercifully pulling into a spot just in front of the biggest of the white buildings we've passed, a place with THE RAMSAY ARMS painted in bold brown letters on one side.

Seb opens his door and steps out, then turns to fold the front seat forward, offering me his hand with a "Milady."

I blush as I put my palm against his, allowing him to help me out of the car.

"Thanks," I mutter, and he gives me a wink before leaning against the open car door, elbow cocked.

He really is just . . . ridiculously good-looking, and when I glance over at the other side of the car, I see Sakshi already on the sidewalk, practically melting as she stares at him.

Perry is next to her, his face still red, his arms folded tightly over his chest. "So are we going in, or are we standing here while Google Earth grabs pictures?" he asks, nodding at Seb, and Sakshi elbows him hard in the ribs.

"Peregrine!" I hear her say, which is how I know it's serious—she doesn't use his full name except in cases of emergency.

Perry scowls, rubbing the spot, then shoots Seb another dark look.

But Seb only flashes me another smile. "Shall we, Roomie Quint?" he asks, offering me his arm, and after a beat, I take it.

CHAPTER 13

"MY NAME IS ACTUALLY MILLIE," I TELL HIM AS WE walk toward the pub. "Flora just calls me by my last name because—"

"Because she's trying to keep you at a distance," he finishes. "Classic Flo. No one gets to be her friend until they've jumped through roughly a hundred rings, most of them on fire."

"That is not . . . even remotely what I was going to say," I tell him, glancing toward Flora.

She's sashaying toward the pub. There really is no other word for the sway she puts into her hips, or the careless way she leads, knowing we'll all follow.

And then I realize I'm basically staring at Flora, and shake myself out of it, focusing on the ornate wooden door in front of me.

The pub is basically everything I've ever imagined a Scottish pub would be—and believe me, I have spent a lot of time imagining Scottish pubs. I have a Pinterest board and everything.

There's a dark carpet, pattern too faint to make out after so much time (and, I'm guessing, so many feet and spilled pints), cozy booths, and a bunch of mirrors that also act as whisky and beer ads, the brands painted around the frames in chipped paint. I also spot a few paintings of the Highlands, complete with stags and the occasional kilted dude.

But I barely have time to take it all in because Saks is already pushing me toward a circular booth in the corner while simultaneously pointing Perry toward the bar.

"Get the first round," she hisses at him, and Perry scowls.

"Why do I have to do it?" he whispers back. "They're the rich ones. Well, the rich*er* ones."

"Perry!"

I'm not sure exactly what it is about just saying his name like that that's so effective on Perry, but he sighs and heads for the bar as instructed.

"I'll have a soda!" I call after him, but I don't think he's listening.

The boys who accompanied Seb to Gregorstoun are already in the booth. Well, the blond guy is. The other two dark-haired guys, who look like twins, are playing darts, and Saks and I slide in. Flora and Seb sit on either side of all of us, like royal bookends.

Clearing her throat, Saks leans forward a little, tilting her head down. "So, Seb," she says, "do you miss Gregorstoun?"

He grins at her. "Not particularly, but then, the scenery wasn't as lovely when I was here."

Sakshi smiles back, playing with her hair, and Perry chooses that moment to come back to the table, somehow managing to hold multiple glasses at once. Must be a skill they teach boys up here.

"Millie," he says to me, and I take the glass of soda from his hands. Apparently he heard me, because everyone else has a beer. Well, everyone but Saks, who has a pear cider, the sweet smell wafting over to me as she spins her glass in her hands.

Seb takes a swallow of his beer and cringes. "Jesus, mate, what is this?" he asks.

Perry slumps into the booth. "Local specialty, they said."

"Sheep piss?" Seb asks, then shakes his head, getting out of the booth. "Going to see if they have a Stella or something."

As he walks off to the bar, I watch Saks watch him, a glint in her eye.

"He doesn't seem like quite as much a mess as he once was?" she offers, and Flora snorts, picking up her own glass of dark beer.

"He's just getting better at hiding it," she says, and Saks gives a cheerful shrug.

"In any case, still worth a shot. And then," she adds, patting my hand, "we'll find you a cute local boy." She winks, long eyelashes fluttering. "Haven't you always wanted to learn what's under a Scotsman's kilt?"

I turn my glass of lukewarm soda around in my hands, giving Saks a weak smile. "Intriguing as solving that mystery might be, I am actually not interested in dating anyone right now."

"She didn't say dating," Flora pipes up, leaning forward so that her jumper falls off her shoulder, revealing a hot pink bra strap. "But there's no harm in sampling the local wares on a more casual basis, Quint. Live a little."

I fight the urge to glare at Flora, because I feel like I do that so much, my face might get stuck that way. Instead, I say, "Not interested in sampling, either. I just broke up with someone."

Technically, Jude and I didn't break up, since we technically never "went out," but it's the easiest way to explain what happened between us.

Hi?

I can still see it sitting there on my laptop, but I push the thought away.

These people don't need to know all about that sad story. I'm just hoping it's an acceptable excuse for enjoying my soda in peace and quiet rather than playing Tumble in the Heather with some random local.

But Saks makes an exaggerated sad face at me, corners of her mouth turning down, lower lip poking out. On anyone else, I'd think she was making fun of me, but everything Saks does is a little outsized, so this seems sincere.

"Poor lamb," she says, patting my hand again. "What was his name?"

Ah. Here we go. I did spend some time thinking of this moment before I ever left for Scotland. How I was going to talk to people about the whole bi thing. I wasn't out or in in Texas, really. I mean, Lee and Darcy knew, Jude obviously knew, but it wasn't a thing that had come up. Before the whole thing with Jude, I'd only dated a couple of boys before, Matt Lawrence freshman year (for a whole two months), and Diego Lopez my sophomore year (*four* whole months). But in Scotland, I decided that if it came up, I was going to honest about it. Casual, even. Like this was my chance to fully start being me, I guess.

So I just shrug. "*Her* name was Jude," I say, and Flora's gaze flicks over to me for a second before she goes back to studying the other patrons with that carefully schooled bored expression she's so good at.

"Oh, so when you do decide to get back out there, we need to find you a lass instead of a lad, understood." Saks is cheerful now, grinning as she sits up, and I can't help but laugh a little as I shake my head.

"Lads are good, too," I tell her. "I am pro both lads and lasses in the general sense, but not interested in either at the moment. I came here for school, not romance."

"You can do both, you know." Flora again. She's leaning back against the booth, arms folded over her chest. "Last time I checked, Gregorstoun wasn't a nunnery."

"It might as well be," Saks says, looking back over at Seb, who's still standing by the bar. There's a blond girl next to him now, and as we watch, Seb leans against the bar, giving her a grin so potent it should be classified as a weapon.

Flora follows her gaze and then snorts as she lifts her pint to her lips. "You can do far better than my brother," she says once she's drained about a third of the glass. Impressive, and also very unprincesslike.

"Better than a prince?" Saks scoffs, and Flora nods.

"Better than a prince who's a git, yes. I adore Seb, obviously, but I wouldn't wish him on any woman."

Someone has turned on music in the pub now, and an old Kylie Minogue song drifts through the darkened pub.

I take a sip of my soda, wondering when we can leave, when a boy suddenly appears at our booth.

Looking at me.

He's cute enough, with dark hair flopping over his brow, and he offers a hand to me. "Wanna dance?"

I glance around.

Surely he can't mean me? I'm sitting at a table with two goddesses, but me, the short brunette wearing a DON'T TAKE ME FOR GRANITE! T-shirt is the one he wants to dance with?

I give him an awkward smile, shaking my head. "No, thank you."

But apparently they don't give up easy up here, because he reaches out to take my arm. "You sure?"

"Fairly sure!" I reply, glancing around me. Saks and Perry are talking to each other in low voices, completely oblivious to what's going on, and Flora is just watching, probably because she's bored.

"C'mon, luv," the boy cajoles, and I'm just about to get up because honestly, at this point, dancing with him might be easier than continuing to argue, but to my surprise, Flora leans across the table.

"Is 'no' some kind of foreign concept here in Sheep Shagger Land?"

She asks the question with wide eyes and a sort of feigned curiosity, but there's a bite behind the words and a glint in her gaze that the boy clearly sees, too. His face flushes, red blotches suddenly springing up on his cheeks.

Taking his hand off my arm, he steps back. "Easy, darling," he says, palms out. "I was only asking her for a dance."

"Right, but you kept asking after she'd said no, which is, I suppose, where my confusion comes in."

"Flora," I say, but now Seb's friends are looking over, both the dark-haired guys and the blond, Gilly, and there's this . . . spark in their eyes I don't like.

"I don't want any trouble," the boy says, and now he's also seen Seb's friends.

But it's Flora I watch, her lips curling as she says, "Then you picked the wrong people to mess with, mate."

With that, she puts two fingers in her mouth and makes the most piercing whistle I've ever heard. I wince, shoulders going up to my ears, and my eyes go to the door. Weird as it sounds, I'm almost wondering if some kind of Royal Guard Dogs are going to burst in, dragging this unfortunate boy away. Wolf-hounds, maybe.

But the whistle isn't summoning trouble of the canine variety. Instead, all three of Seb's friends suddenly present themselves. They all have slightly flushed faces, and they're all definitely a little more rumpled than they were when we first came in.

At the bar, I see Seb glance over, and his lips purse with dis-taste for just a second before he gives a shrug, tosses back the rest of his beer, and then . . . bops the blonde on the tip of her nose with his index finger.

Instead of snatching his finger off like she should so obvi-ously do, the blonde actually giggles, shifting her weight and tilting her head so that her hair swings in front of her face just so.

"Oh, for heaven's sake," Saks mutters, watching them, but then Seb is swaggering over, hands in his pockets.

"Seriously?" he asks, nodding at the boy. "Just one bloke?"

"He was bothering us," Flora says, and I look back and forth between the two of them.

"He really wasn't—" I start to say, but Gilly cuts me off.

"Four to one, it's just not sporting, Flo."

"Indeed," one of the dark-haired boys says. "This seems beneath us."

Thoroughly confused now, I look around the table. "Wait, what are we talking about?"

But again, I might as well not even be here. "Beneath you?" Flora echoes. "Dons, you're banned from the Balmoral Hotel because you tried to fly your underwear from the flagpole."

"I did not try," Dons replies with all the solemnity he can muster. "I succeeded. Or came near enough. Spiffy was there, and—"

"I'm sorry, can I just go now?" the guy who started all this asks, jerking his thumb back toward his table. "Because I deeply regret coming over here." He gestures at me. "No offense, but you're not even that hot."

"So much offense?" I reply, and both Flora and Sakshi scowl at the guy, Flora's fingers tightening around her pint glass.

Almost as one, Spiffy, Dons, Gilly, and Seb look where the guy is pointing.

"Ah, you've got mates!" Gilly says happily, clapping his hands together. "Well, in that case . . ."

And with that, he throws a punch.

The guy staggers back, his drink crashing to the floor, and the other guys at his table all shoot to their feet while Seb and his friends grin.

Seb even throws me another wink. "Sorry about this, love," he says, and then there is a full-on fight happening.

The dude has rallied from Gilly's admittedly pretty weak punch, and he grabs Spiffy around the middle, pushing him into an empty table as the bartender squawks.

"Oh god," Perry whimpers, while Sakshi starts pushing at me.

"Quick, we have to get out of here!" she cries. "Before someone gets their phone out!"

I feel like I just tipped straight into Crazytown, and I stare at Saks, baffled. "Someone should get their phone out," I tell her, "and call the freaking cops."

But Saks just keeps pushing at me. "No, they're going to take pictures, you ninny!"

On the other side of the pub, Spiffy is trying to yank a set of decorative bagpipes off the wall while Seb may be the first man I've ever seen attempt to use a cardboard coaster as a weapon.

I turn to Sakshi, gaping. "*That's* your major concern right now?"

"Quint!"

I twist in my seat to look at Flora on the other side of Saks, and she's lifted her pint glass, grinning, her eyes nearly sparkling.

Then her arm goes back, empty pint glass cocked.

"Duck."

Oh, look, another day, another mess from Prince Sebastian of Scotland. Honestly, why don't they just keep him locked up in a tower room in one of their five billion castles? Isn't that what these royal types do? Anyway, here are the blurry shots of Seb punching some poor pleb who probably made the mistake of lifting his eyes to the royal visage. Note Princess Flora over there on the right, throwing what looks like a pint glass. Maybe they should get adjoining tower rooms, only be taken out for special occasions. They can take Peregrine Fowler with them. He's the ginger bloke in picture number three, cowering under the table. Second son of the Earl of WhoTheEffCares, Gregorstoun student, and wannabe Royal Wrecker, if you ask me. Pretty sure that's the Duke of Alcott's daughter with her hands over her face, but no idea who the other girl is.

("Quelle Surprise," from *Off with Their Heads*)

CHAPTER **14**

THE FACT THAT WE'RE HAVING THE MEETING IN THE chapel and not Dr. McKee's office seems . . . less than great.

I haven't been in Dr. McKee's office on the ground floor, but the one time I passed it and the door was open, it looked . . . cozy. And the scent of strong tea had wafted out the door.

The chapel smells like snuffed candles and furniture polish, which, I'm learning, is much less soothing.

The fight at the pub hadn't just been a local village scandal, but apparently made it into the papers as well. I haven't bothered to look because the last thing I want to see is a blurry creeper shot of me cowering in the booth as punches and pint glasses were thrown. We'd made it back to the school okay, but the very next morning, Flora, Sakshi, Perry, and I had all had notices to meet Dr. McKee in the chapel.

Seb and his friends are long gone, of course, happily consequence-free, I bet.

Meanwhile, I've spent the entire morning trying not to throw up, visions of me being booted onto the next plane to Texas running through my head. How could I have been so stupid? I should've just stayed in my room.

Except, I remind myself, I did it for Saks. My folly was noble at least.

I turn to her now and whisper, "Guess the whole 'marry Seb' thing is out the window now, huh?"

To my surprise, Sakshi shakes her head. "No, but I realize now my plan will need some recalibrating."

"Right," I reply faintly before turning my attention back to Dr. McKee.

She's standing in front of the altar, her hands clasped, her shoulders straight, and next to me on the pew, Flora sighs.

"This is so dramatic," she says in a low voice. "So very like Mummy."

And that's when I realize this little meeting that I thought would just be with us and Dr. McKee is much bigger than I'd understood.

"Wait, 'Mummy'?" I ask Flora, my eyes going wide. "As in your mother? As in the queen of this freaking country?"

Turning to me, Flora raises an eyebrow. "Why do you think we're in here?" she asks. "This is the only part of the school that can be accessed without going through the rest. My mother hardly wants to advertise her presence."

Saks is sitting on the other side of me, and now she leans all the way across me to grab Flora's shoulder. "We're having a meeting with Her Majesty?"

Shrugging off her touch, Flora rolls her eyes. "She'll be here in a Mum capacity, not a royal one."

Sakshi's eyes are huge, and she looks down at her lap. "This isn't even my best uniform."

"All our uniforms are the same," Perry says, but Sakshi shakes her head.

"No, Perry, I have one for regular days and one that I had tailored to fit better. This isn't the tailored one, Perry. *This isn't the tailored one!*"

Before Sakshi can have a total breakdown, the side door to the chapel opens, and a woman walks in, trailed by two men in suits and sunglasses. Just behind them, there's a woman in a bright red suit and the highest, thinnest heels I've ever seen, tapping away on a tablet.

Saks, Perry, and I all scramble to our feet, but Flora stays slumped in the pew, her arms crossed over her chest.

Queen Clara looks a lot like Flora and not much like Seb. Same golden hair and whisky eyes, same way of looking at you like you smell bad.

I fight the urge to give myself a quick sniff check, and instead stand very still as the queen moves forward, holding out her hand to Dr. McKee.

The headmistress takes it, giving a quick curtsy that I try to memorize. One foot behind the other, a kind of quick up-and-down bob where she never bends at the waist but does lower her head. It comes naturally to Dr. McKee, but when the queen approaches me, my knees tremble so much that just standing feels like a challenge, never mind pulling off a freaking curtsy.

Honestly, I'm a little surprised to be this rattled. I've dealt with rich kids here for the past couple of weeks, made friends with two *very* rich kids, and my roommate is a princess. But they're still all just kids, like me. A queen, though? *That* shakes me up.

Perry bows his head. Sakshi executes a flawless curtsy, and while mine is nowhere near as good, I try my best.

Apparently my best is not that great because the queen's lips thin slightly as she gestures for us all to sit.

She stays exactly where she is, ramrod straight at the end of the pew.

"This is not what I had intended to do today, Flora," she finally says. "In fact, I had all sorts of plans, didn't I, Glynnis?"

The woman with the iPad glances up and scurries over, her footsteps tiny, probably because the skirt she's wearing doesn't allow for anything more. Everything about her is bundled up tight, from her killer suit to her intricate updo.

"The Royal Schedule did have to be rearranged some, yes, Your Majesty," she says. She smiles then, but it's not a nice smile, and at my side, I feel Flora tense up.

"Oh, what a shame," she says. "So sorry to have kept you from your usual Saturday of cutting ribbons and kissing babies, Mummy."

It's all I can do not to turn and gawk at her, but then, I guess Flora knows exactly how much she can get away with when it comes to her own mother.

The queen presses her lips together again, her hands folded in front of her. "Flora, one of the reasons we decided to send you to Gregorstoun was to curb some of your more . . . irrational behavior."

"You sent me here as punishment," Flora counters, and the

queen sighs, just the littlest bit. It's weird to think that in addition to running a country and being a ruler, she's also just . . . a mom. A mom dealing with a daughter who doesn't know how to stay out of trouble, I guess.

"I'm sorry you see it that way," she finally says. "But I assure you that was not my intent. However, with the wedding coming up—"

"Oh, is there a wedding coming up?" Flora asks, widening her eyes with fake surprise. "I haven't heard a thing about that. Has anyone alerted the media?"

The queen sucks in a deep breath. "Flora—"

"I'm not an idiot, Mummy," Flora says, sitting forward, her fingers curled around the edge of the pew. "The wedding is why I'm here. You want me out of the way until it's done."

"And if I do," Queen Clara counters, her voice suddenly gone hard, "can you blame me? After you've caused yet another scandal that's embarrassed us all?"

The silence that falls feels heavy and awkward, and even Glynnis looks up, a little crease between her brows. Next to me, Flora goes still, and I see her knuckles turn white where she's gripping the pew.

"No," she finally says. "I suppose not."

"What about Seb?" I blurt out, and everyone looks at me, the queen included.

My face flames hot, and I stammer out, "I—I mean, Prince Sebastian. Just. He did the actual punching and stuff."

"Sebastian is being dealt with," the queen says, "as are his foolish friends for allowing themselves to be . . . weaponized for your nonsense, Flora."

I wrinkle my nose at that, glancing over at Flora. "What does that—" I start, and then I remember. Flora and Seb's furtive conversation, her asking if all his friends were there. The way she whistled the boys over. Had she somehow engineered this whole thing?

"I, however, am not so foolish," the queen goes on. "And while I'm sure you thought this was a flawless plan to get yourself kicked out of Gregorstoun and sent back home, I have been your mother far too long to dance to your tune so easily, young lady."

Drawing herself up to her full height, the queen signals for Glynnis, who comes clicking over on her high heels.

"Dr. McKee has very graciously agreed with me that expulsion is hardly a fit punishment here," the queen says as Glynnis types away on her iPad. "In fact, expulsion is simply out of the question for you full stop, no matter what other schemes you may plan. You are at Gregorstoun for the remainder of the school year, and that is final. If, however, you decide to test me on this . . ."

A subtle flick of Queen Clara's fingers, and Glynnis is leaning over, the iPad offered to Flora, who's still sitting on the edge of the pew, doing her best to look bored.

That expression falls right off her face when she sees whatever is written on the iPad, though, and I lean a little closer, trying to read it myself, but Glynnis pulls it back before I can.

"You wouldn't," Flora finally says, and her mother gives Glynnis another one of those finger snaps.

"I would," she answers. "I will. A complete revocation of

royal titles and privileges until your twenty-first birthday. A bit fairy tale, perhaps, but desperate times call for desperate measures."

We all sit there, taking that in. Flora looks a little gray, and even Saks has gone somber and quiet. Personally, I don't know what "royal titles and privileges" entail, but it seems intense.

Clearing her throat, Dr. McKee signals for us all to stand. "Well, I think that sorts things out," she says.

But at that moment, Sakshi leans over me and Flora both, bobbing into another curtsy and saying, "Your Majesty, I'm not sure if you remember me, but I'm Lady Sakshi Worthington. My father is—"

"The Duke of Alcott," the queen replies, still holding herself stiff. "Yes, I'm aware. I had hoped you'd be a better influence on my daughter, Lady Sakshi, given what a role model your mother has always been. And yet here we are."

Sakshi's mouth opens and closes, and at her side, I see Perry tugging her back to her seat.

"No one influences me, Mummy," Flora says, throwing up her hands. "I'd think you would've at least worked that out by now." Then she shoots a look at Dr. McKee. "And now you have another fun thing to add to the recruitment materials—'visit the local pub where Princess Flora got into her thirty-fourth brawl!'"

With that parting shot, she sashays out of the chapel.

The queen gives a nod to Dr. McKee and then she and Glynnis head out as well, leaving me, Saks, and Perry with our headmistress. Now that the queen is gone and I don't feel as terrified, I step closer to Dr. McKee and ask, "Are we . . . in trouble?"

Am *I* in trouble is what I mean. As in Scholarship Trouble.

But Dr. McKee just takes a deep breath before patting my arm. "One of the most important lessons here at Gregorstoun is how to course-correct after making a mistake. You made a mistake yesterday, but I'd hope you have indeed learned from it."

I nod so hard it's a wonder my head doesn't go rolling off. "Oh, totally," I assure her. "Much learning. Course-correcting like a boss."

Dr. McKee smiles at that, but it's a little sad, and then she reaches out and pats my arm again. "And, Miss Quint?" she says. "Maybe be a little more selective in whom you call a friend."

I'm still thinking that over as I head back to our room. Did Dr. McKee mean Flora when she told me to be careful who my friends were? Because Flora and I are definitely not friends. We're barely acquaintances.

I open the door to find that acquaintance standing by her bed, pulling things out of a carryall with a fancy gold charm dangling from the handle, her back straight.

I'd left for the chapel before Flora, so I hadn't realized she'd already packed up. She must've been supremely confident that her plan was foolproof, and I can't help but scoff a little as I shake my head, making my way to my own bed. It's Saturday, and I have reading to catch up on.

And then I remember Jude's message on my laptop. With everything that happened, I totally forgot about it, and I look at my computer now, wondering if I should answer. But no, it's still early morning in America, and Jude never gets up before noon.

Later. I'll get to it later.

Flora turns, her eyes narrowed slightly. "Come to gloat?" she asks, and I bite back a sigh as I rummage through my desk for *The Mill on the Floss*.

"No," I tell her. "Trust me, I'd love it if your plan had worked out."

Book found, I look up at her, tucking my hair behind my ear with my free hand. "You didn't even care if we got in trouble, too, did you?"

Flora turns to her bag, taking out a framed picture and putting it back on top of the dresser. "You wouldn't have. You didn't, obviously."

"But you couldn't have known that," I argue, and Flora just sighs again before rummaging in her bag for something. She plucks out a roll of tape, the pretty kind used in crafts and scrapbooks, pink with little daisies on it.

Then, as I watch, she crosses the room to the dresser and peels off a long strip of the tape, neatly bisecting the top of the dresser into two halves—mine and hers.

"Do you want to put a line across the floor, too?" I ask, and Flora gives me a sickly-sweet smile.

"The thought had crossed my mind. Especially since it's clear we're together for the long haul."

I flop down on my bed, crossing my legs at the ankle. "You know, this place isn't so bad. I don't get why you hate it."

"Because my life isn't here," she replies, tossing the tape

onto her own bed. "My life is in Edinburgh with my family and my friends, and people I actually enjoy spending time with. My brother is getting married in three months, and I should be there, not . . . not hidden away up here like an embarrassing relation."

Put that way, I get why she might be a little pissed, and I open my mouth to say so, but before I can, she mutters, "This is boring. I'm going to go see what Caroline is doing."

And for the second time that day, I watch Flora flounce away.

CHAPTER **15**

"THIS SEEMS BAD."

Saks, Perry, and I stand outside on Monday morning, huddled together against the chill. Normally, this is when we do our laps, but this morning, we've all been told to gather on the shores of the loch behind the school.

There are a bunch of brightly colored wooden boats on the beach there, oars balanced across them, and I have an idea of what today's physical fitness is going to look like.

Sure enough, Dr. McKee comes to stand in front of us, dressed in a dull green tracksuit with the Gregorstoun crest over her heart. Her hair is pulled back in a high ponytail, and her cheeks are ruddy with the cold and, I think, excitement. A silver whistle dangles around her neck, and she's practically bouncing on the balls of her feet.

"Students!" she calls out. "This morning, we have a real treat for you!"

"This is not a treat," Saks says in a low voice, vaguely

mutinous. "Those boats are the opposite of treats, those boats are—"

"Tricks?" I supply, and Saks looks over at me, hugging her arms tight around her body.

"I was going to say 'turnips,' but yes, I see where tricks makes more sense."

"How did turnips make *any* sense?" I ask, but Saks is looking at Dr. McKee now, who's gesturing to the boats.

"As you know," she says, "the Challenge is merely a few weeks away. Consider this your warm-up. You'll be teaming up with your roommate, and whoever makes it across the loch and back first wins."

Ugh. Rowing a boat with Flora?

I look over to see where she is, and no surprise, she's standing between Caroline and Ilse, all three of them managing to make their own Gregorstoun tracksuits look better than they should.

Mr. McGregor steps forward then. He's wearing his usual uniform of heavy sweater and pants of an indeterminate color, his white hair bushy around his head, his beard looking especially dense this morning.

"And the winners of this race," he says, hefting up an ornate wooden box, "will receive *these*."

He flips up the latch to reveal—

"Antique dueling pistols handed down the McGregor family for over—"

"Ohhhh no," Dr. McKee says, moving forward with her hand outstretched. "No, no, no, no one is winning those, Mr. McGregor, despite their . . . obvious value."

Mr. McGregor's eyebrows take on a life of their own as he

scowls at her, but he closes the box with only a little bit of grumbling.

"No, the winners," Dr. McKee says to all of us in a louder voice, "will receive a free dinner at the Bayview Inn restaurant in the village."

"The pistols are probably less deadly," Perry mutters next to me.

I have no desire to win a dinner out *or* a pair of antique pistols, but I like to win on principle, so I'm practically rubbing my hands together in anticipation as Mr. McGregor hands us all ancient life jackets and directs us to the boats along the shore.

Flora flops down into ours without a second look at me, sitting on the bench with her chin in her hands as she looks around.

"Do you want to lend a hand?" I ask her.

"Not really," she replies, and I bite back a lot of comments to that, concentrating instead on shoving us out from the shore.

We were told to wear our galoshes today, and I did, but I can still feel the bite of the cold water through the rubber as I step into the loch.

Jumping into the boat, I situate myself on the bench, taking up my oars while Flora's still dangle in the rowlocks.

Apparently, I'll be rowing us on my own.

And that's fine with me. Boats are not exactly my specialty, but I'm strong enough, and the water is flat and smooth as we glide across it. I feel my spirits lift a bit as I take a deep breath, smelling the mineral scent of the loch, the freshness of the breeze, the—

"You're making the singing face again."

I scowl at Flora, the moment ruined. Out of the corner of my eye, I see a boat passing us, and I row a little harder.

"Can I ask you a question and get a serious answer?" I ask Flora even as I yank the oars with all my might.

On the other side of the boat, Flora rests her chin in her hand again. "Probably not."

That's honest at least.

I pull on the oars, the wood creaking, and our boat barely inches across the lake. The wind has picked up, whipping tiny waves that set us rocking, and suddenly the water just under us seems very dark and forbidding and possibly filled with monsters.

So I take my eyes off that, and put them back on Flora to ask, "What exactly have I done to make you dislike me so much? Other than the Veruca Salt thing, which, given the way you were acting that morning, was fair."

"I don't dislike you," Flora says with a shrug, her giant sunglasses still covering half her face. She's got the collar of her shirt turned up underneath her Gregorstoun-issue sweater vest. Her dull orange life jacket is just a little too big, and her long hair blows in the breeze as I attempt to row us.

"You could've fooled me," I reply, and Flora sighs, leaning back in the boat, her legs stretched out in front of her.

"I just say whatever comes to mind," she says. "Sometimes it's nice, sometimes it's not so nice. Depends, really. You shouldn't take it personally."

I gape at her, the oars still in the water. "So the other day, when you asked if I was going to start crying or singing, that wasn't personal?"

"I genuinely thought you might start crying or singing." Another shrug, this one a lazy, barely-there lift of the shoulders.

"Saying you thought Saks took me on as a 'charity case'?"

"She's always finding someone who's not exactly in her set to befriend. She's practically famous for it. And while you're not truly tragic, you're *not* an aristocrat, so . . ."

I give the oars another yank.

"Okay, how about how you refuse to call me by my name?"

"Quint *is* your name, is it not?"

"It is, b-but—" I start to splutter, then, rolling my eyes, I heft the oars again. "Okay, fine. So none of those things are mean in your view. And I guess having your friends gang up on me in the hallway was also some kind of—"

"What friends?" Flora says, sitting up.

I nod across the lake to where Caroline and Ilse are lazily rowing their boat, clearly not interested in a dinner at the Bay-view Inn.

Flora follows my gaze, squinting across the water. "Caro and Il?" She snorts. "Hardly friends, darling."

"You hang out with them all the time," I remind her, and she tosses her hair over her shoulders, fixing me with a look.

"Are *you* friends with everyone you hang out with?" she asks with a raised eyebrow and a smirk.

I stare at her. "Yes?"

Another scoffing sound, and then she's picking up the oars and sliding them into the water.

She pulls hard, and to my shock, the boat lurches in the water, shooting ahead of Saks and Elisabeth, who are next to us and starting to go in circles.

Actually, as I look across the lake, I see that . . . everyone is struggling. Saks and Elisabeth aren't the only people spinning around aimlessly, and I can see Perry sort of slapping at the water with his oar while Dougal, slouched low in the boat, is clearly texting.

On the other side, there are three boats that aren't moving at all, and when I glance over my shoulder at the shore, I can see Mr. McGregor with his hands cupped around his mouth, shouting something unintelligible at all of us. Maybe encouragement, maybe insults, who can say? We can't hear him over the wind.

Flora keeps rowing, leaning one way, then the other, her movements surprisingly graceful and fluid. Not to mention *strong*. We're really moving through the water now.

Grimacing, she looks over the top of her sunglasses at me. "Want to lend a hand, Quint?"

"Right," I reply, picking my oars back up. The sensation of facing backward makes my stomach lurch a bit, but I row and listen to Flora's instructions, and soon we're at Caroline and Ilse's boat.

I hear Flora drop her oars as the boats bump into each other, sending both rocking on the choppy water, and I turn around to face her and the other girls.

Caroline and Ilse both smile brightly at Flora. "Hiiiii, Flo," they singsong nearly in unison, and Flora smiles back just as cheerfully.

"Hiya, ladies!" she trills, and then, to my horror, she stands up.

"Flora!" I nearly shriek as the boat rocks again, harder this time, but she's got her feet firmly planted, hands on her hips as she stares down at Caroline and Ilse.

"So quick question, my loves," she says, still grinning, but I remember this look from the pub and know that nothing good is coming. "Did you two attempt to bully Quint here?"

The smiles fade from their faces, and Caroline looks over at me as I crouch lower in the boat, trying to tug at the hem of Flora's sweater. "Sit! Down!" I hiss at her, but she just bats at my hand and stays right where she is.

"Hardly bullying, darling," Ilse says. "Just a reminder that she's taking the place of someone . . . more deserving, let's say."

I can't see Flora's eyes beneath her sunglasses, but I can imagine them narrowing. "Who—Rose?" she asks, then laughs. "Please. Rose Haddon-Waverly should be thanking her lucky stars she missed out on being sent here. And in any case, it's not Quint's fault she's smarter than Rose. Granted, my mother's dachshund is smarter than Rose, but the point stands."

Both Ilse and Caro are frowning now, shooting looks between me and Flora, and I slouch more deeply into my life jacket, the sides rubbing my ears, the smell of slightly mildewed vinyl heavy in my nose.

"You don't like Millie either," Caroline blurts out. "You said she was boring and only cares about studying."

That stings a bit, but Flora only shakes it off. "Those things are just *true*," she replies. "They don't mean I don't like her."

"Seriously, you can keep saying that all you want, but it still doesn't make sense," I tell her, but Flora ignores me, keeping her gaze on Caroline and Ilse.

"Apologize to her," she says, and I'm not sure who looks more shocked, me or the other girls.

Ilse huffs out a laugh. "Darling, you can't be—"

"I am," Flora interrupts. "And don't call me darling. Tell Quint you're sorry you were nasty, and promise not to do it again."

"Oh, for heaven's sake," Caroline says, shifting on her little wooden bench. "You're being ridiculous, Flora. You can't *make* us do anything, you know. Princess or not."

Ilse is glancing around the lake now, tugging at the straps of her life jacket. "Caro—" she starts, but Flora and Caroline are still locked in their standoff.

"So you refuse to apologize?" Flora asks, and a muscle ticks in Caroline's jaw.

"Get bent, Flora," she practically spits out, and without missing a beat or dropping her smile, Flora lifts her foot from our boat and presses it down hard on the edge of Caroline and Ilse's.

Everything happens at once. The boat tips, the girls scream, *our* boat tips, and finally my fingers curl around the edge of Flora's shirt, yanking her back from the edge even as our own boat rocks hard from side to side.

Somehow, magically, we stay afloat.

Caroline and Ilse are not so lucky.

The force of Flora's nudge probably wasn't hard enough to tip them over, but their subsequent panic did the job, and both of them bob in the lake, shrieking, their boat upside down next to them.

Grinning, her cheeks pink, Flora shoves her sunglasses on top of her head. "Seb taught me that trick!" she tells me. "I can't believe it actually wor—"

A loud crack snaps through the air, and Flora and I both instinctively duck before looking back to the shore to see Mr. McGregor standing there, one of the antique pistols over his head, a thin trail of smoke spiraling out from it.

From the look on his face, I'm guessing the race is over.

CHAPTER 16

FLORA AND I ARE DECLARED THE LOSERS OF THE
boat race for "unsportsmanlike conduct," which, honestly, seems
pretty fair. We get off pretty easily as far as I'm concerned. No
stocks, no dungeon, not even detention. Our punishment is to
start arranging the gear for the Challenge, and since organizing
camping stuff is one of my favorite things to do, I don't mind.

We're alone, her and me, in our room, with a bunch of tents
and various pieces of equipment spread out in front of us. Our
job is to start putting them in bunches of separate packs.

"Have you ever done anything like this before?" I ask Flora.
It's night in our room, and since there isn't any overhead lighting, things are dim. Cozy, almost.

"What, gone camping?" she replies, picking up the compass
and frowning at it.

"Camping, hiking, gone outside generally . . ."

That earns me a scowl, and she tosses the compass back to
the floor, where it rattles against a bag of tent stakes. "I've gone
shooting."

"Do you see any guns here?" I sweep my hand over the supplies.

Sighing, Flora gets up from the floor, dusting her hands on the back of her skirt. "I don't see what the big deal is. It isn't as though we're going to be in the wilderness all that long. They wouldn't let us. The lawsuits if something happened to someone?" Snorting, she folds her arms over her chest. "This is all meant as a bit of show, a little 'oh, look what an interesting and progressive school we are!' they can put on the brochures alongside 'chosen educational institution of royalty.'"

I look up at her. She's standing by our door, her chin lifted, but there's more than just her usual snobbishness at play here.

"That really bugs you, doesn't it?" I ask. "Being part of the promo materials."

"What?" She glances down at me, pursing her lips slightly.

"It's just that's the second time you've mentioned them using your family as an advertising thing," I say, going back to counting out tent stakes. "So it's clear that bugs, and I get it."

Flora is still standing there with her arms crossed, but she's watching me with a weird look now. "Nothing bugs me," she finally says before turning back to her pile of gear, and I raise my eyebrows at her.

"Nothing?"

"Well, nothing save you at this moment, I suppose."

Ah, okay, we're back to the Flora I know and loathe. Shaking my head with a muttered "Whatever," I go back to arranging my own things into piles. A tent, six stakes, two compasses, two thermoses—

"And even if I were 'bugged,' which I am not," Flora suddenly says, "it isn't as though there's anything I could do about it. This is just . . . part of it."

"What?" I ask. "Being a prop?"

Flora still isn't looking at me, but her movements are jerky as she folds her own supplies. "Hardly a prop," she says. "It's simply that it's irritating and slightly tacky to have people wanting you to be a walking advertisement simply because of your family. I happen to think I'm an interesting person with or without a crown on my head."

Ah, so that's it. It's vanity. That's actually a relief, because for a second there, I had been dangerously close to feeling a little sorry for Flora.

The horror.

"What are some interesting things about you that have nothing to do with being a princess?" I ask, and she looks up from her stuff, eyes slightly narrowed.

"Are you baiting me?"

It's all I can do not to toss a tent stake at her. "No, I'm serious. Look, since we're roommates and about to be partners on this whole Challenge deal, we might as well try to get to know each other better. So please, enlighten me on the Things That Make You Interesting that aren't royal-related."

For a long moment, I think Flora is just going to ignore me and go back to packing. Which might be for the best, really. But instead, she sits back on her heels, hands braced on her thighs, and says, "I'm an excellent shot."

I raise my eyebrows. "Again with the gun talk? And okay, you can shoot clay pigeons or pheasants or . . . I don't know, stags, whatever, but would you ever have the opportunity to do that if you weren't royal?"

That perfect brow wrinkles again. "Well, I . . . I might have. And anyway, that was just the first thing that came to mind. I'm also very good at fashion. Knowing what goes with what, how colors can complement and contrast. Last year, I even predicted that floral would be big again, but not in the spring, in the autumn."

She looks so pleased with herself that it feels mean to snort, but I really can't help it. "Okay, so, again, would you have all this access to fashion and knowing what trends are going to hit if you didn't also have access to a ton of fashion designers because, you know . . . royal?"

Flora mutters a very rude word under her breath before shaking her head and picking up a rain guard. "I don't know why I even bother trying to impress you with my skills since you're so determined to see the worst in me anyway."

"Because literally all you've done is show me the worst," I remind her. "You're snobby, rude, and you nearly got me in a bar fight."

Rolling her eyes, Flora throws the shirt in her pile of things to pack. "Hardly a bar fight. Barely even a scuffle, really. You're exaggerating. And anyway, a thank-you would not go amiss here."

"A thank-you for . . ."

Flora looks up at me, lips pursed. "For defending your honor against that wanker? He kept asking you to dance after you'd said no. Completely inappropriate."

"Except that you were looking for some excuse to throw your brother and his friends into a fight so the school would kick you out."

"Wanting to get kicked out and helping you are not mutually exclusive," she replies with the arrogance that hundreds of years of royal breeding can give a person.

I can't help but laugh, shaking my head a little. "You are such a piece of work." Then I pick up another bag of tent stakes and toss it to her. "Put this with tent thirteen, please."

She does, making a fairly neat stack of things before gesturing for me to hand her another waterproof bag.

I do before saying, "Today wasn't another attempt at getting kicked out, was it?"

Flora doesn't look up, studiously stuffing a compass, first aid kit, and pair of hand warmers into the bag. "Course it wasn't. You heard Mummy. I can't get expelled, and if I try again, I lose royal privileges for a thousand years."

"I think it was four years, but yeah."

"So," Flora says, looking up at me with a bright smile, "you can rest assured my days of attempting to get expelled are firmly behind me."

I nod, but there's something about that smile—and the way it curls up when she thinks I'm not looking—that worries me.

In today's ROYALS: THEY'RE JUST LIKE US EXCEPT NOT AT ALL news, have you guys read up on this "Challenge" thing they do out at that scary boarding school Flora goes to? It's like Outward Bound, I guess, but they basically dump a bunch of posh kids in the middle of the Highlands and make them camp for two nights to, like, Commune with Nature and learn skills? Which seems stupid to me since it's not like these people are ever going to actually be in the wilds of anywhere except Hyde Park, but whatever, rich people, DO YOUR THING.

Mostly, I'm just going to be warmed from the inside at the thought of Princess Flora having to camp for forty-eight whole hours. WHAT IF HER HAIR GOES UNSHINY??? THE HORROR!!!!

("What the Whaaaaaaat?" from *Crown Town*)

CHAPTER **17**

THE MORNING THE CHALLENGE STARTS IS ACTUALLY
sunny.

Okay, "sunny" might be too generous a term, but it's not
raining, and the clouds aren't that thick, so as far as I'm concerned, it's sunny. Scotland Sunny.

And to tell the truth, I'm kind of excited. Okay, maybe a lot
excited.

Yes, having to do this with Flora is less than ideal, but finally
getting out into Scotland? Real Scotland? Not even the prospect
of two days alone with Flora can kill my buzz for that.

Although, as we stand in front of the school waiting to get
going, she's certainly doing her best.

"This is the stupidest thing I've ever had to do," she mutters
against the lip of a Styrofoam cup of tea. It steams in the cold
morning air, fogging up her giant sunglasses. From the neck up,
she's typical Flora—those sunglasses are Chanel, and her hair
has been pulled into a high ponytail, but the ends are curled, and
she's wearing makeup.

From the neck down, she's as hideous as the rest of us are. We've got these khaki pants and long-sleeved T-shirts covered with a heavy vest, our standard-issue Gregorstoun raincoats on top. There are a few more layers in our bags, but mostly, we all look like slightly bedraggled zookeepers.

Still, this is the best outfit for what we're doing, even if not everything fits great. The school didn't have Challenge uniforms for girls, after all, so we're all making do with hand-me-downs except for the boots. I brought my best pair from home, and I wiggle my toes in them now.

"The stupidest thing?" I ask Flora now. "I find that hard to believe."

I wait for the smart-ass remark, but instead, Flora just shrugs and says, "Fair point."

Narrowing my eyes at her, I shift my pack on my shoulders. "Are you sick?" I ask. "Or just freaked out about camping?"

"Neither, Quint," she replies, tossing out the rest of her tea on the gravel. It splashes a group of girls standing nearby. They give startled squawks of alarm, but when they see who threw the tea, they don't say anything.

Princess privilege, clearly.

Flora shoves her empty cup into one of the side pockets of her pack, so at least she's not adding littering to her list of sins.

There's a low rumble as five vans drive up, and on my other side, Sakshi shifts her weight from one foot to the other. "I still don't think this is necessary," she says. "I mean, I feel very self-reliant, and also very in touch with the world around me."

"At least you get to camp with Elisabeth," I say, nodding

toward her roommate. "I'm stuck with Flora, and Perry is with Dougal."

Perry's roommate looms over him, his shoulders so wide I'm surprised he can fit through doors. As we watch, Dougal punches Perry's shoulder companionably, and Perry is nearly knocked off his feet.

He grimaces, rubbing his arm even as he tries to smile at Dougal. Then he looks over at us.

Kill me, he mouths, and Sakshi turns back to me.

"You make good points, Millie."

We load up into the vans. The plan is that we'll be dropped off at prearranged spots several miles from each other. Prearranged by the school, I should say. We have no idea where we'll all be left, and as we rattle over the rough ground, I mutter to Sakshi, "Maybe we won't be far from each other. I mean, we've all got to run into each other at some point, right?"

Saks looks out the window. We're climbing a hill now, the sky still fairly blue overhead, the hills a mix of green, yellow, and gray from all the rock.

"Maybe?" she offers, and I lean past her to look at the series of valleys and dales stretching out below us. Suddenly, from up here, the school receding in the distance, I realize just how far out we really are. Maybe they *can* spread us far enough apart that we won't see each other until Monday.

My stomach starts to twist a little bit. For the first time, it hits me that I'm about to be dumped out in the middle of nowhere and am expected to make my way back to the school in one piece.

And I'll be doing it with Flora.

That's maybe the hardest part to swallow, the idea of me and Flora having to rough it, just the two of us. And from the way she's studying her nails next to me, clearly bored, I'm pretty sure the chances of me being eaten by a bear while she, like, checks her eyebrows in a compact mirror are now super high.

"Are there bears in Scotland?" I ask now, which really seems like something I should've been curious about *before* now, but oh well.

"Not for hundreds of years," Mr. McGregor assures me from up front, but then he starts muttering about his pistols again, so it seems possible he's lying, and oh my god, why did I want to come to Scotland in the first place?

We crest a ridge, and the view through the windshield makes me catch my breath. In front of us, a stony hill climbs into the sky, snow still dusting the top, and to the right, the land sweeps away into a valley. I can make out the glimmer of a stream, and with the sun actually shining, it's like something from a movie.

This, I remind myself. *This is why you're here.*

Mr. McGregor puts the Land Rover in park and nods out the window. "All right, Team A-9, this is your starting point. Up and out, lassies!"

Team A-9. That's me and Flora.

"Right," I say as Flora just sighs and opens her door, practically sliding out of the van.

"Let's get this over with," she mutters, and I bite back a comment about how that attitude certainly isn't going to get us very far.

The point of this whole thing is supposed to be for us to bond, after all, so I'm determined to at least be . . . okay, "nice" might be too strong, but "pleasant." That feels like the most I can strive for at this point.

As Mr. McGregor pulls our packs out of the back, Sakshi rolls down her window, gesturing me over. "*Courage, mon amie,*" she says, offering her crooked pinkie, and with a smile, I wrap my own pinkie around hers, giving it a shake.

"Same to you, Saks," I say. "See you on the other side."

Flora rolls her eyes as she pulls her expensive sunglasses from the top of her head.

"Oh, for heaven's sake," she drawls. "We're not going to war, it's just a wee camping trip."

She does have a point, much as it kills me to admit that, but as I look around, it's hard to see this as a "wee camping trip." The hills look higher than I'd thought, things seem awfully rugged, and as the van drives off, I'm reminded that for the next few hours, it's just me, Flora, and a whole bunch of Scottish wilderness.

That feels less than wee.

Clearing my throat, I turn, looking around me. I'd done camping with Dad, but always in campsites where the place we needed to put up the tent was clear. Also, most of those places had, you know, bathrooms and showers and stuff.

"I guess we should go ahead and start scouting out a spot?" I suggest, and to my surprise, Flora points farther down the hill.

"We should set up over there," she says. "On the other side of the water."

Down the rise, there's a fast-flowing stream, and on the other side, the ground does look flatter and maybe less rocky.

"Wow, that's . . . actually helpful," I say, smiling at Flora. "Good plan."

"Whatever," she says, readjusting her pack, and we head off in that direction. The wind is blowing, and it smells sweet from the grass with this faint mineral tang from the water ahead of us. I lift my face into it, watching clouds rush over the sky, smiling.

"Okay, this is awesome," I say, not caring that I'm wearing someone else's clothes and accompanied by someone who doesn't like me very much.

From behind me, Flora gives a grunt that might be agreement, might just be that camping has already begun to kill her.

I'm fine with either in this moment.

We get to the bottom of the hill, and a little of my *Sound of Music*–y joy leaves me when I see that the stream that looked so manageable from up higher is a lot bigger and faster than I'd thought.

It's also . . . brown. Not gross brown, don't get me wrong. This looks more like a river made of root beer, which is a cool idea, but it means that I can't really see the bottom, so I'm not sure how deep it is.

Already stymied by nature ten minutes in.

"There!" Flora calls out, pointing at some rocks that form an uneven and slippery path across the water. "We can cross there."

"We can *die* there," I reply, pushing my bangs out of my eyes. Flora is still wearing her sunglasses, her cheeks pink from the wind, a few strands of hair coming loose from her ponytail.

But she shakes her head. "No, I've crossed loads of streams

like these. They're never very deep, and as long as you take your time crossing, you shouldn't slip."

She holds out her hand. "Here, tell you what. I'll hold your pack while you cross."

I like the idea of attempting to cross without an unwieldy pack on my back, but I frown at Flora. "Then how will you get across?"

Flora shrugs. "I'm more used to this kind of thing than you may think. Like I said, I've gone on tons of shooting trips, and we haul gear a lot heavier than all this across rougher terrain. It's just a matter of balance, really."

She says it so confidently that I find myself shrugging off my pack. "If you're sure?"

Although I can't see her eyes behind her glasses, I assume she rolls them. "I'm sure I want this part of things to be over as quickly as possible, so hand me your stupid bag and cross the river."

She takes the pack from me, and I have to say, she doesn't even stagger under the weight. Maybe Flora is tougher than she looks.

So I grin at her. "Thanks!"

"Any day now, Quint," she replies, gesturing to the water.

My first step is not as steady as I'd like, my eyes on all that water rushing underneath me. But the second step is easier, and with my hands out to the side, I'm very glad I'm not carrying a bag like a turtle shell on my back.

I'm focused on my steps, and also on the wind, which seems to get louder, the sweeping sound of the river, and the opposite bank, so I'm not sure how long it takes me to cross. It feels like forever, but when my feet finally land on the slippery bank opposite, I'm smiling again. I clamber up a bit, putting the river behind me some before finding the steadier, flatter piece of ground Flora had first pointed out.

Turning to face Flora, I call out, "Your t—"

The words die in my throat.

Flora isn't on the opposite side of the river. She's on the bank, right behind me.

Grinning.

And our packs are nowhere in sight.

CHAPTER **18**

I SHOULD'VE KNOWN.

When Flora asked to hold my pack, I absolutely should've suspected something was up because *obviously*. In what universe would Flora be the sort of person who willingly holds someone else's stuff? But I told myself that maybe she was just trying to be nice, and now it's clear that that kind of thinking is going to be what gets me killed.

Awesome.

"Seriously, Flora," I say, panic beginning to climb up my throat. "Where are our packs?"

She jerks her thumb over her shoulder.

"In the river."

"The river," I repeat, and some little part of my brain is insisting that I must have misunderstood her, that there's no *way* she'd do something this stupid and reckless.

Then I remember who I'm talking to, and oh my god, all our stuff is absolutely in the river.

I look back down the incline toward the rushing water,

and I think, there in the distance, I can see something bobbing along that might be a pack? But even as I go to take after it—apparently thinking I can outrun a river—whatever it was disappears out of sight, and I stop there, my feet muddy, my breath sawing in and out of my lungs.

"That shite was heavy," Flora says. "They've probably sunk already."

I thrust my hands into my hair, pulling it slightly from my head like the sting will make me wake up from this nightmare where I'm trapped in the wilderness with *no supplies* and a brat of a princess, but no. It hurts a little, and I'm still very much awake.

"Why?" I ask, then shake my head. "Why am I even bothering asking that? *You* probably don't even know why you do the banana-pants things you do."

"Banana-pants?" Flora echoes. *Bah-naaah-naaah pahnts.*

"Crazy," I explain. "Insane. So freaking nuts it's hard to believe."

"Yes, I was able to use context clues to piece that together. I'd just never heard that saying before now. Banana-pants." White teeth flash in a broad grin. "God, that's useful!"

"You know what would be useful right now?" I counter. "Tents. A compass. Food. Water. All the things your *bah-naaah-naaah pahnts* ass threw in the river. Do you have any idea how cold it's going to get out here tonight?"

Flora rolls her eyes. "Honestly, Quint, give me some credit. This is a very carefully-thought-out plot. I lose our supplies in the river, and of course later say we were overtaken by the elements, that it was an accident, and one that never would've happened had the school been more careful. That's something you're going to agree with, by the way."

"I definitely am not," I reply, but Flora flicks that away with one move of her elegant hand.

"We're not even going to spend the night out here," Flora continues. "Because!" She reaches into her back pocket, pulling out her phone. "I am going to call for help and tell them what happened. Very tearfully of course."

Just like that, her face changes, corners of her mouth turning down, lips wobbling, eyes suddenly becoming huge and rather sparkly with fake tears. "Never been so frightened in all my life," she simpers. "One moment we were trying to cross the river, the next ev-everything was in the water, and we were so . . . so scared!"

I cross my arms over my chest, glaring at her. "I'm not doing that."

As quickly as it had come on, the whole Victorian Miss act is over, and she's regular Flora again, unruffled, slightly bored. Shrugging, she looks down at her phone.

"I'll just say you're processing the trauma in your own way."

I'm about to make *quite* the comeback to that, but then she frowns, studying the phone in her hand.

"I don't have a signal."

It's my turn to roll my eyes. "Of course you don't. We're in the middle of nowhere."

Her head snaps up, and for the first time, something like Genuine Human Emotion appears on Flora's face.

She's freaked out.

Which is good—she should be—and also terrifying because I'm not sure what a freaked-out Flora even looks like, really.

She's breathing a little faster now, her shoulders moving up and down, and I see her glance behind and below, like she's hoping our packs will just magically not be in the river anymore.

"So this plan is 'carefully thought out,'" I say, giving her the full finger-quotes thing, "and yet you didn't remember that there's no cell service?"

She scowls at that, then turns back to her phone. Maybe she thinks she can give it a royal command to suddenly work or something—who knows with her.

"I thought out the packs part, and I thought out the excuse part, but it's possible the technical aspects . . . eluded me," she says at last, and I have never wanted to throw a person off a mountain more than I want to throw her in this moment.

"The technical aspects?"

"Stop repeating everything I say!" Flora is glaring at me now, and I take a step back, hands raised.

"I know you're not getting attitude with me," I say. "I know that's not a thing that's happening, because that would be non-sensical, given that all of this is your fault."

"'Nonsensical,'" she snorts. "Honestly, Quint." Then she glances around her, pulling her lower lip between her teeth.

"All right, this is not an emergency. We aren't that far from the school, so we just have to . . . walk in that general di-rection until we get back to it. And we'll probably run into some of our schoolmates, anyway, and we can give them the

135

story about being stranded, so yes. Yes, I think this can all be salvaged—oh, dear."

She's looking over my shoulder, her face gone a little pale, and I freeze.

"What?" I ask, scared to look.

"Shhhh!" she instructs, waving a hand. "Just . . . keep your voice down. It's fine."

Her face and those wide eyes seem to say it's very not fine, and I can feel every hair on my body standing on end. "Is it a bear?" I whisper, and she shakes her head.

"Bears have been extinct in Scotland for—"

"*Hundreds of years, I know, and I do not want a history lesson right now!*" I hiss, and finally, unable to take it anymore, I turn.

And Flora's "oh, dear" makes a lot more sense.

CHAPTER 19

"DEER," I SAY THROUGH NUMB LIPS. "THAT'S WHAT
you meant. *Deer.*"

Because that's what's behind me. A *massive* deer with a
bunch of very pointy antlers, looking right at me.

Look, I am no stranger to wildlife. I am a Texas Girl, after
all. I've had a rattlesnake slither across my path on a walk before, my grandfather once pointed out a coyote on the edge of
his property, and I have seen more armadillos than any girl ever
should.

But it's the size of this thing that has my heart pounding and
my mouth dry with fear.

"It's not a deer," Flora says, "it's a *stag.*"

"Not really hung up on appropriate nomenclature right
now," I reply, my lips barely moving. "Mostly interested in not
getting impaled."

The stag huffs out a breath, and I tense up.

Then Flora moves into my peripheral vision, one hand outstretched.

"What are you doing?" I ask, which is hard because again, lips numb at this point with the terror and all.

"The stag is the national animal of Scotland," she tells me, moving forward very slowly, never taking her eyes off the animal in front of us. "And since I'm a princess . . ."

If I weren't so busy trying to will a wild animal not to kill me, I'd make a face at her. "What?" I ask. "You think this thing respects rank? Have you completely—"

"Shhhh!" she murmurs, still approaching the stag, which, I have to admit, isn't moving and is just kind of watching her.

"There's a reason this sort of thing happens in fairy tales," Flora goes on, and I can see a smile start to spread across her face. "The beast clearly knows that he and I are connected by our love of this land."

"That is the dumbest thing I've ever heard anyone say. I'm dumber for having heard it."

Flora waves her free hand at me. Her sunglasses are on top of her head now, those whisky-colored eyes narrowed as she approaches the stag. "It's working, though, isn't it?"

It is, I guess. The stag stays still, no more huffing breaths, and Flora straightens up a little. "There," she says, smug. "Now all we have to do—"

Without warning, the stag charges, and Flora and I both scream, stumbling backward. She pinwheels into my arms, I clutch at her, and the next few seconds are a blur of falling, the smell of a big animal, and then, the sudden cold as we tumble into the river.

The cold is so shocking it punches my breath right out of me, and my brain does a mad scramble of panic between *giant deer!* and *antlers!* And *omgomgsocoldsocoldalsowetwhywhywhy*, and *DROWNING!*

Except . . . not drowning.

I put my feet down and realize that where we landed in the water is only just over my knees. My whole body is wet, though, hair included, and when I look over, Flora is sitting in the shallower water by the bank, her knees up, hair a wet, bedraggled mess over her face, sunglasses hanging crookedly from one ear.

The stag is nowhere to be seen, and Flora reaches up to flick her wet hair out of her eyes, her chest heaving as she scans the landscape.

Then she says, "You know what? It's actually unicorns who are our national animal, not stags. Just remembered."

Teeth chattering, I glare at her. "Well, maybe one will turn up."

After we make our way out of the river, we start walking.

And walking.

I have no idea where we're headed, really, since I wasn't paying a huge amount of attention to our actual location on the drive up. Not that that would help, since I can't remember if the school is to the east or west of where we are now. Stupid, probably, but then I'd assumed I'd have a compass and a map, and also a tent, and also all the things you need to survive a camping trip.

We crest another hill, and Flora stops at my side, looking down at her muddy trousers.

"At least we now definitely look like we've been in distress," she says, and I whirl around on her.

"We *are* in distress."

The sun is slowly sinking down behind the clouds, and with the damp, it's like the cold is seeping even deeper into my skin. We're in the hills in the middle of nowhere, and oh my god, this is totally how I'm going to die, all because some spoiled princess wanted to get back at her mom.

"I thought you said you were done with trying to get kicked out," I say through chattering teeth.

"I am. Mummy was very clear that I couldn't be expelled. But!" She lifts one finger. "This isn't me causing trouble. This is the school not being a safe place for me."

She lowers her hand and shrugs. "Very different, obviously."

I swear, if Flora could use her brain for something other than cooking up various schemes, she'd probably rule the world, but I'm too angry to be impressed.

"Do you understand that this isn't just about you?" I ask her now, wrapping my arms around my body. Flora is standing just in front of me, and she wraps her arms around herself, too.

"Don't be so dramatic," she replies through all that shivering, and it's all I can do not to reach out and strangle her.

"Don't be dramatic?" I echo. "You're actually saying that to me? You, the girl who's willing to bring down a hundred-year-old institution just because she doesn't like living so far from home?"

Flora rolls her eyes, placing her hands on her hips. "All right, first of all, what do you even care? I'm the one with ancestors who went here. I'm the one whose family practically built this place."

"Then why are you trying to destroy it?" I counter. "Dr. McKee is perfectly nice, and she loves Gregorstoun. Or is she just more collateral damage in your nonstop acting out?"

"Now you sound like my brother," she mutters.

I snort. "Seb? He has his own medal in overly dramatic shenanigans, I'd guess."

Flora's pert nose wrinkles. "No, not Seb. Alex, my older brother. He's always going on about how I make things harder for myself, that I'm my own worst enemy. Complete tosh, of course."

"Actually that sounds very untosh to me," I reply. Then I frown. "If tosh means 'nonsense,' which I'm assuming it does."

There's this look Flora does, somewhere between a side-eye and a smirk, and I get it now. "You're picking up the slang at least," she says, and I shake my head, irritated.

"What I'm picking up is frostbite and probably tuberculosis or some other horrible disease."

Tipping her head back, Flora sighs at the sky, her arms out to her sides. "This cannot be the worst thing that's ever happened to you," she says before looking back at me. "I mean, that fringe alone should qualify before this little incident."

It takes me a second to work out that she's talking about my bangs, and when I do, I tug at my hair, scowling.

"Again, not really sure insults are the way to go here given this whole 'strand us in the wilderness and nearly kill us' thing you're currently responsible for."

Heaving yet another sigh, Flora spreads her jacket on the ground and sits on it. "We're not going to *die* here," she insists, crossing her legs. "At most, we'll give them a bit of a fright, Mummy will see this is not at *all* the sort of place where I belong, and then I'll be out of your hair."

She gives me a look out of the corner of her eye. "Isn't that what you want?"

Oh man, she has me there. No more Flora? A room all to myself, or heck, even a room with just a normal roommate who isn't always five seconds away from some imperious bullshit? That sounds amazing. No more Flora, and I could have the kind of experience at Gregorstoun that I'd been longing for. What I'd planned on when I left home.

But I don't think it's as simple as Flora is trying to make it out to be. In fact, I think this little stunt of hers will just make life harder for everyone at the school, so I don't break. Instead, I sit next to her, on the farthest edge away from her.

"I'm actually kind of getting used to you," I tell her. I'm striving for breeziness, but it's somewhat hampered by all the shivering and the fact that my nose has decided to rebel against the cold by getting deeply stuffed up.

"Oh, this is ridiculous," I hear Flora say, and I'm about to retort with a "Which part?" when she moves across the jacket, putting her arm around my shoulder and tugging me close.

CHAPTER 20

HER BODY IS JUST AS WET AND COLD AS MINE, BUT
it's still a little bit of a relief, the warmth of her against me, or
maybe just the shield against the wind.

How does she still smell good even after hiking, falling in a
river, and hiking some *more*?

Another princess privilege probably.

At least it's not raining, but we're still cold and wet and
stranded. The hills and rocks that looked so nice earlier are
seeming a little more threatening and foreign now that night is
falling, and I really, really hope a stag is the only wildlife we're
going to experience out here. They don't have wolves in Scotland anymore, do they?

"I am sorry you got mixed up in all this, Quint," Flora says
at last, and I look over at her, eyes wide.

"Are you actually apologizing for something?" I ask, and she
sighs, her body still tight against mine.

"I simply thought you deserved some kind of explanation.
It's nothing personal."

"Strangely uncomforting when I'm freezing my ass off in the middle of nowhere," I mutter, and Flora shifts next to me. When I look over, she's staring straight ahead.

Finally, she says, "It's not 'acting out,' like you said earlier. Not exactly."

I keep looking at her, even though the angle hurts my neck, and when she glances over at me, her face is so close I can see the light smattering of freckles across her nose.

"It was just very clear from very early on that I wasn't going to be the kind of princess people wanted. You know, the . . . sweet one. With the bows and the bluebirds and all that. I got angry at people too easily, I got bored too quickly. And if I couldn't be that kind of princess, I figured I might as well try to be another one altogether."

She says that like it's a normal thing to think. Like most people are aware of certain archetypes they have to be, and when they can't fit into one, they choose another.

"That's . . . insane," I tell her, and she rests her cheek on her shoulder as she studies me, damp hair swinging. Her lower lip is already starting to jut out, a deep vee between her brows.

"You don't have to pick some *type* to be," I continue, shifting on the rock. It's getting even colder, the wind downright whistling now like we're heroines in a Brontë novel, stuck out on the moors or something. "You can just be you."

Flora keeps staring at me, like she's waiting for something, and I flick my hair out of my eyes. "What?"

"Oh, I was just waiting for the musical number I was sure followed a statement like that," she says, and I look up at the sky, scooting a little farther away.

"Cool, be a jerk. Again. Some more."

To my surprise, that makes Flora laugh, and when I glance back at her, she's leaning on her hands, watching me. "God, you really believe all that, don't you?" she asks. "All that 'you can just be you.' How extraordinary."

"I feel like by 'extraordinary,' you mean 'stupid,' so I'm just going to ignore you now and try to go to sleep."

There's no way that's going to happen up here with rocks and moors all around us, my body temperature dipping way below normal, but if I sleep, I can disappear for a little bit, can pretend I'm not living in this nightmare where a snotty princess has stranded me in the middle of nowhere all as some elaborate act of rebellion against her parents. Who are a queen and a prince, for god's sake.

I lie there on that stupid, rocky ground, my pullover wrapped around me, and feel the anger bubble up in my chest again. I don't know much about Flora's parents, but she has two of them, right? Both alive, both rich, both who make sure she has the best of everything, no matter what she does. She doesn't even want to be here at Gregorstoun, whereas I spent *months* reading about it and researching it, then applying for every scholarship that exists. I think of those nights sitting up at my computer, working on essay after essay, and suddenly, sleep is the last thing on my mind.

"You're the worst, you know that?" I sit bolt upright, still clutching my jacket.

Flora had been sitting at the edge of the jacket, her arms wrapped around her knees, but now she looks over at me. "Pardon?"

God, that just makes me madder, that *paaaahdon?*

"You. Are. The. Worst," I enunciate, pointing at her. "What's so hard about your life? Oh, boo-hoo, you're missing a fashion show. Oh no, your parents want you to have a good and interesting education. What a shame, you have two of them, and they both care about you."

Flora turns more fully toward me, a weird look on her face.

"You . . . don't have two parents?"

Well, this is not a conversation I wanted to have tonight.

"No," I say, rolling back over.

It's quiet, the only sound the wind continuing its whole Wuthering Thing, and then Flora asks, "Which one?"

I don't know if she's asking which parent I have or which parent I lost. I don't actually care. I just say, "My mom died when I was little."

More silence.

Then: "How little?"

Sighing, I roll over onto my back, wincing as a rock digs into my spine. "Two."

Flora's voice sounds different when she says, "That's really quite little."

"It was."

I don't tell her anything else. How much it sucks to have a mom I can't even remember. How I love my dad more than I can say, how Anna is a great stepmom, but she came into our lives when I was already a teenager. How I think my relationship with Dad might be easier if he hadn't had to be All the Things to me for so long. Those are the kinds of things I haven't even been able to talk to my friends about, and Flora is very much *not* a friend. Maybe she's not totally an enemy, either, but still, these are the kinds of things she doesn't get from me. Private things, important things.

"I'm sorry," she finally says, and when I look over at her, she's lying down, too, facing me. And she does look sorry. Or I think she does. She looks *different* at least, and maybe that's enough with Flora.

"Thanks," I say, then awkwardly squirm around on the ground to face her. "I mean. I don't remember her or anything."

"Is that better or worse?"

It's a totally unexpected question, and for a second, I don't know how to answer her, since that's a question I've asked myself a million times, ever since I was old enough to get what not having a mom meant.

"I don't know," I finally tell her. "It's like . . . trying to miss something you never really had. Like if you'd never eaten ice cream, never could eat it, but everyone was like, 'Don't you miss ice cream?' Only. You know. Bigger."

"Because the ice cream is your mum," she says with such solemnity that I actually laugh.

"I guess?"

Flora smiles, too, then, but it's such a different smile. Usually, her smiles are all slowly curving lips, very cat that ate the canary, like she learned smiling from watching soap operas or something. This is the real deal, and it's surprisingly goofy. It lights up her whole face, and I wonder why she doesn't smile like that more often.

It's a good look on her.

And then she props her head on her hand and says, "At the

pub, before the whole unpleasantness, you mentioned liking girls and boys."

Oh, wow, apparently we're going to unpack everything personal about me tonight. Joy.

Clearing my throat, I roll over to study the sky overhead. It's not all the way dark yet, but it's getting there, and I know that when the sun is completely down, it's going to be darker than I can possibly imagine.

"Yeah," I say at last. "Equal opportunity dater."

"Bisexual," she replies, and my face flushes even as I laugh.

"To get technical, yes, bi. Anything else you want to know about me? Social security number? Embarrassing scars?"

She shrugs, still on her side facing me. "If we're stuck out here, I figure we might as well try to get to know each other. And me, too. With the liking girls and boys. Well, not boys, actually. I mean"—she blows out a long breath—"I gave them a *try*, but it didn't take."

Okay, that has my attention.

Once again, I roll over to face her. "Didn't take?" I echo.

Flora traces a pattern on her jacket with one fingernail. "They're just very . . . boy, you know?"

I kind of do, and I nod.

"Do people know?" I ask her, and then, since that seems fairly personal, offer up, "My dad and stepmom do. Most of my friends, too. I thought it might be weird or hard to talk to them about it, but everyone was surprisingly cool."

"My family is not quite as cool," Flora says. "My brothers know, and they're fine with it. Papa would rather not acknowledge that any of his children are sexual creatures, and Mummy is pretending it's simply a phase and I'll eventually do my family duty. Marry some chinless duke with three hundred acres."

She flops over onto her back, one arm stretched out at her side, the other resting on her chest. "Have three or four royal bairns. Give them obnoxious names."

"Venetia?" I suggest. "Florisius?"

Laughing, Flora repeats, "Florisius," then looks over at me.

"Why are you telling me this?" I ask, and she turns her head to look at the sky.

"You shared something personal with me even though I haven't been very nice to you," she says. "It simply seemed like good sportsmanship to share in kind."

Good sportsmanship. How very . . . Flora.

"Well, I appreciate it," I say and then, surprising myself, I add, "Seriously, I do."

She tilts her head in acknowledgment, but I still point at her and say, "Although the sharing of personal secrets doesn't make up for this crap."

"Fair enough, Quint," she says, and I settle back on the jacket, wondering if I'll actually be able to sleep.

And then Flora sits up, pointing. "Are those flashlights or ghosts?"

I bolt upright, spotting the two circles of light bobbing along not too far away, and then I hear the sweetest sound I can possibly imagine—Sakshi's voice saying, "I *told* you we should've set up camp earlier."

Looking over at Flora, I grin. "It's rescue."

Some scaaaaaaaandaaaaaal to report, my darlings!! Shocking no one, The Princess and the Camping Trip (what a crappy fairy tale that would make) nearly ended in disaster. Apparently Flora and her partner got LOST WITHOUT SUPPLIES! They were found by classmates, and from what I'm hearing, the queen herself might be making a little trip up there—AGAIN!!—to see what's going on. First a pub brawl, now a camping disaster . . . Dare I say it? I think Flora's stay at Gregorstoun might be even more fun than Seb's.

("When Princesses Camp," from *Crown Town*)

CHAPTER 21

"AND SO AS YE CAN IMAGINE, NO ONE IN THE MCGREGOR family has e'er eaten a trout again."

"Totally," I murmur in reply to Mr. McGregor's story, even though I only heard about half of it. I'm sitting in the back of a Land Rover with Flora, the two of us—well, three, counting Mr. McGregor—making our way back to Gregorstoun in the darkness. Thanks to Saks and Elisabeth actually having their packs, they'd been able to send up flares, hence the ride from Mr. McGregor back to the school.

"All I'm saying is that you lassies are lucky 'twas a stag and not a trout," he continues before shaking his head sadly. "Poor Brian."

Now I kind of wish I'd listened more, but we're already pulling up to the front drive of the school, all the lights on, making the house glow in the darkness.

I'd sigh with relief at seeing it if Dr. McKee weren't standing on the front steps, her arms folded over her chest.

"Bollocks," Flora mutters on one side of me, and I nod.

"The bollocks-iest."

I'm tired and wet and cold and not really in the mood to try to explain this whole escapade to Dr. McKee.

But when we pile out of the car, she simply says, "We'll discuss this tomorrow," and then turns to walk back into the school.

I look at Flora, who just heaves a sigh before saying, "Well, we'll worry about that later, shall we? I'm off for a shower. I may never get the smell of river water out of my hair."

But the summons to Dr. McKee's office doesn't come the next morning. Or the morning after that. It's not until everyone is back from the Challenge and I've finally started to relax, thinking I might not get called on the carpet for this after all, that Dr. Flyte stops me from coming into my history class and tells me Dr. McKee wants to see me.

And so once again, I find myself sitting next to Flora in front of the headmistress.

This time, we actually get to meet in her office instead of the chapel, and even though Flora was sure her mom would turn up again, there's no royal entourage.

Just us.

And Dr. McKee.

Sitting behind her desk, she watches us with a slight frown. "Ladies," she begins, then breaks off again, shaking her head. "I'm sorry, I'm not even sure how to approach all of this since the stories I've gotten from Miss Worthington and Miss Graham were somewhat confusing and involved a stag?"

Flora nods. "Yes, we were attacked by a stag, and that's how we lost all our things. It was very traumatic. Wasn't it, Quint?"

For all that I had said I wasn't going along with Flora's stupid plan, I find myself nodding. "A stag. Trauma," I say, and Dr. McKee sighs.

"Miss Quint," she says, fixing me with a look. "You wouldn't be lying for the princess, would you?"

How does she know? Is she psychic, or am I just a terrible liar?

But then Dr. McKee begins shuffling papers on her desk and says, "Because Miss Baird's friend, Miss McPherson, insists that Miss Baird told her two weeks ago that she did not plan on staying at Gregorstoun through the autumn and that she had a new plan to get herself sent home. Is that true?"

In the chair next to me, Flora doesn't move, but I feel myself practically creaking as I stiffen up.

"I don't. There wasn't. I can't . . . plan," I manage to get out, and Dr. McKee frowns even deeper, the bridge of her nose wrinkling.

"Miss Quint," she says, and then Flora sits up, clearing her throat.

"Actually, Caroline was telling the truth, Dr. McKee. It was irresponsible and reckless and selfish, and Millie had no idea what I was up to until it was too late. I asked her to lie for me, and threatened her with expulsion if she didn't."

That last part is not even remotely true, and I gape at Flora. Did our few hours all wet and cold break her?

Or is she actually kind of a decent person under all of that bitchiness?

Dr. McKee just stares at Flora, her hands still folded on her desk. When she finds her voice again, it's to ask, "Do you hate it here so much, Miss Baird?"

Flora swallows, and fidgets a little in her chair before answering. "I thought I did," she says. "But it's . . . not so bad. Those girls who came to help us, Sakshi and Elisabeth. They were . . . nice." She rolls her shoulders, uncomfortable. "And Millie—Miss Quint—has been nice to me even though I don't really deserve it. So. I don't know."

She schools her face into that bored expression I've seen so many times. "Maybe there's something to be said for this whole 'sisterhood' thing."

"Might have been more effective without the air quotes, but thank you, Miss Baird," Dr. McKee says.

Then she looks back and forth between us. She's not all that old, Dr. McKee, I realize. Probably only in her thirties. Maybe she has a brother who went here, or a boyfriend or something. Maybe getting to come to Gregorstoun was her dream, too.

I'm actually feeling a little warm and fuzzy toward Dr. McKee when she says, "Laundry duty for both of you for the next four weeks."

"What?" I ask. "But I didn't do—"

"You lied," Dr. McKee says, once again shuffling papers. "To protect a friend, I understand, but that doesn't make it acceptable. Now out, both of you."

"But—" Flora starts, and Dr. McKee lifts one finger.

"Out, or it's laundry *and* bathroom cleaning duty."

We both scramble out of that office so fast there are probably dust clouds behind us.

Once out in the hallway, Flora and I face each other, but

before I can thank her for doing the right thing, she says, "I'll be late for maths. See you later, Quint."

She saunters off, and as soon as she's turned the corner, Saks is rushing up to me, Perry in tow.

"Did they kick you out?" she hisses, and I shake my head.

"Did they kick *her* out?" Perry asks, and I shake my head again.

"No, no kicking out. Just laundry duty, whatever that means."

Both Perry and Saks wrinkle their noses. "That's actually fairly foul," Perry says. "I got it last year for smoking on the grounds. You learn . . . way too much about your classmates doing their laundry."

"Great," I reply. "Really looking forward to that, then."

The three of us head upstairs, and when Perry peels off for his room, I turn in the hall to face Saks. "She called us friends. Dr. McKee."

"You and Dr. McKee are friends?" Saks asks, tilting her head so that her heavy dark hair slides over one shoulder, and I roll my eyes, shoving her arm lightly.

"No. Me and Flora."

"Oh." Saks's face brightens. "Well, maybe you can be!"

I'm not sure how I feel about that.

When I come into our room later that evening, after supper and studying, Flora is already in there in her pajamas, sitting cross-legged on her bed, her wet hair combed out over her shoulders.

For once, when I walk in the room, she doesn't give me a look. She smiles a little, leaning over to towel her hair, and I stand there, looking at her. At our room, which is so clearly split into My Stuff and Flora's Stuff, complete with a line of tape across the top of the dresser.

"Are we friends now?" I blurt out, and Flora raises her eyebrows at me, letting the towel fall to the bed.

"I suppose so," she says. "We've been through a traumatic experience together. That usually bonds people."

"And that traumatic experience was completely your fault," I remind her, and she gives one of those elegant shrugs that I'm beginning to recognize as a Classic Flora Gesture.

"The provenance of the trauma isn't that important," she says airily, and I can't help the giggle that explodes out of my mouth.

"The 'provenance of the trauma'? Okay, seriously, who talks like that?"

But then I remember that's kind of a stupid question. Who talks like that? Princesses, of course. Royalty. Which is what Flora is, no matter how . . . normal she looks sitting there in her jammies.

Getting up from the bed, she walks over to the dresser and tugs at that strip of tape separating my rock collection from her fancy candles.

"There," she says, balling up the tape and tossing it in the bin. "A new start."

I'm not sure something as simple as getting rid of a piece of tape can be the beginning of a beautiful friendship, but I still nod.

"A new start."

CHAPTER **22**

AS FAR AS PUNISHMENTS GO, IT DEFINITELY COULD have been worse. I mean, I'm not sure they could put us in the stocks or anything—me, maybe, but definitely not Flora—but who knows what sort of weird stuff they could come up with here in the Highlands? We could be forced to tend sheep or throw heavy rocks off fields or something. Okay, the rocks thing might not be so bad for me, but still.

So yeah, laundry duty seems a small price to pay for everything that happened during the Challenge.

Flora disagrees.

"This is barbaric," she says, her perfect nose wrinkling as she hauls an armful of wet sheets out of the washer. "Practically medieval."

The laundry room is down in what I guess was once the cellar or maybe where they kept uppity women back in the day, the stone floors uneven underfoot, and the light coming through the ancient windows watery and gray. It's raining. Again.

"History is my second-favorite subject," I say as I dump a cupful of strong-smelling detergent into the other washer. "And I'm fairly sure I don't remember any mentions of fancy washing machines from the medieval period, but I guess I could be wrong?"

Flora shoots me a look at that. Her hair is up in a ponytail, but a few strands have escaped to curl around her face in the humidity of the laundry room. Little beads of sweat dot her forehead, too, but it strikes me that even down here, in the cellar, doing literal drudgery, there's no mistaking Flora for anything but a princess.

"No one likes a smart-arse, Quint," she says, but there's a little smile curling there at the corner of her lips.

And maybe I smile back a little bit even as I say, "You know, this habit of calling me by my last name makes me sound like your servant."

Flora hoots at that, slamming the dryer shut and twisting the dials on top. "Oh god, what a rubbish servant you'd make," she says as the dryer begins to rumble and shake. "You'd probably spill tea on me just for your own twisted pleasure."

I grin now, making my way over to the long low table in the middle of the room, where baskets of scratchy towels wait to be folded. "Actually, when I'm done with school here, I might apply for the job. Just commit myself to a lifelong scheme of revenge against you for what happened during the Challenge."

I'm joking, but Flora's smile dims a little as she comes to join me at the table. When she reaches out to pick up a towel, I notice that her manicure is chipped, two nails ragged like she's been chewing on them.

Princess Flora, a nail biter? Who would've guessed?

"I am sorry about that," she says at last, then looks over at me. "Truly."

Clearing my throat, I shrug. I don't like a sincere Flora. A flighty, pain-in-the-ass Flora is so much easier to deal with. "I know you are," I say. "And we obviously didn't die, so that's a bonus."

"We perhaps died, because this certainly feels like hell, or, at the very least, purgatory," Flora counters, trying to fold a towel. Mostly she's just balling it up, and with a sigh, I take it out of her hands.

"You might have a point, since 'Teach a Princess How to Do Laundry' absolutely feels like some kind of punishment from the gods."

Flora rolls her eyes. "Oh, poor put-upon Quint," she says, and I hold up one finger.

"No, we're going to do this right. Observe."

I pick up the towel, shaking it out and holding it by two cor-ners. "First things first—we hold the towel like this. Then we bring these two corners together."

I show her, and she picks up another towel, mimicking my movements. I have no idea if she actually doesn't know how to fold a towel, or if she's just going along with this because it's a fun distraction from laundry, but in any case, she dutifully goes through the same motions I do until we both have a little square of towel in front of us on the table.

"*Et voilà*," I say with a flourish, then grab another towel off the pile and toss it to her. "Now let's see if the student has learned."

Cutting me a look, Flora picks up another towel, snapping it out in front of her. "It's hardly rocket science, Quint."

She then proceeds to completely bungle folding the towel. Like, I can't even describe what she does because it defies all laws of god and man, and also towels, and I laugh, shaking my head and walking over to her.

"Oh my god, Your Royal Highness," I tease. "You are a royal disaster."

Reaching around her, I pick up the towel, placing it back in her hands. Then, standing behind her, I go to guide her arms in the right movements.

"Corners together," I say again, bringing her hands together with my own.

Only then do I realize just how close I'm standing to her, how her golden hair is falling over her shoulder and practically into my mouth.

How the way we're standing feels awfully . . . close.

Clearing my throat, I back away so suddenly that Flora actually drops the towel. "Anyway, you'll figure it out," I mutter, going back to my own pile.

Flora is watching me, though, her cheeks slightly pink.

It's just because it's warm down here, the industrial washing machines and dryers making everything hotter and steamier than a basement room in a Scottish manor house has any right to be.

We finish folding towels in near silence, and I'm just reaching for a basket of sheets when I notice something shoved under the farthest basket, just at the corner of the table. It's a magazine, an older one that's sort of wrinkled and faded from the damp here in the laundry room, and I guess whoever had laundry punishment last was reading it. I tug it over to me more out of curiosity than anything else, and it's only when I've got it right in front of me that I see Flora's on the cover.

There's big yellow text over her head screaming FLIGHTY FLORA STRIKES AGAIN! and in the picture, she's got big sunglasses on as she makes her way down a cobblestone street, one arm wrapped tightly around her middle, the other held out against the photographers.

Yikes.

I go to shove the magazine back under the basket, hoping Flora is absorbed enough in trying not to mangle more laundry that she doesn't notice me, but of course she does, and before I have a chance to hide the magazine again, she's beside me, taking it out of my hands.

"Ah," she says. "I see someone's been reading up on me. How flattering."

"That's not mine," I reply, tucking my hair behind my ears. "I just found—"

"Oh, I didn't think it was yours." Flora is still holding the magazine, studying her picture, her shoulders back and chin slightly lifted. It's a pose I'm getting used to seeing from her. "Just one of our other classmates, I suppose. Still, it's a good picture. My hair was smashing that summer."

I stare at her. That's all she sees in that picture? She's practically being hunted down a street, the headline is calling her a hot mess, more or less, and she's like, "My hair is good"?

Flora moves back down the table to her own laundry pile, the magazine left between us. It almost feels like a poisonous snake lying there, and I watch it warily.

Then I look back to Flora, who's refolding the towels she'd already done, her movements stiff. "What was that about?" I finally ask. "You 'striking again'?"

Sniffing, Flora tosses her newly folded towel into an empty basket, promptly undoing the work she'd done. "To tell the truth, I don't even remember. I made a lot of mistakes that summer."

She flashes me a smile. "Thank goodness I have so many publications keeping a record for me."

Flora goes to move past me, carrying a basket to the door, and as she does, she lets one hand dangle free, pushing the magazine to the floor, where it lands in a puddle of damp from the wet sheets.

"Oh, dear," she says breezily, heading for the door. "How clumsy of me."

CHAPTER 23

"LAUNDRY DUTY?"

I laugh, getting settled on my bed as I angle my laptop to see Lee better. "Okay, you say that like it's the worst punishment anyone could ever get."

On the screen, Lee flicks his hair out of his eyes. "It's just bizarre," he says. "Can you imagine getting in trouble at Pecos and them making you, like, wash gym uniforms? Haven't they heard of detention in Scotland?"

"It's actually not so bad," I tell him, and am surprised to realize that's the truth. I haven't exactly *loved* doing everyone's laundry the past couple of weeks, but spending time with Flora has been surprisingly unterrible. Whatever thawed between us up there in the hills has stayed unfrozen, and while I still think of Flora as basically a Posh Agent of Chaos, it's been kind of nice getting to hang out, just the two of us.

"Um, what is *that* face about?"

I blink at the screen. "What?"

"You just made a face," Lee says, grinning. "A dreamy face. Have you landed a Highlander, Mill?"

"Shut up," I say, rolling my eyes, but Lee only laughs again, shaking his head.

"No, I know the face of Millie Quint with a Crush, and that was it. I have seen it, I know your secret heart."

"It is not, and no you don't," I reply, but my heart is beating a little faster, and now I'm not just blushing, I'm beet-red. I can see it in the little rectangle at the bottom of my screen.

The door flies open, and Flora bounds in, her golden pony-tail bouncing.

"Oh, thank god!" she enthuses, dropping down on her bed with a distinct lack of royal grace, and on my laptop, Lee squawks, "Who is that? Is that your roommate? I wanna see her—"

"Okay, gotta go, love you, love you, bye!" I trill at the screen before slamming the laptop shut.

I haven't told Lee about Flora, or rather, I haven't told him my roommate is also a princess, and something tells me that as soon as he lays eyes on Flora, he'll know.

Not that there's anything to know because there's not; I do *not* have a crush.

"Who were you talking to?" she asks me now, propping her chin in one hand, a heavy envelope caught between her fingers.

"My dad," I lie, then gesture at the letter.

"What is that?" I ask her, watching as she slides a finger along the closure, the thick paper making a satisfying ripping sound.

"This, dearest Quint, is freedom," she says, and I try to ignore that "dearest," and the funny things it does to my chest.

It's just Flora Speak. Everyone is darling, sweetheart, my love. Sometimes I think it's because she can't remember most people's names.

"Look," she says, tossing the heavy card inside my way.

It's embossed with so many seals and crests, and the calligraphy is so intricate, I can barely read it, so I hold the card out, squinting at it. "Is this in English?" I ask, and Flora reaches out, swatting at me before taking the card back.

"Don't play the rube with me," she says, but she's smiling. "It's an invitation to a house party next weekend up on Skye, hosted by the Lord of the Isles."

I sit back on my bed, toeing off my shoes. "The who?"

"Lord of the Isles," Flora repeats, and I wiggle my toes at her.

"You can keep saying that all you want, I still won't understand who you're talking about."

Sitting up, Flora tucks her legs underneath her. She's got a hole in the knee of her stocking, a shockingly human thing on a goddess, and I suddenly have this weird urge to reach out with my foot and poke it.

That is an urge I very much do not give in to.

Instead, I make myself focus on her face as she says, "You really don't know much about Scotland for someone who willingly chose to live here," and I scoot up farther on my own bed, away from that hole in her stocking, that little circle of pale skin that I can't seem to stop staring at.

"I know enough," I say, a little defensive. "Mary, Queen of Scots. Braveheart. All that."

"Oh, forgive me, you're an expert in all things Scottish." She plays up her accent as that sentence ends, the vowels rolling and growling in her mouth, and I giggle.

"Okay, don't ever talk like that again."

She grins at me, then sits back on her heels, the invitation still in hand. "Fine, allow me to enlighten you. So years and years ago, way before your Mary and your Braveheart, the Isles were their own kingdom more or less, mostly because they were bloody hard to get to from Edinburgh. So they had a Lord of the Isles, who was basically in charge of Skye, the Hebrides, and you know . . . isles."

"Right," I say, even though I'm not sure I 100% know.

"Annnywaaaay," Flora drawls, flopping back on her bed, legs crossed at the ankle, "in the sixties, they had this big uprising there because of oil or some such, and there was a vote to let them bring back their own lord, so now they have one, and that's who's throwing the party. Lord Henry Beauchamp. Apparently they had to hire professional genealogists to find out who was actually in line to be Lord of the Isles, it had been so long since they'd had one. Turned out to be some bloke living on a sheep ranch in Australia."

Outside, it's started raining again, a soft shushing sound cocooning us in our dim and cozy room. "So he's like a mini king," I say, "but of islands, not Scotland."

Flora makes a scoffing noise, fanning her face with the invitation. The gilt seals catch the lamplight, winking at me. "Don't let Mummy hear you say that. It's more like he's a sort of fancier-than-usual aristocrat. They can't raise their own army out there, or completely secede from the country. But they have a few laws that are different from ours, and now they get to keep most of their oil money. Also, they're more fun."

I have calculus homework I should definitely be looking at, but it's nice, sitting here in the gloom with Flora, and I have to admit, learning about this stuff isn't completely terrible.

"More fun than you?" I ask. "Because that sounds dangerous and possibly illegal."

Flora winks at me with a sly grin.

"They're just not as strict," she says. "Like I said, Lord Henry was from the other side of the planet, and his wife, Lady Ellis, was some sort of fabulous party girl in Swinging London. It was all very scandalous from what Mummy has said. Their children and grandchildren make me and Seb look like model citizens."

I smile at that, finally reaching over for my calculus notebook. "Well, that sounds like your kind of thing for sure, then. Can you get away from here for a whole weekend?"

"They'll have to let me go," Flora says with that breezy confidence that's as much a part of her as her hair color or her long legs. "It's basically a diplomatic thing. Terrible insult if the royal family doesn't send a representative when she's so close."

"Is that what you are?" I ask, notebook already forgotten on my stomach. How does Flora always manage to distract me? "A diplomat?"

"An ambassador," she says, lifting her nose slightly. And then her regal bearing falls away into those surprisingly dorky giggles she's prone to. "Anyway, should be a good time, and even if it's not, it's better than this place."

"Can't argue with you there," I murmur in reply, and okay, no, now I'm seriously going to start my homework.

But then Flora says, "But I so enjoy when you argue with me."

I look up, not so much at the words, but at the tone of her voice as she says them. It's . . . soft. Fond.

Affectionate, maybe.

But "soft, fond, and affectionate" describes puppies, not Princess Flora of Scotland, and maybe one of these days, I'll actually start remembering that.

So rather than smile back, I pick up my pen and say, "Well, don't worry. You'll have probably ten million more opportunities to do that in the future."

"Could this weekend be one of them?"

I am just . . . never getting this homework done, I see that now.

"What?" I ask, eyebrows somewhere near my hairline, and Flora crosses her feet the other way.

"Come with me to Skye. You've never been, have you?"

I flick my pen at her, and she raises her hands to defend herself, laughing.

"Okay, stupid question." *Stewpid.* Her accent really is the best.

"I'm just saying, you came to school here to see more of Scotland, but so far, all you've seen is, what? A few airports? A train station? And Dungregor, which is just too depressing to contemplate. So come with me and see Skye. You'll love it."

I chew on my lower lip, shooting a glance at my desk. It's

practically groaning under the weight of my books. I'm behind on my reading for history, haven't even started on my English essay, and my calculus grade is probably slipping as we speak.

On her bed, Flora flops over to her stomach, pushing herself closer to the edge. "Skyyyyyyye, Quint," she wheedles. "There will be so many rooooocccckkkks."

That shocks a laugh out of me. "There are lots of rocks here, too."

Flora's grinning again, that mischievous one with the glint that always spells trouble. "But not magic rocks."

"Now Skye has magic rocks?"

She reaches over to her side and pulls out her phone, tossing it to me. "Look at my wallpaper."

I do. It's a picture of Flora, but a younger Flora, maybe fourteen or so. She's standing between her two brothers. Seb isn't quite as Magazine Handsome as he is now, but the other guy, their older brother, Alex, is definitely chiseled. He's blonder, like Flora, and all three of them are decked out in what was probably very pricey athletic gear. Flora's cheeks are red, her smile broad as she looks at the camera, and behind them is this massive rock, jutting out of the ground and into the sky. All around them is a mix of green grass and stony rubble, and with the mist surrounding the three of them, they could be on another planet.

"That's us at the Old Man of Storr a few years ago. On Skye."

I know she's trying to tempt me with the rock formation, but it's Flora's face I'm looking at when I hear myself say, "Okay. I'll go."

While not as headline-grabbing as the Scottish Royals, the Beauchamp family of Skye is still one of the more interesting clans in the country. Lord Henry and Lady Ellis are known for their gracious hospitality as well as their gorgeous home on the northern tip of Skye. After the restoration of the "Lord of the Isles" titles, the family occupy a space somewhere between the royals and the nobility, although Lady Ellis herself was born a princess in the English royal family.

Princess Flora is especially fond of the family, having been close to Lord Henry's youngest granddaughter, Lady Tamsin Campbell, daughter of the Duke of Montrose. There were hopes of a match between the duke's daughter and Princess Flora's brother, Prince Sebastian, but they seem to have been scuttled last year, and Flora and Tamsin's friendship was rumoured to be a casualty of the breakup.

("Scotland's Poshest Families," from *Prattle*)

CHAPTER **24**

"SO DO I NEED TO BOW TO THESE PEOPLE LIKE I DO your mom?"

Flora shakes her head, pulling out that little mirror with the pink glittery back to check her makeup. "No. Well, yes, sort of, not as deeply. A tiny curtsy will do, and Lord Henry is not all that formal anyway, if I'm honest."

We're in a black SUV, making our way north to Skye. Flora told me that up until the '70s, the only way to get to Skye was on a boat. Now, thank god, there's a bridge. Me and boats do not mix well.

Of course, there's a chance me and this entire weekend won't work, anyway. It's not like I forget Flora is a princess when we're at Gregorstoun—I couldn't if I tried—but this is my first taste of the actual royal life. I've felt weird in Darcy's house for years, and she's just Regular Person Rich. Not *this* kind of fancy.

Sighing, Flora stashes the compact again and settles deeper into her seat. "You're nervous."

I hold up my thumb and forefinger. "Little bit," I admit. "But I know I call Lord Henry 'my lord,' and Lady Ellis 'Your Royal Highness,' because she was born a princess and got to keep that title. And that there are different glasses for water and wine, and there will be a whole bunch of forks to use."

Flora gives me one of those smiles I like so much, reaching over to pat my leg.

"By jove, I think she's got it!"

I roll my eyes, but my cheeks are warm, and the place where she's got her hand feels even warmer.

Stupid, stupid, stupid, I remind myself. A crush on Flora is the stupidest thing I could possibly do, for all kinds of reasons, but ever since the Challenge, things are different between me and Flora. Not just because I know she likes girls, too, but that's part of it, I have to admit. My brain wants to remind me that sexuality aside, Flora is *not* a romantic option for me, but it's hard to remember it when she's looking at me like that, when we're tucked away in the back of a fancy car, speeding through some of the most beautiful scenery I've ever seen. The whole princess thing had never really appealed to me as a kid, but this?

Yeah, this I could get used to.

Then the car is pulling up a long gravel driveway, and I twist my hands nervously.

The Lord of the Isles lives in the first Honest-to-God Castle I've seen since I got to Scotland. I might have thought Gregorstoun was a palace the first time I saw it, but as I climb out of the back of the car and take in the structure in front of me, I realize Gregorstoun is just a really big school. This?

This is a castle.

It's not like something out of a fairy tale, all lovely and delicate. Weirdly enough, that's kind of what I'd been picturing. This is more a medieval fortress, with turrets and high walls, slits cut into the rock for arrows.

"God, it's beastly, isn't it?" Flora murmurs at my side, and I look up at the place.

"It's . . . amazing," I finally say, and she looks over at me, lips slightly pursed. I wish I could see her face better, but she's wearing another pair of those massive sunglasses she likes since, for once, the day is actually bright and sunny.

Reaching down, she takes my hand. It's a friendly gesture, one I've seen her make with other girls at school, but when her fingers curl around mine, a little shiver sparkles through me.

Luckily I don't have too much time to focus on that because there are two very furry horses suddenly bounding down the front steps toward us.

I make a sound that is probably deeply unattractive, a kind of "Yeep!" as the animals approach, but Flora drops to one knee there in the gravel, arms already outstretched.

The dogs—because that's what they are, not some freak species of pony—happily dance around her, pink tongues lolling, and Flora makes all sorts of high-pitched noises and kissy sounds at them as they bask in her attention.

Laughing, she rises to her feet, readjusting her bag on her shoulder, and I look at her, feeling weirdly . . . unsettled.

I have Flora so fixed in my head as prissy and unapproachable, even when I have those moments of wanting to smell her hair, but this Flora? This goofy, "get down in the dirt with the dogs" Flora is new. Or not new exactly, but more like you shifted a drawing another way and suddenly saw a hidden picture inside or something.

It's weird.

But then there are men in khaki pants and gray sweater vests coming out to get our luggage—apparently things aren't all that formal here—and Flora's reaching for my hand again, tugging me inside.

"Come on. If you think the outside is impressive, the inside will floor you."

She's not wrong. We step through the massive stone archway and into a hall that soars overhead and stretches all around us in three directions. Directly in front of us is a massive staircase made of worn stone, leading up to an open gallery. To the right, there's more ancient stone and a long corridor of doors, and to the left is another stone arch that leads to a long hallway full of suits of armor, all lined up against the wall like they're ready to defend the house against invaders.

There's a boy jogging down that hall. Like the guys outside, he's wearing a sweater vest, but it looks better on him, clinging to broad shoulders and a narrow waist. His hair is appropriately floppy for a guy who looks like him, and his eyes are really blue as he gets closer, grinning at us both.

"Flo," he says warmly, scooping Flora up into a hug, and she hugs him back, her hands patting his back.

"Sherbet!"

I blink, wondering if she really did just call him "Sherbet," but then he's setting her down and offering me his hand to shake.

"Hullo, I'm Sherbourne."

Ah, okay. Still not really a name, but not a frozen dessert, either, so I guess I'll take it.

"So this is your first time on Skye?" he asks me, and I nod as he gestures for me to step in front of him and head up the staircase.

"It is, yeah. It's lovely."

Sherbet smiles at me, hands in his pockets as we all walk up together. The stairs are wide enough that the three of us can actually stand side by side, and there's still room for someone to pass us.

"What are you doing here, Sherbet?" Flora asks. "I thought you'd be gallivanting in Greece or something." Flora leans a little closer to me. "Sherbet's boyfriend is Greek, and we're all wildly jealous of the trips he gets to take to visit him."

Sherbet laughs. "Last time I checked, Flora, dating someone from Greece was not a prerequisite for visiting. You could have your very own Greek holiday anytime you want."

Flora mulls that over, tilting her head to one side. "Christmas, then, maybe? After the wedding, of course. I'll talk to Glynnis."

I wonder if I'll ever get used to it, the way things like "a trip to Greece" get the same amount of consideration I'd give to going camping for the weekend. What is it like not to have any sense of money or limitations or time? How does anyone live a life like that?

But then, as Sherbet guides us onto the landing, I remind myself that I'm spending a weekend in a castle, so hey, maybe that life isn't as remote as it seems.

"Flora, I believe you know where your room is," Sherbet says, and Flora slings her bag over her shoulder, grinning.

"The Fruit Punch Room, yes, thanks, Sherbs." With that, she wiggles her fingers at me and says, "I'll come by your room once I've unpacked and freshened up, okay?"

"Sure," I reply, still wondering what "the Fruit Punch Room" might entail, but then Sherbet is opening a door to his left and ushering me into the bedroom.

It's all done in shades of mint green with the occasional darker green accent and a few splashes of deep, rich purple. My bed has an honest-to-god canopy, plus little curtains held back against the massive posts with purple velvet ribbons.

A giant window dominates one wall, and when I walk over to it, I see I have a view of a little garden plus, in the distance, the ocean.

I glance back over my shoulder at Sherbet, who's grinning, hands in his pockets. "It's something, right?" he says, and I figure if a boy like this is impressed by this room, it really *is* something.

"I can't . . ." I say, trailing off and shaking my head before laughing. "Something, yeah," I finally say before turning back to look at the view again.

"It's one of the prettiest rooms in the whole castle," Sherbet tells me, "which I guess is why Flora always picks it."

Turning back, I look at him, surprised, and he winks at me.

"She insisted you have it."

CHAPTER 25

FLORA IS AS GOOD AS HER WORD, COMING BACK to my room after about twenty minutes, wearing an entirely different outfit. I'm still in the black pants and sweater I wore here, but I actually put on some mascara and a little lip gloss, and Flora notices immediately.

"Look at you, Quint," she says, teasing as she tugs me out the door and into the hallway.

"Figured I should bring it if I was going to hang out with lords and stuff," I tell her. "But I still have no idea what I'm going to wear to dinner tonight."

Flora waves that away. "I told you, I'm handling that."

"That's what scares me," I mutter, and she flashes me a sly grin.

"Do you doubt my taste?"

"Not doubt so much as fear," I say, and she gives a bright laugh.

We make our way down the hall, past portraits and little

alcoves with small marble statues, and as we head for the stairs, I ask, "Why is your room called 'the Fruit Punch Room'?"

Without answering, Flora walks to a door a little way down the hall and opens the door, gesturing for me to come over.

I look inside, then almost immediately take a step back. "Whoa."

The walls of the bedroom are so red it almost hurts my eyes, and the bedding is covered with a pattern of fruit trees and grape vines.

"Makes sense now," I say, and she nods.

"When Lord Henry was made Lord of the Isles, the former owners of this house had to hand it over to him. Allegedly they were so pissed that Lord Henry was taking over, they tried to redesign the entire thing before he could get here. But they only managed this one room, making it as ghastly as possible. Lord Henry thought it was funny, so he kept it as is."

"Interior design as revenge," I muse. "I like it."

Smiling, Flora closes the door, and we continue along the hall and down the stairs into the main foyer again. Sherbet isn't there, but there is a man standing in a tweed suit, a cane in one hand, tapping impatiently on the marble floor.

"Uncle Henry!" Flora calls, and the man turns to look at her, his wrinkled face splitting into a grin as he spots her.

"Ah, there's trouble," he says affectionately, and Flora steps off the stairs to give him a hug.

Lord Henry is in his seventies, but moves and stands like a much younger man, his shoulders back, his hair thick and white. And when he looks at Flora, there's a twinkle in his blue eyes. "Wasn't sure you'd make it," he says, bending down to kiss her cheek, and Flora squeezes both his shoulders before pulling back.

"I wouldn't miss one of your dinners for anything, Uncle Henry," she says, then waves at me. "And I brought my roommate, Amelia." She lowers her voice to a stage whisper. "She's American."

"Ah," Lord Henry says, taking my hand and pressing a kiss to the back of it. "As are some of my grandchildren, so I have a lot of affection for your countrymen."

"Lord Henry's daughter, Maggie, married an investment banker from New York."

"She did indeed," Lord Henry confirms. "He's terribly boring, but I won't hold that against all Americans."

With that, he winks at me, and I relax a little. So far, my first look into Flora's World isn't too scary. Sure, we're in a castle, and yes, I've just met a lord, but he's still just . . . a person. A nice person who likes Flora and is welcoming to random Americans in his house.

Then he asks Flora, "You haven't seen Tamsin yet by any chance, have you?"

Flora's smile dims a bit, and she straightens her shoulders, flipping her hair over one shoulder. "No," she replies. "I actually didn't know she'd be here. It'll be nice to see her again, though."

"Ellis wanted the house full of young people for the weekend," he replies. "Says it keeps us young. In any case, if you see her, tell her my wife was looking for her, won't you?"

Flora nods, her expression pleasant enough, but I can tell something is up as Lord Henry wishes us a good afternoon and heads up the stairs.

"Who's Tamsin?" I ask once he's out of sight, and Flora tosses her head, moving toward the front door.

"Lord Henry's granddaughter," she replies, and as two footmen open the heavy doors for us, I trudge after her onto the steps. "Not one of the American ones."

"That wasn't really what I was asking, and I feel like you know that?"

Turning to face me, Flora pulls her sunglasses over her eyes, giving me that appraising look she's so good at.

"Playing Nancy Drew, Quint?"

"Just being nosy, actually," I reply, and Flora's cheeks dimple as she struggles against a smile.

"No one talks to me like you do," she says, and I scoff.

"Honestly, Flora, I think that's half your problem."

Flora snorts at that, but when we move down the stairs, she reaches out and plucks a rose off a nearby bush, twisting it almost nervously.

"Tamsin is a girl I used to date," she says finally. "Not that anyone really knew that. She'd been earmarked for Seb, but that was a no-go, obviously. But then," she adds, pulling a few petals off the rose, "I suppose I was a no-go, too."

She says it lightly, but I think there's actual hurt behind the words, and I know how she feels.

So I step forward, almost laying a hand on her arm before I think better of it. Instead, I ask, "Flora, did she break whatever it is you have in place of a heart?"

Bursting into laughter, Flora swats at me with the mangled rose. "You're the worst," she says, but then she grabs my hand. "Come on, let's go down to the beach."

We spend most of the afternoon down there, just walking and talking. Not about anything all that serious, but still I'm kind of amazed at how easy it is just to . . . talk to Flora. Like a person. She actually listens, for one thing, and seems interested. Maybe that's just a Royal Skill, being able to feign interest in anyone and anything, but it feels genuine.

We enjoy the beach so much that we're nearly late getting back to the house, and then it's a rush to get ready.

I take a bath, marveling at how big the tub is even if the hot water doesn't last nearly long enough to fill up to the top, and when I get out, I discover someone has laid a black garment bag on my bed.

Crossing the thick carpet on bare feet, I tug down the zipper.

Thirty minutes later, I stare at myself in the mirror, trying to reconcile the Millie who likes jeans and boots and rocks with the girl in the gorgeous dress in front of me.

Flora wasn't kidding when she said she could scare something up. The dress is a deep forest green, so dark that it almost looks black, and it fits like it was made for me. The green makes my brown eyes look deeper, bringing out flecks of gold, and my tan is pretty against the rich fabric. I even like the little plaid bow affixed to the waist.

Turning slightly, I hold both sides of the skirt out, unable to keep from grinning at myself. Who knew I liked dresses this much?

There's a knock at the door, and I turn toward it, dropping my skirt before someone catches me posing like I'm about to go on *Toddlers & Tiaras*. "Come in!" I call.

It's Flora, and if I thought my dress was nice, it's nothing compared to hers.

She's decked out in the full Baird tartan, which should look ridiculous, but on her, is almost absurdly beautiful. The purple, green, and black set off her creamy skin and her golden hair perfectly, the black velvet belt around her waist giving her an hourglass shape. There's even a tiara of emeralds and diamonds nestled in her golden hair.

But it's her smile as she looks at me that has my heart suddenly knocking against my ribs.

"Well, well, Quint," she says. "You clean up even better than I'd hoped."

Smoothing my hands down the front of the skirt, I shrug, awkward all of a sudden.

"I can't believe you managed to find something that fits me this well," I say now, turning back to the mirror, because if I'm looking at myself, I won't be looking at her, and that seems like the best idea right now. "Who here is my size exactly?"

Flora is still standing in the doorway, her hand on the knob, and she lifts one shoulder in a shrug. "No one. I guessed and sent an email to Glynnis to have something sent up."

I turn around again, mouth dropping open slightly. "You guessed?" That seems impossible. The dress fits too well and looks too good on me. Flora and I may know each other well by now, but I didn't think we were at the "know your measurements on sight" level of friendship.

"What can I say? I have an eye for these things," Flora replies, but her eyes don't quite meet mine. Then she gestures out into the hall. "Well? Shall we?"

CHAPTER **26**

PEOPLE ARE GATHERING AT THE BOTTOM OF THE stairs as we head down, and I see Sherbet, who waves cheerfully to us.

He's talking to a blond girl in a blue dress, and I glance over at Flora, wondering if this is Tamsin.

But instead, Flora cries, "Oh, Baby Glynnis!"

The girl glares at both of us as we approach and steps away from Sherbet.

"It's Nicola," the girl says, and Flora waves that off.

"I know, but Baby Glynnis is so much more apt. Quint, Baby Glynnis. Baby Glynnis, Quint."

"Nicola," the girl says again through clenched teeth, and I reply, "Millie."

She shakes my hand, and as she does, tilting her head down a little, I suddenly see the resemblance to the woman who accompanied the queen to Gregorstoun.

"Oh, you're *literally* Baby Glynnis," I say, and the girl's hazel eyes shoot up toward the ceiling.

"Ni. Co. La," she says. "But yes, Glynnis is my mother, which is why I'm stuck out here in the backwoods of Scotland instead of being at home."

I wonder what kind of life she lives back "home" that a castle is the "backwoods," but Flora leans in and says, "Baby Glynnis is usually in California with her dad, but I'd heard Glynnis brought her up for a bit."

"Literally standing right here," Nicola says. "Can hear everything you're saying."

"What are you doing on Skye?" Flora asks her, and Nicola jerks a thumb at Sherbet.

"Sherbet invited me, and since I was bored and Skye is far from my mother, I agreed."

Sherbet, apparently hearing his name, waves Nicola back over to him, and as she walks away, Flora leans in close. "For a hot second two years ago, Nicola was the only girl Royal Wrecker," she murmurs. "She and Seb were thick as thieves."

"Thick as thieves in the sexy way or the friend way?" I ask, and Flora's lips tilt up at the corners.

"Friends only, believe it or not. I think it might have been the first time Seb actually had a girl who was a friend. But even without any sexiness, it was quite the scandal. Glynnis nearly lost her job over it. Nicola went back to California, and we haven't seen her since. But Glynnis has always wanted her here, learning the ropes. Glynnis's mum worked for my grand-dad, her dad worked for *his* father. That family has acted as the right hand to the monarch since . . . lord, I don't know, Mary, Queen of Scots, probably? Needless to say, Nicola is less than enthused about it."

Before I can get any more gossip, there's a loud gong, and I glance up to see Lord Henry standing in front of a set of double doors at the other end of the hall. "I'm sure there's some fancy thing I'm supposed to say here," he calls out, "but instead, I'll just say dinner is served, so move your arses already."

Everyone laughs at that, and we make our way to the dining room.

Lady Ellis is as elegant as her husband is charming, and I remember what Flora said about them being scandalous in the '60s. It's hard to imagine, looking at them now, but then, as Lady Ellis passes by her husband to lead us all into the dining room, I see his hand briefly pat her backside.

Okay, then, maybe scandal is not so hard to believe.

Flora must have seen it, too, because she leans in and murmurs, "They are such goals."

I glance over at her. "Are your parents like that?"

She snorts, linking her arm through mine again. She keeps doing that, and it keeps making it harder to remember that I'm not Flora's date this weekend, just her roommate she's brought along as a charity case, more or less.

"My parents sleep in separate wings of the palace. Not just rooms. Wings."

"Isn't that how all royal people do?" I whisper back, and her eyes meet mine.

"It's not how I would do," she says, then she nods toward Lord Henry and Lady Ellis. "It's definitely not what they do. They have seven kids."

"Seven?"

Flora nods. "Seven. And they were basically an arranged marriage."

I wouldn't mind hearing more about that, but we're in the dining room now, and Flora drops my arm, moving toward the head of the table. As a guest of honor, she'll sit up there with Lord Henry, while I'm relegated to somewhere near the middle. Luckily, I've got Baby Glynnis—sorry, Nicola—next to me, so at least there's a familiar face and accent.

"So how are you liking Scotland?" she asks me as a bunch of men in fancy suits bring us plates. I'm so distracted by the ceremony going on around us, I can barely answer her question.

"Um, it's good," I say as a tiny plate is placed in front of me. There's a fish on it, staring up at me with its fishy eyeball, and I swallow hard. "It's . . . you know. Scotland," I say to Nicola, but she's already smirking slightly, tapping one fingernail against the tiny silver fork to my left.

"That one. Also, you don't have to eat it. Just poke it a few times while making conversation, no one will notice."

I don't even want to do *that*—poor fishie—but I pick up the fork Nicole pointed at and give the fish a few half-hearted stabs.

"See?" she says, smiling, and in that second, she really does look a lot like her mom. "You're a pro."

I snort at that, glancing up the table to where Flora sits, having a fairly animated conversation with Lord Henry, who's smiling at her, clearly charmed.

"I will be competing in the amateurs for the rest of time, I'm pretty sure," I reply, and Nicola grins back at me, turning to her own sad, dead fish.

"I wish I could get back in the amateur division, believe me."

There are multiple wineglasses around me, but I pick up the one that seems like water and take a cautious sip. Yes, water, okay, good. "How long are you staying here for?" I ask, then wave a hand to amend, "I mean in Scotland in general, not here at the castle."

Nicola heaves out a sigh that ruffles her glossy bangs. "I leave after the wedding. Mum needs an extra hand, or, let's be real, an extra pair of eyes."

I raise my eyebrows at that, but Nicola just waves me off. "It's boring shop talk. So you're from Texas, right?"

We chat a little bit about back home—me about Houston, Nicola about San Diego—both of us agreeing that Scotland is gorgeous, but awfully cold for girls used to a sunnier locale. And before I know it, the plates are being cleared, and I've done it—survived my first royal dinner.

From there, we move into the ballroom just off the main dining room, and as a string quartet starts up, my stomach sinks. I'd been relieved to get through dinner unscathed, but dancing, too?

I watch the couples moving across the ballroom floor. Lord Henry and Lady Ellis are elegant, and even Nicola acquits herself well, dancing with Sherbet.

And then I scan the people gathered at the edges of the ballroom, looking for a girl who might be Tamsin. I'm not sure why I feel this deep need to see Flora's ex, but I do. Maybe I'm just curious as to what kind of girl could dump Flora. Is she a goddess, too?

I keep looking. The tall brunette in purple? Maybe her? Or—

I feel an elbow at my side, and turn to see Flora smiling at me. "Well?" she asks. "Are you ready to take a turn around the room? There are several blokes looking for a partner, it seems like."

There are a few guys hanging back, but the idea of trying to dance has me shaking my head and nearly backing up into a potted plant. "Oh, no, I don't . . ."

"You don't what?"

"I don't dance," I finish, feeling sweaty and a little sick at the very thought. "I'm, like, catastrophically bad at it."

A glint comes into Flora's eye, and I know I'm in trouble.

Then her hand lands in mine. "We'll just have to remedy that, then, won't we?"

CHAPTER **27**

FLORA DOESN'T DROP MY HAND AS SHE LEADS ME
down one hallway, then another. We pass tall windows that look
out onto the gardens, but I can't see anything except our own
reflections, and I'm struck by how wide-eyed I look, and how
very un-me I am in my dress. But maybe this is me? Just another
version of me I didn't know was in there.

We come to a pair of glass doors with ornate golden handles,
and Flora tugs at one, opening the door. A wave of warm air
and the smell of green, growing things washes over me.

"What is this?" I ask, and she pulls me into the room, shutting the door firmly behind us.

"An orangery," she replies, and I glance over at her. She's
dropped my hand by now, and I chafe my palms up and down
my bare arms, even though I'm definitely not cold. In fact, if we
stay in here much longer, I might start sweating.

"I like when you say things like that as though they're actually words," I tell her, and Flora laughs, walking over to a
nearby potted tree that, yes, has a few oranges on it.

"An orangery," she says, placing one gloved hand under the fruit and modeling it like she's a game show hostess. "Those of us from colder climes had to have special places to grow certain things, and oranges were once considered a luxury item."

"Ahhhh," I say, walking over to another tree. "So if you were really, really fancy, you had a special room in your house just for growing oranges."

Flora inclines her head with a gracious nod. "Ergo," she starts, and we both finish with, "an orangery."

I laugh a little, shaking my head, and wander deeper into the room, which is all glass walls and potted orange trees. The floor under my feet isn't the usual flagstone and marble I've seen in the castle, but a cream-colored tile, and in the center, there's a mosaic of a giant orange with a few white blossoms attached. Overhead, the ceiling is painted to look like a bright blue Mediterranean sky.

"This is a very weird room to have all the way up here in the wilds of Skye," I murmur.

Suddenly I realize Flora is right next to me, her own head back to study the ceiling, and I don't know if it's all the plants or her perfume, but something smells sweet and delicate.

"Lady Ellis had it built when she moved up here," Flora says, still studying the ceiling. "When I was a little girl, and we played hide-and-seek, I always hid in here."

I look over at her, my arms still folded tight across my middle. It's dim in this warm, scented room, the only light coming from sconces placed at intervals around the hexagonal room, and it strikes me that this is kind of . . . romantic.

Clearing my throat (and tearing my eyes away from Flora's sharp jaw), I look back at the ceiling.

"You must've really sucked at hiding, then. Everyone would've known where to look for you."

She shrugs, that Flora Shrug that's both elegant and careless and seems to sum up Everything Flora. "I never worried about it all that much."

That makes me laugh. "You never worried about hiding during hide-and-seek?" I shake my head. "That is ... very you."

That grin flashes. "Isn't it just?"

And then she's taking my hands, pulling me to the center of the room, right over that gigantic orange. "Now, enough stalling. Let's dance."

"So which one of us leads?" I ask, and Flora gives me that look I'm getting used to. That one where she lifts her chin while looking down at me at the same time.

Now it doesn't seem haughty to me, though. Now I see it as the joke she means, and I smile when she says, "Me, naturally."

We stand there in the conservatory in our poofy dresses, and I slowly place my hand in Flora's. My other hand lands on her bare shoulder, her skin warm and silky.

I fight the urge to stroke my thumb over the delicate rise of her collarbone, reminding myself for what has to be the thousandth time that Flora is the least safe of crushes for more reasons than I can count, but that's hard to remember when she puts her hand on my lower back, pulling me close.

There are acres of skirts between us, and it strikes me that whoever came up with the waltz prooooobably didn't imagine two girls doing it together.

Flora looks down at all that silk and tulle and giggles. "Oh, dear."

I go to step back, but her hand tightens on my waist, keeping me from going too far. "This is stupid," I say, cheeks red. "You don't have to—"

"But I want to," she says, and her head comes up, her eyes meeting mine.

I wish I could say I got the hang of it immediately and that there were zero crushed toes or awkward spins, but that would not be the truth. I'm not a *total* disaster, but let's just say that *Dancing with the Stars* is nowhere in my future.

Still, it's nice, turning in circles in the conservatory with Flora, the smell of orange blossoms heavy in the air, her tiara winking in the soft glow of the lamps. And it's nice being with her, as much as I hate to admit it.

"You're a natural," she says, and I look up, frowning.

"You're messing up my count." I'd been doing the whole one-two-three, one-two-three thing in my head, not that it had seemed to help all that much.

She rolls her eyes. "Don't count. Just feel."

"Okay, talk like that is for sexy dances, not the waltz," I say, and one corner of her mouth lifts in that slinky, feline smile she does.

"Are you saying this isn't sexy?"

I blink at her.

Is she flirting with me? And if she is, is it just because Such Is Flora, or is she feeling as intrigued by this whole thing as I am?

No, can't let myself think that, can't go there at *all*. One heartbreak per year should be more than enough for me. And that's all Flora could be, really.

Heartbreak.

We come from entirely different worlds. I don't even know how to dance, much less how to address a duke by his title or what fork to use. And I think of all those tall, glossy-haired girls surrounding Flora. Caroline. Ilse. Probably Tamsin.

Me? Definitely not tall. Or glossy.

Not to mention, I'm pretty sure that getting your heart broken by a princess is a whole new level of awful.

Maybe that's why my feet suddenly trip us up, my heel coming down on the back of my skirt.

I think the Flora I first met would've made some rude remark about what a klutz I am, but this Flora—this new, dangerous Flora—just laughs. "Okay, maybe that's enough waltzing."

It's enough everything. It's too much *everything*.

I can't do this.

Dropping her hand, I move away from her and look back to the orange trees. "So was it just oranges they grew in here or other things, too? Lemons? Limes? Was there some kind of vast citrus empire they were running out of fancy houses back in the day?"

I glance over my shoulder to see that Flora is watching me with a funny look on her face, head slightly tilted. "Quint, are you babbling?" she asks at last, and if I thought my face was hot before, it's probably on fire now.

"Just trying to learn new and interesting Scottish facts!" I reply, smiling too big. "And speaking of, why don't you show me some of the. Um. Paintings outside. In the hall."

The hall is also dim, but it's cold and intimidating, not romantic, so that is for sure where I want to be right now.

I don't even wait for Flora to agree before I head for the doors, determined to put . . . whatever this was behind me.

CHAPTER **28**

"IS THIS ROCK SUFFICIENTLY MAGICAL?"

I'm standing on the top of a massive green hill, staring at a shard of stone thrusting up toward the sky. Wind is whipping my hair out from under my beanie, and my cheeks sting. It started raining on us about fifteen minutes into this hike and only just stopped, so I'm vaguely damp and clammy.

And I am also *delighted*. When Flora told me at breakfast that there was something she wanted to show me, I didn't imagine anything like this.

"The most magical," I confirm to Flora, looking at the Old Man of Storr.

Flora hadn't lied about this part of Skye being almost unbearably beautiful and also very rock-filled. It feels like being on another planet, almost, everything bare and craggy, loose rubble under my feet. Even the other tourists brave enough to make this climb on a windy, wet morning don't take away from the beauty of the place or the sense that I'm somewhere completely different and unknown.

Grinning at me, Flora leans down to pick up a loose pebble, bouncing it in her hand. She's wearing a red jacket and black pants, her own hair also stuffed underneath a hat. Her nose is red, too, but she still looks nearly magazine-ready.

Such is Flora, I guess.

Then she gestures to the rock, calling out over the wind, "So tell me about it!"

I screw up my face, trying to shove my hair back out of my eyes. "What, the rock?"

"Yes, Quint, the big magic rock. Give me all the rock facts in your ginormous brain."

Self-conscious, I dust my hands on the back of my pants, glancing up at the shard. "Well, it's made of two types of rock," I start, and Flora sits on the ground, drawing her knees up to her chest and wrapping her arms around them. It's a very un-Flora-like pose, and I almost giggle at it, her sitting there like a bright and eager student.

"Louder!" she calls, and I roll my eyes.

"Two types of rock!" I repeat. "In layers, see?" I point, and Flora nods. "So that means the rock is fairly fragile and susceptible to weathering, and that's what happened here. All the wind and rain and years just kind of . . . whittled it into this. This big rock."

Flora squints a little as she studies the huge, jagged piece of stone, then she says, "See, legend has it that there's a giant buried under this hill, and that's his thumb, sticking up out of the ground."

"Well, that story is much better than 'giant rock made slightly less giant by erosion,'" I admit, and Flora laughs, standing up.

"I think I like your science-y version better, if I'm honest."

We stand there for a second, grinning at each other, and suddenly last night in the orangery comes rushing back to me. The way I felt dancing with her. How the air around us seemed different, charged.

And even up on top of a mountain in the north of Scotland in October, my skin suddenly flushes hot.

That feeling only intensifies when Flora slips her arm through mine and bumps my hip with hers, saying, "So I delivered on all my Skye promises, yes?"

"And then some," I tell her.

Nodding back at the Old Man of Storr, she steps away and holds out her hand. "Give me your phone, I'll take a picture of you by it."

Feeling self-conscious, I move in front of the rock, pulling my hair out of my eyes before clasping my hands in front of me.

Flora laughs. "Okay, Quint, try to actually look like you're having fun."

"I *am* having fun," I retort. "I'm just terrible at posing for pictures."

With an extravagant sigh, Flora comes to stand next to me, throwing her arm around my shoulders and pulling me in tight. "Fine. We'll selfie it, then, shall we?"

She holds my phone out, her face pressed to mine, and I can see us in my phone screen, her smile dazzling and bright, my own a little more hesitant.

"Quint, you're insulting the giant under the ground with that face," Flora says through her smile, and I laugh.

That's when Flora snaps the picture.

When we get back to the castle, it's already getting dark, even though it's barely evening. The wind has gotten colder, too, and Flora and I tumble out of the car that had taken us to Storr.

"Hand me your phone," she says, and I do it without thinking because Flora is that good at issuing commands.

"Back in the land of Wi-Fi," she mutters to herself, and I remember setting up my phone with the castle's Wi-Fi yesterday. The network was called "IT'S THIS ONE GRANDDA," so I assumed one of Lord Henry's grandkids had set it up for him.

Flora's fingers tap over the screen, and I make a grab for the phone with a laugh. "What are you doing?"

"Posting this amazing shot of us to your Instagram because I know you won't," she replies. "Or if you do, you'll forget to give us the filter that makes us the prettiest."

"Right, because you need a filter for that," I say, the words just tumbling out, and Flora looks up at me, nose crinkling.

"Are you calling me pretty, Quint?"

My face flames hot, and I make another grab for the phone, but Flora is already turning away with a triumphant "Ha!"

She hands the phone back to me then, and there we are on my Instagram, windblown and laughing, the Old Man of Storr barely in the shot. Then I read the caption.

Two "stone"-cold foxes at Storr!

"That is . . . a terrible geology pun," I tell her, but I'm grinning like an idiot.

"Oi!" Flora cries with mock outrage. "Points for trying at least!"

I slip my phone back into the pocket of my jacket. "Don't you have to be careful about that kind of thing?" I ask her. "Putting pictures of you up on the internet and stuff?"

Flora takes off her sunglasses, polishing them with the ends of her scarf. "A bit. I'm not allowed to have any social media, of course, and I'm sure at some point, someone will find that shot on your page and it will end up on one of the blogs or in a magazine, but . . ."

She shrugs. "It's not exactly a scandalous picture, and I wanted to take it. So I did."

"*I wanted to, so I did,*" I say. "Basically your motto."

Flora lifts her chin at that. "Oooh, I might see about having that officially added to my crest!"

She turns away then, missing the way my mouth drops open a little bit. Right. She *has a crest.* Because princess.

Shaking my head, I jog to catch up with her, and the two of us are almost to the front steps when a voice says, "There you are."

We stop there in the front courtyard, the fountain burbling to our left as a tall brunette walks down the front steps. She's wearing black pants tucked into high glossy boots and a white blouse with an honest-to-god tweed vest. Even though it's dim outside, an expensive pair of sunglasses rests on top of her head, pulling her hair back from her face.

And it's a good face. High cheekbones, straight nose, really great brows.

"Tam," Flora says, pulling up short, and I am in no way surprised that this gorgeous creature in front of us is Flora's ex.

Tamsin's eyes slide to me in all my grubby, mountain-climbing glory, and I pull off my beanie, attempting to smooth down my hair, but I can feel my bangs sticking up and off to the side.

"Hi," I say with a little wave. "So I'll go on in and let you two—"

Flora threads her arm through mine, and she draws me closer to her side, effectively freezing me in place. "No, stay," she says. "Tam, this is Quint—Amelia, I mean."

"Millie, really," I say, offering Tamsin my hand, and after a beat, she shakes it with a faint "Hullo."

"Quint's my roommate at Gregorstoun," Flora adds, and Tamsin looks back to her, her arms folded loosely over her chest.

"It's still hard to imagine you there," she says with a little smile, and Flora finally lets go of my arm to flick her hair out of her eyes.

"It's not so bad," she says. "The company is interesting at least."

Something flickers over Tamsin's face at that, but then she gives a little laugh. "Good to know. I was hoping I'd get to see you this weekend. I was hoping—"

"Well, you did get to see me, so lucky for you," Flora interrupts, and then her hand is on my arm again, tugging me toward the house.

We head up the front steps and through the massive door, Tamsin's eyes on our backs, I'm pretty sure, and only once we're inside does Flora let out a long breath, reaching up to take off her hat and ruffle her hair.

"Well, that was awful," she mutters, and I reach out, laying my hand on her arm.

"I'm sorry," I say. "Trust me, I know how awful that feels."

"Dastardly Jude," Flora says in response, and I can't help but giggle a little.

"The very same. But if it's any consolation, it's totally Tamsin's loss."

Flora looks over at me, and it might just be a remnant of the cold, but I could swear there's a blush high on her cheekbones. "It is, isn't it?" she says at last, and when we head upstairs to our rooms, I don't think anything of slipping my arm through hers again.

CHAPTER 29

WHEN WE GET BACK FROM SKYE, DR. MCKEE IS waiting for us in the front hall. I wonder if she's going to ask us about our trip or maybe hit up Flora for information on Lord Henry—the school is always on the lookout for wealthy donors, Saks says—but instead, she says, "Welcome home, ladies. I hope you had a lovely time on Skye. One of my favorite places in Scotland."

"It was gorgeous," I say, meaning it, and Dr. McKee gives me what I think is a genuine smile.

Then she says, "In your absence, we've decided to make a few changes. Miss Quint, for the rest of the school year, you'll be rooming with Miss Worthington. Miss Baird, Miss Worthington's roommate, Miss Graham, will be taking Miss Quint's place in your room."

We stand there in the hall, not saying anything for a beat, and I have this horrible, jolting thought that Dr. McKee heard about us dancing at Skye. That she somehow *knows* that it's like the ground has shifted underneath me and Flora just the tiniest bit.

It makes me want to squirm with embarrassment, and I don't even look over at Flora when she says, "For heaven's sake, why? Quint and I were just getting to be friends. Isn't that the point of being roommates?"

Dr. McKee's smile tightens just a bit. "The point of being roommates is learning how to share space with other people in a congenial and respectful manner. Friendships are a lovely bonus, but not the point, no."

This still feels weird to me, and I think Flora might keep fighting, but instead, after another long pause, she only shrugs. "Fine," she says, and then she turns to me.

"Well."

"Well," I echo, very aware of Dr. McKee watching us.

"Suppose I'll see you in class, Quint."

"Yeah, same," I reply, and I wonder if we're supposed to shake hands or something.

But Flora just turns, heading up the stairs with her bag. When she's out of sight, to my surprise, Dr. McKee reaches out and rests a hand on my shoulder.

"This is for the best, Miss Quint, I assure you. And this decision is not a reflection of your behavior at all, but more a . . . let's say a precautionary measure."

"Against what?" I ask, my fingers numb around the handle of my duffel bag.

"I told you," she says. "You need to be careful in choosing friends here at Gregorstoun. Miss Baird is a lovely person, and her life is very glamorous indeed, but you never struck me as the person to get her head turned by that. It's part of why you were assigned to be her roommate in the first place. And now . . ."

Cheeks hot, I heft my bag a little higher. "And now my head seems turned?"

"Flora's mother thought it might be better for her to live with someone who's not quite as attached to her," Dr. McKee says, and okay, then. So that's the real answer—this isn't just a school decision, it's basically a royal decree.

I remember Flora saying her mom thought her liking girls was a phase. Is that what this is about?

And if it is, what does that mean?

Moving rooms doesn't take nearly as long as I think it will. That's the deal we make, that I'll go to Sakshi's room while Elisabeth moves into Flora's, and as I stack up the last of my books, Flora sits on the edge of her bed, watching me.

"She's an actual child, you know. What's-her-name. Lady McHorseyHorse."

"We're not supposed to use titles here," I reply, "so it's Miss McHorseyHorse."

Flora snorts in response, and I slide a bookmark into the latest Finnigan Sparks novel before adding it to my stack. "Upside, you won't have to look at so many rocks anymore, probably. Just plastic horses."

"I like rocks," Flora says, and I look over at her, eyebrows raised.

"You do not," I say, and she flicks her hair over one shoulder.

"I am growing and evolving under your influence, Quint."

She's joking, but there's still something in her face, something that makes me feel sadder than moving rooms should warrant. I'm getting to room with Saks, after all, and I love Saks. A month ago, I would've been thrilled at this switch.

So why am I so bummed out now?

I glance at my phone and see I have a few notifications. When I pick it up, I open to the picture of me and Flora, the one she posted just yesterday, and see a handful of comments. There's Lee with *GIRL, WHAT?? ALSO: BABE!!!* and right under him, Saks has chimed in, *MEGA BABE*. It's funny, seeing the two of them together there in the comments, two friends from two very different parts of my life, and I wonder what it would be like if they met one day.

I'm still trying to picture it—Lee and Saks hanging out—when I notice the last comment.

HeyJude02: You look so happy.

Looking at the picture, my cheeks pink, my mouth open as I laugh, Flora's face right next to mine, I really do look happy. Really happy. Because I *am* happy.

Or was until I realized I'd be switching rooms.

Without letting myself overthink it, I reply to Jude's comment.

☺

Okay, as far as replies go, an emoji isn't much, but I figure it's something.

Clearing my throat, I pick up the last of my things. "So I'd say this has been fun, but it's really only been a little bit fun, and mostly annoying," I say, and Flora tilts her head, looking up at me from underneath her lashes.

"Liar," she says, and I make a big show of rolling my eyes.

"Maybe the fun outweighed the annoying, but only in, like, tiny, microscopic amounts."

"Keep telling yourself that, Quint," she replies, and then she gives a little laugh, shaking her head. "This is so silly. I'm going to see you every day even if we don't live together anymore, so let's not get maudlin here." She waves one hand. "Go. Get settled with Saks and tell Miss Horsey I'm awaiting the pleasure of her company."

"Will do," I say, and I make myself walk out without a backward glance.

CHAPTER 30

"SAKS, CAN YOU GIVE ME SOME GOSSIP ON THE royal family?"

We're lying on Sakshi's bed, technically studying for our upcoming history test, but my mind has been a million miles away.

If I'm honest, I've been out to lunch ever since Skye two weeks ago. Things between me and Flora have been pretty much the same—we get along, we chat, we sit together at lunch—but that moment in the orangery has been playing on a loop in my head. And not just that, but the whole weekend, really. Giving me her favorite room. Picking out the perfect dress for me. Is this just Flora trying to be nice now that we're friends, or—

Okay, maybe this is why Dr. McKee decided I should room with Saks instead.

I come out of my reverie to see a long expanse of Sakshi's thigh peeking out from beneath her skirt as she leans down to rummage under her bed.

"Poppet, I thought you'd never ask," she says, coming back up with a stack of magazines. She flops them onto her green bedspread, grinning.

"Where did you get those?"

Saks sits up on her bed, crossing her legs. "I have my sources."

She pulls the first glossy issue off the stack, setting it down with a thwack on the bed between us. The word "MAJESTY" is printed on top in curling letters.

"This is the latest issue," Saks tells me. "And there's a whole feature on Flora's brother Alexander and his fiancée. Her name is Eleanor Winters, she's American, we're *obsessed*."

Flicking open the magazine, she points to a picture of a blond woman with her cheek on Prince Alex's shoulder as they stand in a garden. "Right," I say, remembering Lee telling me about that. "I sort of know about her."

"And this is her sister, Daisy," Saks goes on, flipping another page. This one shows a redhead in jeans and T-shirt, her arm linked with a handsome guy also dressed way down. "She's dating the chief Royal Wrecker, Miles Montgomery. Well, he was chief Royal Wrecker, he and Seb had some kind of falling-out, not one hundred percent sure it's been sorted. Miles went to America to win Daisy back, so the story goes, and this is them there. We're slightly obsessed with her, too."

"They're still fighting," I say. "Seb mentioned this guy. Said he was dead."

Clucking her tongue, Saks flips another page. "That's a shame. The rumor was he was a calming influence on Seb. He'll need that now that I've declared him a lost cause."

I look up at her, tugging at the ends of my hair. "Wait, what? Since when?"

She reaches for another magazine, this one dated just last week. Opening it to a page showing Seb in a soccer jersey, she taps the picture with one hot pink nail. "Midlothian Hearts," she tells me, like that makes sense.

Seeing my confusion, Saks clarifies, "A football team. My father is a passionate Arsenal supporter." Shaking her head, she sighs. "Like Romeo and Juliet. Daddy would never approve of my marrying a *Hearts* fan, even if he is a prince."

I stare at her for a long beat before laughing and pressing my forehead to her shoulder. "Saks, I really love you," I tell her, and she beams at me.

"Thank you, darling. It's mutual."

Then she reaches into the magazines and pulls out a slightly trashier-looking one. "So you know all about Seb already, really."

"More than I wanted to."

"And you lived with Flora, so I guess you know all you need to there."

Feigning a casual air, I pick a magazine out of the stack. "Never hurts to learn more."

Saks tilts her head down, fixing me with a look, but she doesn't say anything. Instead, she takes the magazine I'm holding back, tosses it aside, and hands me another one.

"This was a special issue all about Flora for her sixteenth birthday," she says, and sure enough, there's Flora on the front, smiling in a plaid-lined trench coat. She's accepting flowers from an old lady in the crowd, and over her head, the headline reads, "Sweet Sixteen!"

"Neat," I say, and then I try to shrug, but I'm pretty sure it looks like I have a muscle spasm in my shoulder. "I'll look through this, I guess."

Sakshi rolls her lips together, holding back a smile, and then she pats my arm. "You can keep it."

An hour later, I'm alone in the room, lying on my bed, reading every word of that magazine. It's a total puff piece, a tribute issue to how great Flora is, but it's still kind of cool, seeing so many pictures of her throughout her life.

Flora in a christening gown.

Flora and Seb as toddlers, hand in hand and weirdly solemn in fancy clothes.

A surprisingly awkward Flora at around twelve or so, braces winking as she grins at the opening of a children's literature exhibit.

Plenty of Flora surrounded by very pretty girls as she gets older.

Those are the ones I keep staring at. Maybe they're all just friends, but some of them were probably more than that, and as I look at shiny head of hair after shiny head of hair, thin, long legs in designer jeans, perfect figures in ball gowns, I am suddenly painfully aware of the fact that I'm wearing old leggings and a hoodie that reads GEOLOGY: IT'S GNEISS!

There's a knock at the door as it opens, and I shove the magazine under my pillow, flipping over onto my back with a paperback copy of *The Mill on the Floss* in hand.

"Hey!" I say to Flora, who stands in the doorway, watching me suspiciously.

"Quint," she says. "I wanted to see if you wanted to study downstairs, but . . . What were you doing?"

I wiggle the book at her. "Reading." Not actually a lie, after all.

She keeps staring at me, but finally seems to accept that answer, walking over to the bed and dropping down on the edge.

Then she frowns at me.

"What does your shirt say?"

"It's a pun," I tell her, tugging at the hem. "Gneiss/nice. See, that's a *real* geology joke."

I wait for an eye roll, but instead she looks over at the rocks on the dresser. "I see you've settled into your new room, then."

"It rocks," I say solemnly, and she bursts into those giggles that are so unprincesslike, but so cute.

Then, surprising me, she gets up and walks over to the dresser, tapping her nails along a few of my specimens.

"I never asked," she says. "Which one is your favorite?"

It's started to rain outside—again, some more—and the lamplight in the room is dim and cozy.

Feeling more than a little awkward, I get up and walk over to her. Flora is taller than me by several inches, just the right height for me to lean my cheek on her shoulder.

Not that I'd ever do that.

Instead, I pick up the hematite. "This one, probably. Hematite. It's magnetic, for one thing, which is super cool. And I got this one when my dad took me to Yellowstone in the sixth grade, so it's special."

"What about this one?" Flora picks up the piece of rose quartz, holding it in her palm.

We're standing close together, so close that when she tilts her head to look down at the rock, the ends of her hair brush over my fingers as I tap the quartz.

"That one's just pretty," I say. "It doesn't have any other special qualities."

Flora's lips curve up. "I happen to think being pretty is a very special quality."

"You would," I huff out on a laugh, but then I look up, and our faces are just . . . right there.

Her lips are right there.

I can smell the lemony soap she uses, can feel the soft, warm exhale of her breath on my face, and if I moved closer—

The blooping sound from my laptop telling me someone is trying to Skype me has us both jumping back, and I shake my head, face hot as I pick my computer up off my bed, answering the call.

It's Dad, and I smile at him, trying to seem normal.

"Hey!"

"Millipede!" he replies, and then Gus's face nearly obscures the camera as he attempts to say hi, too.

Laughing, I sit on the edge of my bed. For the next few minutes, Dad and I chat about things back home while Gus babbles and attempts to show me at least three new toys.

When I end the call, Flora is back near the door, watching me. "You miss them," she says, and I fiddle with the ends of my hair.

"Yeah? As most people do when they're away from their

families. And I won't get to see them until Christmas break."

Her brow wrinkles. "Don't you have some other holiday before that, you Yanks?"

"Thanksgiving," I say, flopping back on my bed and wincing as the magazine rattles. Luckily, Flora doesn't appear to hear it.

"But we can't afford for me to go back then *and* at Christmas, so we're just waiting."

"Do you want me to buy you a ticket?" Flora asks, like she's offering to lend me a pair of shoes.

"I . . . what? No," I stutter out. "I couldn't accept that."

"Why ever not?" Flora asks, and I stare at her. There for just a second, we'd had a moment over that rose quartz. A moment when I forgot she was a princess and just thought of her as a beautiful girl.

But she's also a beautiful girl who would toss a transatlantic plane ticket at someone like it wasn't anything.

In other words, not a girl for me.

The magazine currently hiding under my pillow should remind me of that.

"It's just . . . that's too big, Flora," I tell her now, picking up my book again. "Way too big. You can't just throw money at people."

I can feel her still looking at me, and she eventually gives an airy "Whatever, then."

Lowering the book, I scowl at her over the top. "Flora—"

"No," she says, waving a hand. "Just thought I'd offer. Consider it forgotten."

But I don't miss the way her eyes slide back to me when she thinks I'm not looking.

CHAPTER **31**

"IF THIS IS SOME KIND OF DELAYED HAZING RITUAL,
you're all fired from being my friends," I say, cautiously feeling
my way down the hall. Sakshi has both hands clamped around
my eyes while Perry holds my hand.

"No hazing," he promises, "although I'm kind of surprised
we didn't get that here, come to think of it."

"This place does seem like a peak hazing locale," Sakshi
agrees, and I would roll my eyes if they weren't covered.

They came up to my room a few minutes ago, promising a
"surprise," and I should've known better than to offer myself
up to them. Whatever this is, I have a feeling Flora is involved.
It's been a week since our conversation about the plane ticket,
and while she hasn't brought it up again, I know Flora doesn't
give up that easy.

Maybe that's why I went so willingly with Saks and Perry.

I have a basic sense of where we are. We went down to the
first floor, and I can hear the wheeze from that one radiator
near the art studio that's always acting up, but other than that,

I am firmly Without a Clue as to what we're doing down here.

I am, however, really certain that if we get caught, we will never get out of detention.

"Whatever this is," I warn, "it better be worth it."

"It is," Perry promises, and then my nose picks up the smell of . . . sweet potatoes?

Yes, sweet potatoes with that burned-sugar smell of marshmallow, and over all that, the savory scent of sage.

"Guys," I start, but then Sakshi drops her hands, and I blink.

We're in the art classroom, and there, spread out on the desk, is a miniature Thanksgiving feast. I spot a small roast bird that's not a turkey, but smells great, and a couple of china dishes, one heaped with macaroni and cheese, the other holding the beloved sweet potatoes with marshmallows. There's also a pie and an ancient silver candelabra illuminating the whole thing, but my eyes are drawn to one thing and one thing only.

The girl standing behind the desk, beaming at me.

"Surprise!" Flora trills, clapping her hands together. She's wearing jeans and a sweater, her hair loose around her face, and she's smiling at me, a real smile, and I am surprised.

Not by the miniature Thanksgiving she's made for me, though.

No, what surprises me is the sudden, jolting, and undeniable realization that even though I didn't want to, I've fallen for an actual princess.

Flora's smile drops slightly, her hands lowering. "Are you not pleased?" she asks, looking down at the food. "Did I get it wrong?"

I have to swallow before I'm able to speak. "No," I reassure her, stepping forward. Out of the corner of my eye, I see Perry and Sakshi exchange a glance.

"No, it's perfect," I go on. "I mean, three actual weeks before Thanksgiving, but still. This is . . . I'm speechless."

That smile lights up her face again, and my heart thuds so painfully in my chest I'm surprised no one can hear it. My head is spinning and my throat is so dry that I happily gulp down the can of soda Flora hands me.

I immediately regret that decision when a sort of flat bubble-gum taste hits my tongue, and I pull back the can to frown at it.

"Yeurgh."

"That's Irn-Bru, Scotland's national drink, missy," Flora says, all faux-offended as she takes the can back from me, and when our fingers brush, I swear I feel sparks.

But I make myself give her a look and say, "Didn't you also think the stag was Scotland's national animal? And look where that got us."

"Look where it got us indeed," Flora counters. "We're friends now. We wouldn't have been without that stupid stag."

She has a point, but all I can think is that that must be where all this started. It wasn't the laundry or the dance in the orangery or looking at my rocks together—it was that night up there on the hill that led to this moment, me realizing I'm into her. I should've seen it then, the way things changed between us.

We eat the rest of our tiny feast happily enough, Flora regaling us with the tale of how she got all this food here in the first place.

"I don't know how Glynnis managed to find someone who

could make this," Flora added, picking up the spoon in the sweet potatoes and poking around at the dish, "but the woman is a superhero."

And then Flora's gaze shoots to me, her teeth dimpling her lower lip.

"Bollocks. Is that too big, too? Having a royal liaison track down food? I know you said the plane ticket was a lot—"

I reach over and touch her arm, shaking my head. "No, that was just . . . using available resources. It's different from throwing money at something."

Flora nearly preens at that, lifting her chin with a smug smile. "So I thought."

Across the desk, I see Saks and Perry glance at each other, something passing between them, but I ignore it.

For now, things feel . . . homey. Nice.

Almost normal.

And then there's a flash in the window.

Interesting (I guess, if you're into that sort of thing) news to report out of Scotland today. Princess Flora has managed to keep her nose clean for the last six weeks or so, shocking everyone, I'm sure. Maybe that draconian school they sent her to is working? Or maybe it's something else. Apparently there's a mole up there in the Highlands, and not the fuzzy kind. A student has been leaking info on Flora to the press, and according to the source, Princess Flora has gotten very cosy with her new roommate, some girl from Texas named Amelia Quint. So cosy, in fact, that they are roommates no more, according to our source. A few weeks ago, the princess and her new pal were separated into different rooms. Could be they're just friends, but the source seems to think they're more. Anyway, here's a blurry shot of the two of them eating . . . Thanksgiving? With some other people? Who the f*** knows.

Personally, I hope for Flora's sake she is dating an American girl who might actually have sense, but then I wouldn't wish Flora on my worst enemy, so it's a real toss-up here.

("Princess Flora Does Some Stuff, I Know You'll All Click on It, I Need to Eat," from *Off with Their Heads*)

CHAPTER **32**

THE PHOTOGRAPHER THEY FISH OUT OF THE BUSHES is younger than I'd imagined most paparazzi to be. Maybe he's new, which is why he made the rookie mistake of having his flash on.

Despite Dr. McKee telling all of us to clear the halls, it feels like the whole school gathers there in the foyer to watch her and Mr. McGregor talk to the local police, as the photographer sits in the back of a police car. I hear the word "trespassing," and Mr. McGregor, red-faced and fairly bristling with anger, mentions "tarring and feathering" at least four times.

Next to me, Flora is very quiet and very still as she watches.

"They took the SD card from his camera," I tell her. "And it's not like he got anything all that exciting. Unless a bunch of teenagers eating yams would sell papers over here or something."

But Flora shakes her head, long hair swishing against her shoulder blades. "He'll have sent the pictures on already. He took them on his phone, not with the camera."

She looks over at me. "That's their trick. Show up with a big expensive camera, everyone assumes that's what you've used, so no one thinks about the phone." She turns back to stare out the massive front doors at the scene on the front lawn. "It's rather ingenious of them, really."

With that, she turns to head up the stairs, and I follow after her, grabbing her elbow.

"Go tell them that!" I say. "About the phone. Maybe he hasn't sent—"

But Flora is already moving away. "That's sweet, Quint, but I promise you, it's a done deal."

I watch her vanish up the stairs, and Sakshi comes to stand next to me, following my gaze.

"This is why her mother wanted her to have a security detail up here," she tells me. "Flora sells more magazines than her brothers put together."

"Even more than Seb?" I ask, and Sakshi nods before twirling a strand of her long dark hair and turning to face me. Well, to look down at me, what with her being an Amazon and all.

"Do you like her, Millie?" she asks.

Gah. My throat feels tight suddenly, my face probably bright red as I gesture vaguely. "Yeah. I mean, we're definitely getting along better now, so—"

"No." Sakshi's hand comes down on mine, covering the back of it. "I mean . . . do you *like* her?"

Cutting her a look, I pull my hand back. "Isn't this the kind of thing we should be asking in notes? The kind with boxes, check yes or no?"

She smiles at that, but there's real concern in her face when she looks at me. The corners of her mouth turn down, her eyes narrowing just a little. "I just don't want you to get hurt."

It's close to what Darcy said about Jude, that I was setting myself up for heartbreak, and I don't like that comparison.

"Trust me, neither do I," I reply.

We all hang out downstairs until the police car drives away and Dr. McKee comes in, briskly clapping her hands and telling us to disperse. Everyone follows her order, but I hang back, waiting until the hall is mostly clear to approach the headmistress.

"Dr. McKee?" I ask, and she turns, eyebrows raised like she's surprised to see me there.

"Yes, Miss Quint?"

"What's going to happen with that guy?" I ask, nodding out toward the front doors.

Dr. McKee turns to follow my gaze, reaching up to pat at her chignon. "Oh, I assume they'll take him to the station in the village, put the fear of god into him, and send him back to Edinburgh or Glasgow or wherever he came from."

"Is the queen going to hear about it?" I ask, and Dr. McKee pivots on her heels to face me fully.

"That's none of your concern, Miss Quint," she says, which I take as a yes. Will that mean more security people around? Flora will hate that.

But I don't say anything, just nod and give Dr. McKee my best Humbled and Quailed face before jogging up the stairs.

I open the door to see Flora sitting on my bed.

Holding the magazine about her that I'd shoved under my pillow. And, stupidly, kept there ever since.

She looks up when I come in, and as I close the door behind me, she holds up the magazine.

"Bedtime reading?"

"Saks had it," I say. "A-after Skye, I was curious about your life and the people in it, so I asked for help, and—"

"And then decided to get into the lucrative side business of spying on me for the tabloids?"

The words are so unexpected that I take a step back. "What?"

Flora tosses the magazine to my bed, standing up and folding her arms over her chest, one hip cocked slightly. She looks every inch the Mean Girl I'd tagged her as on my first day, and I realize that I'd forgotten just how cold she can be when she wants.

"That photographer was up here because someone has been leaking information. I just checked the various blogs dedicated to tracking every breath me or my brothers take, and what do you know?" She pulls her phone out of her pocket, wiggling it at me. "Story after story about me, about you, about us going to Skye, about what went wrong at the Challenge. And now I see you've been reading up on me."

I'm still gaping at her. "Do you . . . honestly think I'm calling up Scottish tabloids and telling them things? Flora, I wouldn't even know how to do that. American, remember? Also, unlike you, I don't steal my phone back from the main office every five seconds. I only have it on the weekends, and you're around me most of—"

"Then why were you reading about me?" she asks, her voice getting louder, and I don't know if it's shock that she'd actually think I'd do something like rat her out to the press, or if my head is still spinning from the fake Thanksgiving and finally understanding how I feel about her, but I hear myself shout back, "Because I like you!"

I have never seen a Shocked Flora, but that's who's standing in front of me now. Her mouth drops open slightly, and I throw up my hands, determined to let this now be as embarrassing as possible.

"I have a crush on you," I go on. "A stupid and hopeless crush, and honestly, I am *very* disappointed in myself about it, but there it is. I like you. I wanted to read that magazine so I could learn more about you, and also look at pictures of you because you're pretty, and this is *the* most embarrassing thing that has ever happened to me, so enjoy watching it, I guess."

Only once all the words are out do I realize I didn't do the nervous stuttering thing, that moment when all the words I want to say form a logjam of awkward in my mouth. I just spat it all out directly in her face, and oh my god, I just told her . . . everything.

She's still staring at me, her arms still folded across her chest.

"You like me," she repeats, and completely defeated by my humiliation, I shrug, both palms up.

"I do. It's so dumb, but I do."

Flora drops her arms, reaching up to tuck her hair behind her ears. "Why is it dumb?" she asks, and I look at her, my heart seeming to speed up and slow down all at once. I'm so aware of it thudding there in my chest, in my throat, in my ears.

"What?"

Stepping closer, Flora murmurs, "Why is it dumb, Quint?"

And then . . . holy crap, she's kissing me.

Flora's hands are cold on my cheeks, or maybe it's just that my face is hot, but I can feel each of her fingertips on my skin, pressing in like a brand, and my own hands come up to catch her wrists. It shouldn't be a big surprise that Flora is such a stellar kisser, but my knees didn't get the message because they're trembling like I just did four laps around the school.

And underneath my fingers, I can feel the steady pulse of Flora's heartbeat, a reminder that I'm not the only one feeling shook here.

Smiling against her mouth, I pull back a little, and she grins at me, that real smile that probably shows too many teeth to be a Proper Princess Smile, but the one that is definitely my favorite.

Then it fades from her face, and a trio of wrinkles appears between her perfectly groomed eyebrows. "Oh god, is this too much?" she breathes. "Is it too soon, do you need more time? I can give you more time, if you want, I just . . . I just felt like I had to kiss you, so I did."

Pulling back even more, I raise my eyebrows at her. "Are you, Princess Flora Ghislaine Mary Baird, actually saying you might have rushed into something? Like, you're admitting that?"

She presses her forehead to mine briefly, and I wonder why the scent of the same soap we all use here smells so much different on her skin than it does on mine or anyone else's. "Did I rush in?" she asks, and I take a deep breath before shaking my head.

"No. No, for the first time since I met you, I think you might have had perfect timing."

CHAPTER **33**

SOMEHOW I'D FORGOTTEN WHAT IT FEELS LIKE TO be in deep smit for someone.

With Jude, there was that weirdness carrying over from how long we'd been friends, from keeping it kind of secret, from still trying to figure out what the whole thing meant. With Flora, there's just . . .

Well, there's just moments like right now as we do our laps around Gregorstoun, and she glances over at me with a bright smile, cheeks pink, hair sticking to her face even though it's freaking freezing, and my heart feels so big in my chest I can hardly stand it.

"Are you going to sing this time, Quint?" Flora teases, turning to jog backward, and I nod at her.

"Maybe. If you fall and bust your ass, I'm definitely going to sing a song about that and the perils of hubris. Like an Oompa-Loompa."

"What is it with you and the Willy Wonka references?" she

asks, turning back to jog like a normal person, and I slow down a little, Flora falling into step with me.

"Maybe 'Veruca Salt' can be our always," I joke, and she laughs.

Then, as we approach a rise in the path, she reaches out and grabs my hand, pulling me behind a rock formation to press a quick but heated kiss to my mouth, and yeah.

Maybe I haven't forgotten what this feels like, because I'm not sure I've ever felt *anything* like this.

Pulling back, she studies my face for a long moment, then runs her thumb over my lower lip, sending a shower of sparkles through my blood.

Then I lean in to kiss her, and this time, there's nothing quick about it.

I happen to think Flora and I are being very discreet about this new thing between us, but I'm immediately disabused of that notion at lunch as Sakshi and Perry sit on either side of me, almost simultaneously. They're good at that, so good that I sometimes wonder if they've practiced.

"Spiiiillll," Saks sings out, opening her bottle of mineral water while Perry reaches over me to steal the roll off Sakshi's tray.

"Or don't," he tells me, glaring over at Saks, "because it's none of our business."

Saks rolls her eyes. "Honestly, Perry, don't be such an old lady. Millie is our friend, and we support her happiness, which means we need to learn all about it. So. Spill."

Blushing, I roll my shoulders and continue pushing beans

around my plate. "There's not much to spill," I say, and Saks heaves out a huge sigh, ruffling her hair.

"Not much to spill? Millicent—"

"It's Amelia, and you know that."

"You're dating a *princess*," Saks goes on like I didn't even say anything, fluttering one hand by her face, and I'm surprised by how much hearing those words feels like a punch to the gut.

"No," I say, shaking my head. "That's not what—"

"That's absolutely what's happening," Sakshi argues, and even Perry nods, his mouth full of bread.

"It really is, Millie," he says, and I look back and forth between them.

"I like Flora," I say in a low voice. "And she likes me. But what that means is . . . still something we're figuring out."

Saks wrinkles her nose a little. "Oh, darling," she says. "It doesn't work like that. Not with this crowd."

I see Flora walk into the dining room then, and there's that silly little trip in my chest at just seeing her.

Saks follows my gaze, then giggles, nudging me with her elbow. "Oh, you smitten kitten, you," she teases, and I shove back at her.

"Staaaahp."

"She doesn't deserve you," Perry says, but he's smiling, too, and Saks reaches across me to pat his arm.

"That's so loyal, Peregrine," she says, and he grins back at her, and I suddenly realize I'm not the only smitten kitten at this table.

But then Saks shifts in her chair, picking up her fork and

adding, "You know they found out who was telling reporters about Flora, right? It was Elisabeth! My former roommate turned Flora's roommate, can you believe it?" She shakes her head. "Of all the people it could've been, it was a horsey girl."

She lowers her voice. "Apparently she found out the papers paid well for Flora tidbits, and she wanted some fancy new . . . what was it, Perry? A saddle?" She shrugs. "I don't know, I don't like horses, much to my father's horror."

"Isn't she, like, twelve?" I ask. "Some sixth grader was selling gossip?"

Picking at her own beans on toast, Saks glances at me. "I told you, darling," she says. "Whole other world."

Later that afternoon, I'm sitting in my room with Flora. Sakshi has cleared out to give us some privacy, and I'm on my bed while Flora sits at the desk, both of us working on our papers for Mrs. Collins's lit class, but every once in a while, we peek up over our laptops at one another until finally, Flora puts her computer down with a thump and launches herself across the room to lie on my bed.

Giggling, I close my own laptop, leaning down to brush her hair back from her face. It's still a weird feeling, just reaching out and touching her like that, but I like it.

Flora does, too, I think, as she rolls onto her back to look up at me, her lashes long around those golden eyes.

"You're distracting me," I tell her, and she shrugs, reaching up to tangle her fingers with mine there by her shoulder.

"What's the fun of having a schoolmate you snog if you don't distract her from schoolwork?"

The words are light, teasing, but they make some of that golden glow I was feeling dissipate.

Schoolmates who snog.

Friends who kiss.

But Flora isn't Jude, I remind myself, and I lean down, still a little shy as I kiss her.

But Flora is definitely not shy, kissing me back with her hand at the back of my head, and soon it's not so much kissing as it is making out, my paper and laptop and own name pretty much forgotten.

It's not just the kissing (although I like that a lot) but all of it.

The way Flora's fingers always dance over any piece of exposed skin, turning places I never thought of as all that sexy—the insides of my elbows, the spaces between my fingers, my forehead—into pulse points of want.

How her usually imperious *"Quint"* sounds so different when it's whispered against the damp skin of my neck.

Or how she makes *me* so different. Bolder and braver, quicker to touch her in all the places where she wants to touch me.

This is one of those times when I feel like I can't *stop* touching her, even with all our clothes on, and I probably would stay there wrapped up in her forever if my phone didn't suddenly chime.

Lifting my face from Flora's, I wrinkle my nose. "That's my phone."

Still draped across the bed, her face pink, Flora pushes her hair back. "So?"

"So it's in the main office?" I say, and Flora gives me that smug smile.

"Is it?"

Groaning, I get off the bed as my phone beeps again, clearly coming from the top drawer of my desk.

"I just thought you'd want yours, too," Flora says, pushing herself up on her elbows, and I open the drawer.

"Thank you for including me in your life of crime," I say, but Flora is, not surprisingly, completely unapologetic.

I see now that the chimes are from my email, the personal one I still keep, not the one the school gave me, and they're both from Lee.

Guilt hits me a little at that. I haven't talked to Lee in a couple of weeks now, even though I'd been meaning to. It's just things had gotten so—

And then I see the subject lines of the emails.

The first one: WHAT THE ACTUAL HELL MILLIE

And the second: YOU ARE DATING A PRINCESS WHAT

Opening the first email, I see Lee has left me a link to some blog called *Off with Their Heads*. Charming.

It's got a picture from our "Thanksgiving"—guess Flora was right about the guy having taken it with his phone—but also, there's my name.

My name right there.

And the second email has another blog post, this time with Lee adding his own commentary.

Millie, you have been HOLDING OUT. I knew you had a crush, BUT ON A PRINCESS? WHO IS YOUR ROOM-MATE???? What is going on? Email me immediately. Email me YESTERDAY.

"Who's Lee?"

I turn to see Flora right behind me, surprising me.

"My best friend," I say, distracted as I mess with my hair. "How do people already know this stuff?"

Flora lifts one shoulder, heading back to my bed. "They always do," she says before settling back down with her laptop. "And honestly, I'm glad this time. Maybe now Mummy will understand that I'm gay, not 'going through a phase.'"

I look over at her, wondering if I can explain how weird this makes me feel, seeing my name on some random blog. I'm . . . nobody. I've never been mentioned on the internet in my life except for that time I came in second in my district's geography bee in seventh grade.

But of course Flora wouldn't get that at all since she's been in the public eye since before she was born. Literally. There was a whole part in that tribute magazine full of pictures of a pregnant Queen Clara.

And I get what she means, about this maybe finally forcing the issue of her being publicly out.

So I just put my phone back in the desk drawer, promising myself I'll email Lee later.

I sit back on my bed, pulling my computer over, and Flora turns to look at me.

"Okay?" she asks, and I nod.

"Yeah," I say. "It's just . . . weird."

Flora doesn't say anything for a minute, then she sits up, placing both of her feet on the floor, her hands braced on the edge of the mattress.

"Do you want to come home with me this weekend?"

"What, to Edinburgh?" I ask, and when she nods, I add, "To the *palace?*"

"That is my home, yes. My mom's throwing this little party for Alexander and his fiancée, and I just think . . . well, once you spend a little more time with my family, things like that"— she gestures to my phone—"might not seem so odd. We're all frightfully boring, after all."

"So I'd be your . . . date. To this party."

"If you want to be," Flora says evenly. "Or you can be my good friend and former roomie, Quint, come to keep me out of trouble."

I snort at that. "Date would definitely be more believable than Person Who Keeps Flora Out of Trouble."

Another smile and she crosses her legs at the ankles, swinging her feet. "Is that a yes?"

I think about Queen Clara and the last time I saw her—the only time I saw her—and Seb with the whole pub brawl thing. So far, my impressions of Flora's family haven't been great, but maybe she's right. Maybe if I'm in and among them, this won't all feel so . . . bizarre.

"It's a yes."

CHAPTER **34**

THE TRIP TO SKYE WAS ONE THING, BUT THIS—HEADING
to the actual palace with Flora for a weekend—is a whole
other deal. For one, we don't drive down. A car takes us from
Gregorstoun to Inverness, where we get on a train, but not
just any train. The Baird family has their own train car, decked
out with the family crest everywhere and seats that are comfier
than any I've ever sat in. Flora sits next to me, our fingers
intertwined as we watch the countryside rush by, and I'm
thrilled and happy and pants-wettingly terrified all at the same
time. When Flora and I went to Skye, it was just as friends.

Now we're definitely more-than, but is it maybe too soon
to be this . . . official? This isn't just some family visit, after
all. It's a party for the upcoming royal wedding. Will I go to
the wedding with Flora as her date? And speaking of weddings,
how will that work one day for Flora? I mean, it's way too soon
to be thinking about getting *married*, but is there a title for a girl
who marries a princess? Is there—

"You have your Thinky Quint Face on."

I glance over to see Flora leaning on the armrest close to me, her lips slightly pursed, eyes narrowed.

"Because I am Quint, and I am thinky," I tell her, but when she leans over to kiss me, it chases all those thinky thoughts away.

When the train pulls into Waverly Station, there's a car waiting for us.

There's also a handful of photographers. Not the sea of flashbulbs I was expecting, but still, I feel very aware of the fact that I'm wearing jeans, a sweater, and sneakers, and that I probably should've gone with something other than a ponytail for my hair.

Flora let me borrow a pair of her sunglasses, and they feel too big and too silly on my face, but I'm glad for them as we get into the back of the town car.

"Oof," I say once the door has shut behind us and we're winding our way through a narrow street, passing a sea of touristy shops. "I have never been so aware of people looking at me."

"How dare you? They were looking at *me*," Flora replies, but she's smiling when she says it, and I laugh, fluffing out my bangs and attempting to smooth back my hair.

"We are going to have a chance to look a little nicer before I meet the other royals, right?" I ask, and Flora nods, already typing away on her phone.

"Glynnis is in charge of this entire thing, so we might actually have hairdressers meeting us at Holyrood."

She's kidding.

At least I think she is.

But I don't have time to ask because the car is suddenly pulling up to the palace, turning through big wrought-iron gates, and it's all I can do not to press my nose against the window as Holyrood looms into view.

"Oh man," I breathe, taking in the warm-colored stone under the afternoon light. "It's so . . ."

"It is," Flora says happily, and when she reaches out to squeeze my hand, I feel that same mix of giddiness and terror that accompanied me on the train ride down.

Glynnis is waiting for us in the drive, as shiny and polished as ever, and I notice Nicola standing a few feet away. She's not quite as put together as her mom, but she still looks nice in a button-down shirt and cute skirt.

"Hi again," I say to her, waving, and she waves back before walking over.

As Flora and Glynnis confer about something, Nicola leans close and says, "This is going to be a lot more intense than Skye, but I promise no one is as scary as they seem."

"What does that mean?" I ask, but she just pats me on the shoulder with a sympathetic look before going back over to her mom.

"Amelia," Glynnis says, gesturing me over and snapping at a footman lingering near the car.

"Ralph here will see you to your room," she says before leaning in and saying to the footman, "the Darnley Suite. If the garment bag is not in there, call Charles and tell him to call me."

"Roger, madam," he says, and I'm not sure if he's telling her he understands or if he's correcting her on his name.

In any case, it all sounds vaguely like code.

Then Glynnis turns her attention back to me. "Celeste will come to do your hair at three, then Veronica will be in to do your makeup at four. Once you're dressed, I'll send someone up with a selection of jewels."

I swallow hard. "Jewels?"

The word cracks somewhere in the middle, and my hand goes to my throat, remembering that collar of diamonds Flora wore up on Skye. Will I have something like that? I . . . cannot be trusted with something like that. I'll spend the whole night with my hand on my neck, making sure an object that costs the same as my dad's house—if not more—hasn't plunged into my soup bowl.

Glynnis sees my gesture and laughs a little, shaking her head. "Only some earrings—nothing too valuable."

Somehow I think me and Glynnis don't have the same idea about what "valuable" means, but I'm relieved enough to nod and say, "Sounds great!"

"Emeralds," Flora says to Glynnis, who nods, making a note on her ever-present iPad.

"Go on," Flora tells me, nudging my hand. "Rest up, and I'll see you at five for drinks in the pink drawing room."

When I stare blankly at her, she adds, "Someone will come get you, don't worry about it."

With another smile, she's off with Glynnis and Nicola, and I'm left to follow Ralph-or-maybe-Roger to my room.

I don't actually have a lot of time for gawping at my surroundings, and we go up a series of back staircases and down a bunch of narrow halls, twisting and turning until I'm at a room that's not as pretty as my room on Skye, but still way nicer than anything I've ever seen.

And sure enough, there's a garment bag laid out for me on the bed.

Unzipping it, I see the ball gown I wore on Skye.

"Hi there," I tell it, stroking my hand over the fabric and remembering that dance in the orangery with Flora. Maybe this dress is a good luck charm?

I definitely feel like I'm going to need one.

CHAPTER **35**

IN A WEIRD WAY, IT'S LIKE THE NIGHT AT SKYE ALL over again.

Me in my green dress, Flora in another ball gown, this one gold instead of tartan, another castle, more people in strange old-fashioned uniforms.

It should feel the same, and maybe for Flora it does. This is the kind of thing she's used to, after all. But for me, everything is different.

Flora slips her arm through mine as we approach a pair of huge gilded doors, and I take a deep breath.

Flora glances over at me. "They're just people," she says. "End of the day, same as anyone else."

Looking over at her, I raise both my eyebrows. "Do you actually believe that?"

"Oh god, no," she replies immediately, giving a little shudder. "Bloody terrifying, the whole lot of them, me included."

That makes me laugh, and when she reaches out and briefly takes my hand, I give it a quick squeeze back.

Flora may have been joking, but there's no doubt that this particular *Meet the Parents* moment is more intense than the usual.

Not that we've been totally open about what we are, of course.

If we even are anything.

Please. Me? Royal Girlfriend? The idea is so ridiculous I want to laugh.

Except that when Flora's hand drops from mine, my fingers almost instinctively curl around the empty space, wanting to hold on to her longer. And that feels . . . a lot more than friendly.

But then the doors open, and I don't have time to overthink things anymore.

This is the family's private drawing room, but it's still crowded. All those ball gowns and kilts take up a lot of room, I guess, and I feel shaky and sweaty.

Then I hear, "Ah, here she is."

I've never met Flora's older brother before, but I recognize Prince Alexander as he stands and crosses the room to hug Flora, kissing both her cheeks.

Then he turns to me.

I have a moment of panic. I know I'm supposed to curtsy to the queen, and that means I should probably curtsy to a prince, too, but how deep? Not as deep as I'd curtsy to the queen, right?

I put one foot behind the other, ready to dip, but Alex stops me with a shake of his head and a smile. "No need for that when it's just family," he says, reaching out to instead shake my hand.

Flustered, I shake back, then look over at Flora, who's smiling.

There's a pretty blonde just behind Alex, and I realize this must be his fiancée, Eleanor. Another American in this mess is kind of nice to see, so I probably give her too big of a smile as I reach out to shake her hand, too.

"Hi, I'm Millie. Amelia. Either, really."

"Eleanor," she replies. "Ellie. Either, really, as well."

Her smile is genuine and warm, and I wonder if I can maybe just spend the entire night talking to her and Alex and not deal with any other royals.

"You're from Texas, right?" Ellie asks, and I nod.

"Yeah, outside Houston. How did you know that?"

Alex squeezes Ellie's hand, giving her a small smile. "Ellie makes it her business to know most everything," he says. "I'd be lost without her, always trying to remember names and who's from where."

"You'd be fine," Ellie tells him, but Flora looks over at me and mouths, *No, he wouldn't.*

Is this how it can be here? Just . . . kind of normal? The regular family stuff?

Then I look at the massive paintings on the wall, the fancy weaponry, the suits of armor, and remember that, no, nothing here is normal, and I should probably keep that in mind.

Leaning in close, Alex says to Flora, "Auntie Argie wants to talk to you about something. I'd get that over with as soon as possible if I were you."

Groaning, Flora rolls her eyes and then turns to me. "Let me go deal with that. You'll be fine on your own for a few, right?"

I look around at a sea of glittering jewels and champagne glasses. "Oh, yeah," I say weakly. "Business as usual."

And then she's gone in a cloud of silk and expensive perfume, and when I look over to talk to Alex and Ellie, they're gone, too.

Leaving me just . . . standing there.

"Heeeey, so you have the glazed expression of a person dealing with this whole shebang for the first time."

I glance over to see a redhead who looks vaguely familiar, and she offers me a macaron on a napkin. "Take it," she urges. "The sugar will help."

She's American, too, and I suddenly remember this is Ellie's younger sister, Daisy. I guess she's over for this pre-wedding party, too, and I let her push the treat into my hand, but I don't eat it, looking out instead at the crowd of people milling around, at all the jewels sparkling in the lamplight. "I did a dinner thing," I tell her. "Up north. There were fancy people there, but . . . this seems different."

Nodding, Daisy takes a bite of her own macaron. "Yeah, the Full Palace Experience is something. But hey, you haven't embarrassed yourself, or caused a fight at a polo match—"

"Or insulted a duchess," a boy adds, coming up to stand next to Daisy. He's a little taller than she is, with sandy hair and a face meant for that *Prattle* magazine Flora likes so much. I'm pretty sure he's one of Seb's friends, and, if the way Daisy slips an arm around his waist is any indication, he's also her boyfriend.

"That was one time," she tells him, holding up a finger. "One. Uno."

"Is there a prerequisite for how many aristocrats one has to insult before it can be called 'an Incident'?" the guy counters, and Daisy looks up, clearly pretending to think it over.

"Three," she decides. "Three pissed-off duchesses, and it's a problem. One is a fluke."

He smiles at her, and it changes his face slightly, making him look younger, cuter. And also head over heels in love.

Daisy's got it just as bad if the way she's looking at him is any indication, and I find my own eyes searching out Flora across the room. Are we that obvious? Maybe not?

"Ohhhhh, so *you're* Flora's crush!"

I startle slightly, turning my head back to Daisy, who's grinning at me. "What? No, we're roommates. Or we were."

"You can't be both?" she asks before turning back to the boy at her side. "Miles, light of my life, pain in my ass, will you go get me and . . ."

"Millie," I supply, and she nods.

"Great, Millie. Would you go get Millie and me a couple of drinks, please? The nonalcoholic kind, please."

"That was *also* one time," he mutters, but he presses a quick kiss to her temple before heading off toward the refreshments table.

"Seriously, spill," she says as soon as he's gone. "Because Ellie and Alex were gossiping about Flora having it bad for someone. And, I have to say, I'm relieved because you look so normal and nice? This family needs more normal and nice. I'm *normal*, but nice still eludes me a little. Sorry, is this too much?"

I shake my head. "No, I'm relieved, too. Just that there's someone else who gets how weird this all is."

"It is vast oceans of weird, my friend, for sure."

For a moment, we just stand there, staring at all the people milling around. And then Daisy nudges me with her elbow, nodding toward Miles as he stands near the bar with Spiffy and Dons.

"But sometimes," Daisy says, "you meet someone who makes it all worth it."

I try my best to smile at her, but I clearly don't do so great with it because Daisy reaches out and touches my arm now, her lips pressing together with sympathy. "Except it's different when your person is just, like, the chips and salsa as opposed to the whole enchilada."

Glancing over at her, I raise my eyebrows. "The chips and salsa?"

Daisy wrinkles her nose. "Okay, yeah, don't tell Miles I called him that. I don't think he'd see it as a compliment."

"It's a solid metaphor, though," I admit, and Daisy grins, proud of herself.

"I thought so. But anyway, point is that even being with Miles felt weird at first, and he's just the best friend. Watching my sister go through this with Alex . . ." She shakes her head. "She says he's worth it, too, and I believe her, but I get it. Or I guess I get it as much as anyone can."

That's actually nice to hear, even though I'm not sure she does get it. Watching it and experiencing it are two different things. But she's still the first person who at least gets that it's weird. Perry and Saks have lived in this world for a long time, too, so they don't have that same sense of it that I do, that this is . . . just not how people live, not really. It's their world. It's Flora's world.

But it's not mine.

But Flora? *She's* mine. Or at least she is for right now.

I feel Daisy's hand on my arm again, and she leans in. "Try not to overthink it. That's the best advice I can give. Just . . . go with the flow."

Looking around the room, at the expensive gowns and glittering jewels and actual swords affixed to the walls, that doesn't seem possible, and I say so. "Has anyone in this room ever gone with the flow in their lives, you think?" I ask, and Daisy follows my gaze before shaking her head.

"Probably not, no, which is why they need us."

Miles returns, holding goblets of water, and as he hands them to us, he apologizes, saying, "I know this is not the most exciting of beverage options, but it's all they have that isn't booze."

"'The most exciting of beverage options'—*how* am I attracted to you?" Daisy mutters, but she takes the water anyway before nodding at me and saying, "This is Millie. She's Flora's crush."

"I know," he says, surprising us both. "I read about that earlier." Then he offers me a genuine smile. "Congrats and all that."

"You read about it?" I ask. "Where?"

Thanks to a clever school chum with an iPhone, PEOPLE has these exclusive shots of Princess Flora of Scotland cozying up to her American roommate, Amelia Quint. The Princess and the Texan have been rumored to be more than friends recently, but these pictures of them kissing seem to put to rest any doubts as to the nature of their relationship.

However, don't get your heart *too* set on this being the new Royal Romance now that Flora's brother and his own American Girl, Ellie Winters, are getting closer to tying the knot.

"Flora was mad for Tam," a source tells PEOPLE exclusively, referring to Lady Tamsin Campbell, once thought to be paired with Prince Sebastian, "and they'll probably end up back together in the end. Flora only chucked her because she freaked out when it got too serious. Honestly, most of us think this thing with the roommate is just a ploy to make Tam jealous."

Poor Amelia!

("EXCLUSIVE: FLORA AND GAL PAL HEAT UP THE HIGHLANDS!" from *People*)

CHAPTER **36**

I SIT ON THE LITTLE TUFTED BENCH IN THE DIM HALLWAY,
staring at my phone.

It's not a bad picture of me with Flora. In fact, I look kind
of . . . good in it. Not as good as Flora, of course, but then,
I'm not superhuman. It's cute, though, us hand in hand there by
the rocks, smiling at each other. The next picture captured that
moment when Flora pushed my hair back from my face, and
okay, that one I can't really look at because my heart-eyes are
kind of ridiculous.

But I keep looking at that line about Flora "chucking" Tam.
Flora told me Tamsin broke up with her, not the other way
around. Is that true? I think back to seeing Tam back on Skye.
She'd seemed cold and standoffish, yeah, but had that actually
been hurt, not snobbery?

"There you are."

I glance up to see Flora coming down the hall toward me, her
dress belling out prettily as she walks. How many dresses like
that does Flora own? I wonder.

Reaching out to me, she takes my hand. "We're about to go in for dinner. It'll be just like at Lord Henry's, so we won't get to sit together, but I've made sure you're near Daisy so you'll have someone to talk to at least, and—what is it?"

I really wish I didn't have one of those faces where everything I'm thinking is immediately obvious, but such is my curse. It was my mom's, too, Dad tells me.

"Can we go somewhere and talk for just a sec?"

She looks over her shoulder back toward the ballroom, but then she nods, tugging me up from the bench and farther down the hall. "It'll be a bit of a scandal if we're late, but I for one am all right with that." Flashing a smile at me that makes dimples appear in her cheeks, she adds, "You've clearly been a good influence on me, Quint—I haven't caused a ruckus in ages."

We pause at the end of the hall, and her smile turns into something like a smirk. "Should probably rectify that," she murmurs, and then she leans over, kissing me softly. Even though my head is still reeling, I can't help lifting my hand to her wrist, holding her hand against my face for just a little longer.

When Flora pulls back from the kiss, she laughs lightly, running her thumb over my lower lip, sending a shower of sparks through me. "Why such the serious face?" she asks, and I try to make myself smile back, but I'm not sure I do such a great job at it.

Still holding my hand, Flora opens a heavy door there at the end of the hallway, and a blast of cold air hits me. She's taking me out onto the rooftop terrace I spotted before, so we can have this super-awkward conversation in a very romantic location.

Great.

We step outside, and I'm already shivering. Flora is, too, but she's still grinning at me. "I know it's not quite the season for this," she says, "but it's one of my favorite spots. Look how gorgeous Arthur's Seat looks from here."

I glance over to my right, and sure enough, the craggy hill reaches up to the stars, lit from the lamps in the park below, a darker shape against the navy sky.

"I knew you'd like this place," Flora says, a little smug. "Volcanoes and all that. Advanced rocks, really."

My throat feels tight as I look at Arthur's Seat, and just for a moment, I think about forgetting the whole thing. Just kissing her again, telling her I love it here—and I do—then going back in to the dinner.

Turning around, I face Flora, my hands clasped in front of me, and she blinks, her shoulders stiffening a little bit. "Quint?" she asks. "Seriously, what's wrong?"

"Did you dump Tamsin?" I ask, and Flora blinks.

"What?"

I take a deep breath. "Tamsin," I say. "You acted like she broke up with you. Like you got how I felt about the thing with Jude, but . . . is that not what happened?"

Flora wrinkles her nose. "Why does it matter?" she asks, and my heart sinks.

"So . . . that's a yes, then. You broke up with her."

"Only because she wanted to be almost absurdly secretive about us," Flora counters. "Which made me feel slightly rejected, so to *my* mind—"

"That's not the way the world works, Flora," I tell her now, stepping closer. "You can't just say, 'Well, to *me*, it was like *this*,' and have it actually *be* that."

Flora waves a gloved hand. "Quint, this is ridiculous. Tamsin has nothing to do with us."

"But she does," I say, "because that was this . . . this thing we had in common. The thing that made it feel safe to like you."

Flora looks as baffled as I've ever seen her, one hand on her hip, her head tilted to one side. "Safe? What does that even mean?" Sighing, I look up at the sky above us. It's clear tonight and cold, stars twinkling in the inky black sky, Arthur's Seat rising to my left, and I almost shake my head at all of it. Up here on the terrace at a palace with a princess under a starlit sky by an ancient volcano, like a fairy tale I never thought to imagine.

"I don't want to be your distraction," I say at last. "I *can't* be that again. Someone fun to hang out with until the person you really want comes back."

"Is this about Dastardly Jude?" Flora asks. She's got her arms folded tightly around her middle, and I don't think it's from the cold. She's so beautiful standing there in her golden dress, her diamonds and emeralds glittering, but just like the stars and the palace and the entire night, it's a reminder of how different her life is from mine.

"Maybe?" I say. "And let's get real here, Flora. The Tamsins and Carolines and Ilses of the world are much more your type," I finally say. "I'm short, I say 'y'all,' I have no idea how anyone plays polo—"

Flora's face is cold now, her shoulders back. "That's what you think my type is, is it? You think I'm only interested in girls like Tamsin?"

"I think the princess and the scholarship kid looks good on paper, but is too hard in reality," I reply, and Flora waves a hand again.

"You're not even on scholarship anymore, for heaven's sake, and honestly this is so—"

"Wait, what?"

I move closer to her, the night breeze tugging strands of hair from my updo. "What do you mean I'm not on scholarship anymore?"

Some of Flora's coldness fades away, and she shifts her weight, her eyes sliding from mine. "I . . . may have paid your tuition for the rest of the year," she says.

"You just . . . paid for school? And didn't tell me? Didn't *ask* me?"

Her gaze meets mine again, lower lip poking out just a little. "Oh, yes, so very sorry to have done something nice for you. What a villain I am."

But I shake my head. "No, Flora, that's not the point, the point is you did it without asking if I wanted you to. I earned that scholarship. I worked hard for it. It was important to me, but you just saw it as . . . what? Something embarrassing? Something a little grubby."

"Yes," she says now, turning to face me. "That's what you want to believe, isn't it? That I couldn't bear to date someone not of my class."

Shaking her head, she backs off in a swirl of skirts and perfume. "Honestly, Quint, if that's what you think about me, then I'm not sure why you ever liked me in the first place."

I don't know what to say to that. Somehow this has all gotten so twisted and out of hand so fast that I'm not even sure what to be mad about anymore. But I *am* mad. And hurt and confused.

Flora, however, is just mad. "Anyway," she says on a sigh. "This entire scene is unnecessary and, frankly, boring. Why don't we go back inside, and you can run off and hide in your room or something? I'll have a car take you back to Gregorstoun in the morning."

"Flora, can we—" I start, but she's already moving for the doors, her skirts swishing over the stone, her tiara glittering.

Just like that, she's gone, back into the palace. Back into her life.

And I'm left outside.

CHAPTER **37**

I WAKE UP THE NEXT MORNING WITH GRITTY EYES AND the beginnings of a massive headache. And that's nothing compared to the ache in my chest. The idea of going downstairs for breakfast and sitting across the table from Flora makes me want to hide under the covers. What even happened last night? Were we fighting about Tamsin or about the scholarship?

But then I remind myself that if our first fight can go that badly, maybe it was never meant to be. Maybe it was always going to end like this.

I finally manage to get up, but when I make my way to the family's private dining room, it's empty except for a few of Seb's friends, Daisy, and her boyfriend. The boys just glance at me as I walk in, but I see Daisy give me a sympathetic smile, and I wiggle my fingers at her before going over to the buffet and grabbing some breakfast.

Scottish breakfast isn't exactly my favorite at the best of times, but right now, when I can't imagine ever wanting to eat again, it's especially unappetizing. Still, I put some mushrooms, a grilled tomato, and a slice of toast on my plate before heading to the table.

When I sit down, I see Daisy nudge Miles—well, kick him under the table, seems like—and he clears his throat with a "Right," before leaning over and saying, "Millie, I'm so sorry about mentioning the story last night. I just assumed you knew, or didn't care, or that . . . Well, all of us have gotten very used to seeing things about ourselves in the press, true or not, over the years, and I forget that's not the case for everyone."

"And you're a prat," Daisy helpfully supplies, to which Miles sighs, closing his eyes briefly before adding, "And also, I am a prat."

Smiling in spite of myself, I poke at my mushrooms. "You're not," I tell him. "It wasn't a big deal."

"It seems slightly biggish," Daisy says, "because we heard you're leaving this morning?"

"It isn't about that," I say, which is technically the truth. "It's just . . ." I eat a mushroom to avoid talking for a second. "Not for me," I finally say, waving my fork around. "This whole thing. Leaving it to the professionals."

Daisy opens her mouth to say something to that, but now it's Miles's turn to kick her under the table, and glaring at him, she rubs her shin.

I shove some more toast in my mouth and make apologetic sounds before basically bolting from the dining room.

When I get back to the bedroom I was staying in, I see my things have already been packed. The royals are clearly very efficient at booting you out once your time is up.

This time, there's no help with my bag, no one at all in fact until I step out the back door and see Glynnis waiting for me.

"There you are," she says. "The car just pulled up."

Sure enough, there's a black car idling in the drive.

"When will Flora be leaving?" I ask, but Glynnis only gives me that tight smile, her lips crimson.

"Her Royal Highness will be returning to school here in Edinburgh. With the wedding coming up, it's really best to have her closer to home now."

The morning is cold and gray, and there's a mizzle falling that suits my mood as I stand there in the portico, waiting for the car to come around. If I had known that last night might be the last time I'd get to talk to Flora . . .

The thought makes my throat go tight, but the last thing I want to do is start crying in front of Glynnis. I have a long trip back to the Highlands during which I can fully indulge in self-pity, after all.

To my surprise, Glynnis lays a manicured hand on my sleeve. "I'm sorry to see you go, Amelia," she says, and weirdly enough, I think she might mean it. "I thought you might be a more permanent fixture."

I don't know what to say to that, so I just give an awkward shrug, trying to smile. "Not exactly cut out for the royal thing," I tell her, but Glynnis only gives me a little pat, her smile turning just the slightest bit sad.

"Well, off you pop, then," she says, gesturing to the car, and I shift my bag to my other shoulder, nodding. Off I pop indeed.

Back to Gregorstoun. Back to normalcy. Well, as normal as that place gets, I guess.

The car smells like expensive leather plus the faint burning scent of the heater on blast, and I'm already tugging off my scarf as I settle into the back seat when a movement catches my eye.

There are big windows looking out on this private drive from the second story, and I see Flora in one now, still wearing her robe, her hair loose and messy around her shoulders. Her face is a pale oval against the thick glass, but I'd know her anywhere, I'm pretty sure.

It's so weird to look at her and know that I might never see her again—almost certainly won't see her again—except in magazines or on TV sometimes. But isn't that for the best? She was never really mine, and this whole thing was like a dream I stumbled into. A fairy tale where she was the princess in the tower and I was . . . Okay, I wasn't the frog, exactly, but close enough. And one day, Flora will find her princess, too.

It just won't be me.

Another flash of red from her robe, and she's gone.

The train back up to the school is nowhere near as nice as the ride down was. This time, I'm in a regular carriage, sitting next to a stranger, and I'd be lying if I said I didn't spend most of the ride looking up stories about Flora on my phone.

I'm quickly realizing this is going to be the worst part of things—with Jude, I just had to deal with her at school and on Facebook. With Flora? I'll have a lifetime of being able to pull up multiple pictures of a Girl I Used to Like.

Once the train gets to Inverness, I call the school to send Mr. McGregor to pick me up and bring me back to Gregorstoun.

I'm expecting another story about Killer Trout, or the McGregor Legacy, Cruelly Stolen, but all Mr. McGregor says as I climb into the car is "Chin up, lassie," which nearly makes me cry all over again.

It's raining now, and the school that once looked so beautiful and special to me just looks dismal as we pull up.

Once I'm inside, I make a beeline for Sakshi's room. The door is cracked, so I don't knock—I just push it open and call, "Hey, I'm back—"

Only to be confronted with the sight of Sakshi and Perry entwined on her bed, kissing.

I squawk, and *they* squawk, flying apart—both of them fully and completely dressed, thank god—and scrambling off the bed.

"Millie!" Saks cries. "We were just . . . Perry and I are—"

"I know what you were doing," I reply, and then, as awful as this whole day has been, I clap my hand over my mouth, giggles erupting out of me.

And then they both start laughing, too, their clothes rumpled, their hair a mess.

"Are you shocked?" Sakshi asks, threading her arm through Perry's. They should look so mismatched as to be ridiculous, Sakshi so glamorous and gorgeous, Perry so . . . neither of those things, but instead, they just look right. Perfect, really.

Laughing, I throw myself on both of them, wrapping them into a hug that's made tougher by the fact that Saks is so much taller than me and Perry, but we manage it.

"No, not shocked, bloody well thrilled," I say, and Perry guffaws, patting my back hard.

"Spoken like a true Scottish lass, now," he teases, and I pull back, still smiling at both of them.

"Who would have thought?" Sakshi asks on a sigh. "All three of us finding love at Gregorstoun of all places."

I try to smile. I really do.

But I can feel it wobbling on my face, my eyes stinging, and suddenly there are tears rolling down my face.

"Peregrine," Saks says, pointing to the door. "*Out*."

Fifteen minutes later, Saks and I are sitting on her floor, a tube of chocolate digestive biscuits half-destroyed between us.

"Oh, darling," Saks says, breaking a cookie in half, "I am sorry."

I want to protest and tell her no, everything is fine, I'm fine, it's all deeply, deeply fine, but that would be a lie, so I let her pull me close to her, my head on her shoulder. "Flora always was a heartbreaker," she says, stroking my hair, but I shake my head, pulling away.

"No, that's the thing. She didn't break my heart, Saks. I . . . I think I might have broken hers."

Sakshi's dark eyes go wide. "Oh, dear," she murmurs. "That might be a first for Flora."

Tilting my head back to stare at the ceiling, I groan. "You're supposed to be making me feel better," I remind her, and she pats my arms again, all fluttery fingers.

"Of course, of course. I mean, how could you know Flora had a heart to break? And it's probably her due. Like I said, she's always had quite a reputation as the love-them-and-leave-them type."

I think of Flora making me a fake Thanksgiving, of her picking out the perfect dress for me. Of how happy she seemed to have me at her side in Edinburgh.

My eyes are stinging again, and I wipe at them with the back of my hand. "She's a lot more than anyone thinks she is," I say at last. "She's funny and smart and kind. Well, not always on that last one, but she tries, is the point. And she's just got that hard shell because her insides are marshmallows, basically, so she has to have a protective coating, you know? But once you get past that, she's just . . . she's . . ."

Saks is still sitting against her bed, and she's watching me now with her mouth hanging open a little bit.

Self-conscious, I stand up, dusting off the back of my jeans. "She's just a lot greater than anyone knows," I finally finish up, and Saks leans forward, asking me the question I was really afraid she was going to ask.

"Then, darling, why did you leave her?"

CHAPTER **38**

THE NEXT FEW DAYS ARE SOMEHOW EVEN WORSE
than I'd thought they'd be.

The school feels empty without Flora in it, and, as I expected,
I spend way too much time Googling her.

I even set up an alert, which feels like a special kind of
pathetic.

Dad knows something is up whenever we Skype, but I just
blame my general sad-sackness on school, the weather, and being homesick, which is kind of true. Being home at Christmas
seems really nice now, and I start marking the days off with a big
red pen on my calendar.

I've got twenty-nine more days to go when I trudge back
up to my room after class one afternoon, tossing my bag on
my bed.

With a sigh—I am a champion sigher these days—I open
my laptop. There's an email from Lee, a missed Skype call from
Dad, and . . .

Another Hangout message from Jude.

This one just says, *Was thinking about you today. Hope you're having fun up there in Bonny Scotland!*

She sent it just three minutes ago, and without letting myself overthink it, I type back.

Hi. Yup, things are good here.

Her reply comes back an instant later.

Plenty of unicorns?

Smiling, I type back, *A surprising lack of, sadly.*

That's a bummer!

I stare at the screen, wondering what to say next, when another reply comes in.

I miss you.

The cursor blinks at me. Those are definitely welcome words from Jude, and I realize I miss her, too.

But . . . not like I did a few months ago. I miss my *friend* Jude, not my almost-sort-of-girlfriend Jude. Because while what I felt for her was real—and while seeing her back together with Mason sucked a whole lot—it was always a tightrope with Jude. I never knew what we really were or how she really felt, no matter what she said about being an us.

Flora hadn't called us an us, but we'd *felt* like one.

My fingers move quickly.

I'm not mad anymore. About what happened this summer. I don't even know if I was mad, I guess. Hurt? I don't know. But I'd like us to be friends again if we can.

And then, after a pause, I add, *But just friends this time.*

This time her reply takes a while in coming.

I'm sorry, Millie. Honestly. Really, really sorry.

And I'd like to be friends again, too. ☺

I go to reply with a smiley face in return, but there's more.

Besides, I see you have a very fancy new girlfriend now, lol.
GLOW UP. ☺

My fingers hover over the keys, wondering if I should tell Jude about what happened with Flora, but before I can, there's a knock at the door.

BRB, I type to Jude, then hop off my bed to answer the door.

It actually takes a beat for my mind to absorb just who I'm seeing.

It's Seb.

He looks a little worse for wear, his shirt a bit wrinkled, his jaw patchy with scruff, but it's definitely him, leaning against the doorjamb.

"Roomie Quint," he says with a faint grin.

"Brother Seb," I reply, and his grin deepens.

I shake myself out of my shock and usher him inside.

I quickly realize I have no idea where he's supposed to sit, given that the only options are the bed—nicer, bigger—and my desk chair—probably more appropriate. In the end, I don't have to offer because Seb makes the decision himself, sitting heavily on the end of my bed, his elbows braced on his spread thighs.

"So," he says on a long breath. "This is buggeringly awkward, but I'm here to talk about you and Flora."

"I assumed that was it," I tell him, taking a seat in my desk chair and slinging an arm across the back.

Seb nods, but he's still looking around the room. "Who're

you rooming with now?" he asks, taking in Sakshi's bed with its brightly colored pillows and striped sheets.

"Saks," I reply, and he nods again, rubbing a hand over the back of his neck.

"She around? Wouldn't mind—"

"No," I say flatly, turning to face him more fully. "So can we get this over with?"

Seb leans back at that, his expression faintly surprised. "Get what over with?"

"Whatever this is going to be," I say, wishing I were closer to the dresser so I could fiddle with one of my rock samples. The hematite maybe. Ugh, but no, then I'd just remember showing it to Flora, and—

"You think I'm upset with you?" Seb asks. "Here to do some sort of patronizing brother thing?" Snorting, he shakes his head. "Trust me, love, I'm rubbish at that. I'm here because . . ."

Trailing off, he sighs and looks around again. "You wouldn't happen to have a drink around here, would you?"

I blink at him. "As in booze? No, I, a seventeen-year-old, do not have *booze* in my *dorm room*."

Seb mutters a rude word under his breath and slumps slightly before asking, "Are you in love with my sister?"

I don't know how to answer that, and my instinct at first is to deny it. To tell him that Flora was a great friend and roommate, but that's it.

But then I realize: I don't want the first time I admit, out loud, that I'm in love with Flora to be to anyone *but* Flora.

And I say so. "That's private."

Seb's blue eyes widen at that. "So that's a yes."

"It's a none of your business," I shoot back.

Outside in the hallway, there's the usual murmur of sounds I've gotten used to here at Gregorstoun. The sound of feet on floors, the murmur of voices, the occasional howling of the wind. Inside the room, I can practically hear the ticking of Saks's alarm clock.

"If that's all you came here to ask me," I say now to Seb, picking up the notebook I've left on the bed, "then I guess you have an answer. And I have homework to do, so—"

"She's miserable," Seb says. "Without you. I've never seen her like this before."

That's a direct hit to the heart, and I swallow hard before saying, "Well, I'm not exactly dancing through the streets, either."

"Then why did you leave?"

I look up at him, my fingers fiddling with the hem of my shirt, and he lifts one elegant hand to add, "And don't say that's private. I mean, it is, I'm sure, but I'd still like to know."

I think about getting into the whole thing about Tamsin, about the tuition, about how I am in no way cut out to be a princess's girlfriend.

But in the end, I just say, "We were too different. It was too hard. I get where I was fun and . . . convenient, I guess, but she's never going to end up with someone like me."

"Bollocks," Seb says, sitting back with his hands braced on his knees. "Absolute bollocks."

Blinking at him, I clear my throat before saying, "It is not bollocks. It's the truth. I mean, look at me."

"I'm looking," he replies, "and I see a perfectly lovely girl who my sister is completely mad for, and who's throwing away a good thing because she's not brave enough to give it a shot."

"That's unfair," I say, but Seb only shrugs, patting his shirt pockets for something.

He pulls out a cigarette, and I lean forward, plucking it from his fingers and tearing it in half, tiny shreds of tobacco falling on the floor.

To my surprise, that makes Seb grin. "See?" he says. "You're exactly what she needs. You say you're not cut out for the royal life, but look at you. Not scared of me, survived an entire weekend in a castle, looks good in tartan, and, from what Flora has said, smart as a bloody whip."

"She said that about me?" I ask in a small voice, and Seb leans forward again, putting a hand on my knee.

"She's a bit of a screwup. We all are. Well, all of us except for Alex. But she cares about you. She let you in. She trusted you." His hand squeezes just a bit. "Now return the favor."

With that, he stands up, idly scratching at his chest with a muttered "*Now* I'm going to go find a drink."

And then he's gone, leaving me sitting there, his words running through my head.

Crossing the room, I go over to the dresser and pick up the rose quartz, feeling its cool weight in my palm. I remember Flora's face when she looked at it as we stood so close. I remember the way her hand felt in mine when we danced on Skye. I remember . . . everything.

And then I'm putting the quartz down and heading to the door.

I don't walk down the hall so much as march, and taking a

deep breath, I steel myself and rap my knuckles on Perry's door, knowing I'll find Saks there.

Sure enough, she opens the door, her black hair pulled off her face in a high ponytail. "Millie!" she exclaims, her eyes bright. "Is it true Seb came to see you? What did he say? What did *you* say? Was it awkward? Did you tell him I've moved on? Did he—"

"Saks," I say, holding up one hand. "We can get into all of that later. For now, I need your help."

She blinks, leaning against the door frame. "With what?"

Saying it is going to make it real, which is vaguely terrifying, but I know now it's the only thing I can do.

"I screwed up," I say on a long breath. "Like, monumentally. With Flora."

Saks nods. "Yes, we know."

Scowling, I put one hand on my hip. "Okay, great, glad everyone's in agreement that I blew it."

Another nod, this time with a sort of exaggerated sad face. "You really did."

I roll my eyes. "Noted. But that's not what I need help with."

Straightening my shoulders, I look up into Sakshi's face. "I'm going to get her back."

CHAPTER **39**

I HAVE NEVER SKIPPED SCHOOL IN MY LIFE. I'VE also never sneaked out, or "borrowed" a car, or lied to an adult, but this morning, I'm doing all of those things in one fell swoop.

I mention all of this to Saks, who twists in the passenger seat of the car Perry is driving, her brow creasing into a frown. "But you're doing it for a good reason!" she says, then reaches over and takes Perry's hand, a smile lighting up her beautiful face. "True love."

True love. Right.

But that thought just makes my stomach twist, too. Flora. I'm going to see Flora again, and I'm going to tell her how I feel.

Yeah, way scarier than the idea of getting caught with the groundskeeper's car.

When Perry said he had a way for us to get to Edinburgh, I expected an elaborate train and bus schedule, so him pulling the ancient Land Rover around to the back of the school where Saks and I were waiting was something of a shock. Perry swears Mr.

McGregor had said he was free to use it whenever he wanted, but I'm not sure if something said after four pints counts.

So now here I am, in the back seat of a borrowed-but-also-possibly-stolen car, and oh my god, this is insane.

"Should we maybe talk about how exactly I'm going to get to see Flora?" I ask. There's a tear in the fabric seat, and the metal floorboards are rusted. Are we even going to make it to Edinburgh in one piece?

Saks waves an elegantly manicured hand. "All under control, darling. You forget, I'm the daughter of a duke, and that counts for something. I'll present myself at the palace, with you and Perry as my guests," she goes on, scrolling through her phone, "and I'll say . . . Oh, bollocks!"

"Okay, pretty sure mentioning testicles is not going to get us very far in the palace," I say, but Saks shakes her head, a stricken expression on her face.

"No, bollocks because the royal family isn't at the palace today. There's some new museum exhibit opening about Scottish royal weddings, and they're all going to that this morning, then there's a procession down the Mile. Dammit! I knew I should've looked at their social calendar, but I was quite"—another hand wave—"swept up in everything, I suppose."

"Glad you find my love life so sweeping," I mutter, leaning forward to take Saks's phone from her hand. Sure enough, there's the announcement about the museum exhibit, complete with Flora's name in bold type.

"We're halfway there," Perry says, glancing over at Saks. "We can always get to Edinburgh and hang out for a bit. They have to go back to the palace eventually."

They do, and they will, I'm sure, and that's a great plan, just grabbing some lunch there in the city and waiting.

Or . . .

Swallowing hard, I hand Saks back her phone. "By the time we get there, the parade will be starting," I say. "We can just go there."

Saks twists in her seat, her dark eyes wide. "Millicent Quint," she breathes. "Are you telling me—"

I give a firm nod. "I am."

Squealing, Saks claps her hands, and Perry looks over again, clearly confused, his knuckles white on the steering wheel. "What?"

"Big Romantic Gesture!" Saks cries. "Millie is going to declare her love in public! Oh my god, I think I might start weeping."

"And I think I might start vomiting, so please don't," I say, settling into the back seat, an entire colony of butterflies in my chest. Maybe that's what makes the drive go by so much faster than I'd thought, because before I know it, we're pulling into the city.

Parking the car, Perry gestures for me to get out. "The parade is going down the Mile," he says, "so all you have to do is get to the front, wait for Flora to pass by, and tell her you love her."

I stare at him, my palm suddenly sweaty on the handle. "Right," I say, but it comes out a croak, so I clear my throat and start again. "Right."

"Easy peasy!" Saks says, then, thank god, she opens the door. "I'll come with, though, just to make sure."

"Well, I'm not missing out," Perry says, turning the car off, and I smile at the two of them, feeling a little choked up all of a sudden.

"Y'all are really good friends, you know that?" I say, and they both grin at me.

"Of course we do," Saks says, and then we're heading down one of the little side streets and up toward the Mile.

There's a series of barricades set up, and a crowd has already gathered around them in the cold autumn air. We're toward the back, but I can hear pipers and drummers, and when I rise up on my tiptoes, I can see the royal family making their way down past St. Giles's.

Flora is in the middle of her brothers as they make their way through the crowd, her hair pulled back from her face. She's smiling and shaking hands, taking the occasional bouquet of flowers and thanking people before handing them off to a man in a black suit.

Just looking at her makes my chest ache. She's so good at this, even though she'd swear she's not. But I can see the way people look at her, can tell from her smile that it's sincere. She's never looked more like a princess to me, even when she was all decked out in the tiaras and sashes.

But she's not just a princess.

She's *my* princess.

Aaaaand she's way too far away for me to get her attention.

Turning back to Sakshi and Perry, I shake my head. "This is stupid," I say. "I can just email her or—"

"NO!" they shout in unison before glancing at each other and doing those soppy smiles they do all the time now.

Then Perry grabs my hand. "Millie, this requires a big gesture. Emails are not big. Emails aren't even medium-sized."

"My boyfriend is right," Saks says, and then, yes, once again, the cutesy smiles. They actually touch noses, and it would be gross if I didn't love them both, but Sakshi quickly shakes herself and says, "Not the time. Anyway, what Perry said. You are winning back the woman you love, and that means an email simply will not do. So."

Reaching down, she plucks a bouquet out of a little girl's hands. When the little girl, her hair as bright as Perry's, opens her mouth to protest, Saks rummages through her pink Chanel purse, pulling out her wallet and phone before handing the bag to the little girl. "Fair trade," she says, and the girl, clearly having good taste, takes the purse eagerly, flowers forgotten.

"Saks," I say, but she shakes her head.

"It was last season anyway. Now, take these flowers and go get your princess."

The flowers in my hand are a little wilted, the purple blooms definitely worse for wear, but there's a bright ribbon around the stems in the Baird family plaid, which seems like a good sign.

And after a moment, I reach into my pocket for the smooth and shiny lump of rose quartz I slipped in before we left the school.

The crowd is thicker now, surging near the barricades, and the Bairds are moving down the Mile, closer to where I am, but unfortunately, I'm stuck all the way at the back of the crowd, and being the size of a sixth grader definitely doesn't help.

Luckily, I have Sakshi.

"PARDON!" she calls out loudly, her bright smile in

contrast with her sharp elbows as she pushes her way through the crowd. Perry stands behind me, the caboose in this engine getting me to the front of the line, and I duck my head, following behind Saks as best I can. As the crowd parts, I hear some of the murmurs start up.

Most of them are about how gorgeous Sakshi is, which is valid, but I hear my name a couple of times. *Amelia. Millie. That's her. That's the girl dating Flora.*

And this time, the words don't make me want to cringe or hide out of sight. They make me want to hold my head up. Yes, that's me.

Millie, the girl dating Flora.

We're nearly to the edge of the barricade now. It's cold out, gray and windy, and I nearly trip on the cobblestone when I hear Saks trill, "Flooorrraaa!"

There's still six feet of Saks hiding me from sight, but I hear Flora's reply of "Sakshi!"

And then suddenly, Saks is gone, and I'm standing there at the barricade facing Flora, a bunch of flowers in my hand.

The smile Flora had been wearing for Saks falls away, her expression going guarded for a second until she looks down and sees the flowers.

One corner of her mouth lifts slightly, a patented Flora Smirk, but her eyes are suspiciously bright as she glances back up. "Are those for me?"

"They are," I say, holding them out. "I stole them from some kid. Well, Saks did, and they're not as pretty as I would've wanted, but beggars can't be choosers, right? Or . . . stealers can't be choosers, I guess."

The crowd is starting to back away from me a little now, and I see Flora's bodyguards watching us cautiously. From just behind Flora, Seb rises up on his tiptoes to see what's going on.

When he spots me, he breaks out into a grin, and maybe that's what gives me the courage to rush on.

"Flora, I'm so sorry. About everything. About not being brave enough or . . . or tough enough or whatever it was. Because I . . ."

I have never been more aware of people looking at me, and even though the rest of the royal family is moving on, the crowd's attention feels very focused on me and Flora right now. But I realize that there's only one person's attention I care about right now—Flora's. As long as she's looking at me, I don't care about anyone else.

"I love you, Flora," I say, and even though there's a crowd around us, and bodyguards and other royals, it feels like it's just us. Like we're back in our room at Gregorstoun, or out on the moors under the stars. "And yes, sometimes you make me crazy, and we're definitely going to have to talk about the whole high-handed thing, but . . . it's worth it. You're worth it."

Flora laughs at that, the real kind that shows her teeth, and her hand is tight in mine.

"I'm sorry, too," she says. "I should've told you the truth about Tam, and I definitely shouldn't have paid your tuition without telling you, but . . ." She shrugs. "What can I say? I'm a mess."

"You're not," I immediately reply, then I rethink that. "Okay, you are, but you're kind and sweet and lovely, and did I mention the whole 'in love with you' part? Because seriously. In love."

"So I'm your sort of mess, then," she says, and I reach into my pocket, pulling out the rose quartz.

"You are," I tell her, pressing the rock into her palm. She looks at it for a long moment before lifting her head to meet my eyes.

"This is a very fine rock," she says at last, her voice a little tight, and I grin back at her.

"You already have all the fancy jewelry in the world," I say, "but I can keep you supplied with actual rocks. And read maps for you. And there's a whole world of laundry out there you don't even know about. Towels were just the beginning."

"Well, how can a girl resist such an offer?" Flora says, tossing her hair a bit, and my heart feels so big in my chest, I'm surprised I don't burst.

"Kiss her, lass!" a man shouts from the crowd, and Flora bursts into giggles, covering her mouth with one gloved hand even as tears sparkle in her eyes.

"Is he talking to me or you?" she asks, and I step forward, shaking my head.

"I don't know," I tell her, laying my palm against her cheek. "But it's good advice, so I'm going to take it."

And I do.

ACKNOWLEDGMENTS

As always, thank you so much to the fabulous team at Penguin, who knocks it out of the park on every book. I feel very lucky to get to work with such brilliant ladies!

To my editor, Ari Lewin, and my agent, Holly Root: They don't let you put GIFs in acknowledgments, which is a real shame, because I need a lot of Real Housewives GIFs—you know, the ones where someone is crying and being messy in a fancy dress, and other, more responsible people are holding her up?—to express all y'all do for me. Thank you for helping these books—and me!—be the best we can be.

Thank you so much to the readers who've come along on this wild and woolly (literally! sheep!) journey into the Royals 'verse with me. Your enthusiasm has meant the world to me.

Thank you to my family, as always, for everything.

And last, but never least, for all the girls like Millie who are still figuring themselves out, or the girls who, like Flora, feel pretty damn secure in who they are and who they want to be with: This one is for you, with love.

Turn the page to read an excerpt from
Her Royal Highness's companion novel

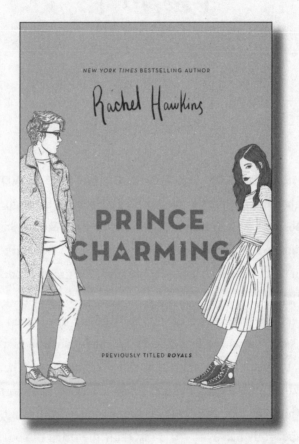

First published in the United States of America by G. P. Putnam's Sons as *Royals*, 2018
Published by Penguin Books, an imprint of Penguin Random House LLC, 2019

Chapter 1

"SOME OLD LADY JUST CALLED ME THE C-WORD."

I glance up from the magazine I'm paging through. Isabel Alonso, my best friend and fellow cashier at the Sur-N-Sav, leans back against her register and snaps her gum. Her dark hair is caught up in a messy braid, black against the green of her apron.

"Just now?" I ask. The store is more or less deserted, which has been the case since the giant Walmart opened up on the other side of town, so Isabel and I are the only cashiers working today. I haven't had anyone in my line in over an hour, hence the magazine. Still, I can't believe I was absorbed enough to miss something actually exciting—if super rude—happening.

Isabel rolls her eyes. "It's my fault the price of sour cream went up."

"That seems fair," I tell her with a solemn nod. "You are a fabulous dairy heiress, after all."

Isabel turns back to her register, punching buttons at random. "We have got to get new jobs, Daze. This is humiliating."

I don't disagree, but when you live in a small town in north

Florida, your options are kind of limited. I'd wanted to get a job at the library last fall, but that hadn't worked out—no funding—and one summer of helping out at Vacation Bible School had cured me of the desire to work with little kids, which meant babysitting or working part time at the local preschool was out. So it was all Sur-N-Sav all the time.

Although now, looking at my phone where it's propped against the register, I see that my time at Sur-N-Sav is up.

"Ah, three o'clock, the most beautiful time of day," I say happily, and Isabel groans. "Not fair!"

"Hey, I've been here since seven," I remind her. "You wanna leave early—"

"You have to take the early shift," she finishes, waving a hand at me. "Okay, Mrs. Miller, got it."

Mrs. Miller is the manager of the Sur-N-Sav, and Isabel and I have gotten very used to her lectures over the past year.

Sighing, Isabel leans next to her register, chin propped in her hand. Her nails are painted three different shades of green, and a simple beaded bracelet slides down one slender wrist. "Four more weeks," she says, and I repeat our favorite mantra.

"Four more weeks."

At the end of June, Isabel and I are bidding a not-so-fond farewell to the Sur-N-Sav life and heading out to Key West for Key Con, then plan to spend a week bumming around the town. Isabel's brother lives there with his wife and Isabel's ridiculously cute baby nephew, so we have a free (and parent-approved) place to stay. To say my entire life is revolving around this trip might be something of an understatement. Not only will we get our geek on, but we will also get to do fun Key West things. Snorkeling,

3

the Hemingway House, all the key lime pie a gal can hold . . . yes, this trip is going to make my entire summer, and Isa and I have been planning it for almost a year now, as soon as the con was announced. Our favorite author, Ash Bentley, is going to be there talking about her Finnigan Sparks series, plus there are at least twenty different panels Isabel and I want to check out—on everything from women in space operas to cosplay design. It is geek heaven, and we are beyond ready.

"You need to come over this weekend so we can start planning outfits," Isabel says, straightening up and punching random buttons on the register as Whitney Houston wails about the greatest love of all over the sound system. "I still haven't decided if I'm cosplaying as Miranda from *Finnegan and the Falcon* or Jezza from *Finnegan's Moon*."

"Ben would probably prefer Jezza," I say. Ben is Isa's boyfriend, and has been for roughly eleventy billion years. Okay, since eighth grade. "Lot less clothes on Jezza."

Isa screws up her face, thinking. "True, but Ben's not even going to be there, and I don't know if I'm ready to show a quarter of my butt cheeks to all of Key West."

"Fair," I acknowledge. "Besides, being Miranda means you get to wear a purple wig."

She points a finger at me. "Yes! Miranda it is, then. Who are you going to go as?"

Smiling, I start shutting down my register. "Cosplay is your thing," I remind her, "so I'm just going as me. Boring Girl in T-Shirt and Jeans."

"You are a disappointment to me in every way," Isa replies, and I shake my head.

The doors slide open, another senior citizen shopper strolling in as I finish with my register and take the cash drawer to Mrs. Miller's office. At most grocery stores, clerks count the money themselves, but years of working with teenage employees has given Mrs. Miller trust issues, and to be honest, I'm happy to leave that chore to someone else anyway.

That done, I make my way across the store, noticing as I pass the magazine racks lining the register lanes that a bunch of them have been turned around, the ads on their backs, rather than the covers, facing the customer.

This has to be Isabel's doing. I walk up to a rack and turn the nearest backward magazine to face me. I see a quick flash of blond hair and bright teeth, and then my eyes land on the headline, printed in bold yellow script: "TEN THINGS YOU NEVER KNEW ABOUT ELLIE WINTERS!"

I wonder if any of the ten things would surprise *me*. I doubt it, though.

My sister has lived a life pretty free from the scandalous, almost as if she knew she'd end up on the cover of magazines. I'm almost tempted to flip through, but then decide that "A," it would be weird and "B," Isabel *did* go to the trouble of trying to hide the magazines from me in the first place.

"It was nothing bad this time," she calls out now. "Just figured you didn't need to see!"

Giving her a thumbs-up, I continue toward the door at the far side of the store.

My stuff is in the break room, a truly tragic space made up of orange walls, green plastic chairs, and a scratched laminate table. At some point, someone had carved "BECKY LOVES

JOSH" into the top of it, and every time I sat there on my break, reading or studying, I wondered what became of Becky and Josh. Were they still in love? Had Becky been as insanely bored here as I was?

Although, hey, at least Becky was never confronted with pictures of her sister on the front of tabloids.

Or being in the tabloids herself for that matter.

Ugh.

The whole prom debacle is still this mix of anger and hurt, a thorny ball lodged right in my chest, and thinking about it is like poking a sore tooth. You forget just how much the tooth aches until you focus on it, and then suddenly it's all you can think about.

Which means I can't risk thinking about it now, or I might start crying in the break room at the Sur-N-Sav, and there is nothing on earth more depressing than that scenario. That's like movie-where-the-dog-dies levels of pathos, so yeah, not doing that.

Instead, I heft my beat-up patchwork bag onto my shoulder and head out the door.

The blinding brightness and heat of the late-May afternoon is intense as I walk outside and into the parking lot, and I squint, reaching in my bag for my sunglasses, my mind already on what I'm going to do for the rest of the afternoon. Mostly, it involves draping myself over the AC vent in my room and reading the new manga I picked up from the bookstore yesterday.

"Dais."

And there's that sore tooth.

Great.

Michael is leaning against one of the yellow-painted concrete pylons in front of the store, one ankle crossed in front of the other, dark hair falling in his eyes. He's probably been practicing that pose. Michael Dorset is a *champion* leaner, one of the best, really. In the Olympics for Cute Boys, he'd take the gold in the Hot Lean every time.

Lucky for me, I am now immune to the Hot Lean (trademark pending).

Sliding my sunglasses onto my face, I hold up a hand at my ex-boyfriend.

"Nope."

Michael's face curls into a scowl. He has these really soft features, all round cheeks and pretty brown eyes, and I swear he's taught his hair to do that thing where it falls juuuuust right over his forehead. A month ago, I would've been a puddle of melted Daisy at that face, would've reached out to push his hair back from his forehead. Michael Dorset had been my crush since ninth grade. He'd always hung out with a way more popular crowd than I had (I know, shocking that my glasses and *Adventure Time* T-shirts didn't make me a bigger draw), and then last year—*finally*—I'd gotten him.

"I screwed up," he says now, shoving his hands in his pockets. He's wearing the skinniest jeans known to man, jeggings if I'm being honest, and he's got one of my ponytail holders around his wrist. The green one.

Fighting the kindergarten urge to rip it off, I shift my bag to my other shoulder. "That's an understatement."

It's *hot* in the parking lot, and I suddenly realize I'm still wearing the little green Sur-N-Sav apron that goes over my clothes. Michael is all in black, as per usual, but doesn't seem to be sweating, possibly because he's like 0.06% body fat. This is the last place I want to have this discussion, so I move past him and toward my car.

"C'mon," he wheedles, following. "We need to at least *talk* about it."

The asphalt grits under my sneakers as I keep walking. Even though we're not that close to a beach, sand magically appears here, pooling in cracks and potholes in the parking lot.

"We did talk about it," I say. "It's just that there wasn't much to say. You tried to sell our prom pictures."

Fun part of having a famous sibling—you yourself somehow become *kind of* famous.

But it seems like you just get the annoying parts of fame, like, you know, your boyfriend selling private stuff to a tabloid.

Or trying to.

Apparently the royal family had people on the lookout for that kind of thing and shut it down pretty quickly, which, honestly, just made the whole thing ever weirder.

"Babe," he starts, and I wave him off. I'd *liked* those stupid pictures. Thought we looked cute. And now every time I look at them, they're just another thing that got weird because of Ellie.

I think that's what pissed me off most of all.

"I was doing it for *us*," Michael continues, and that actually makes me stop and whirl around.

"You did it to buy a 'super-sweet' guitar," I say, my voice flat. "The kind you'd talked about forever."

Michael actually does look a little sheepish at that. He shoves his hands in his pockets, shrugging his shoulders up and rocking back on his heels. "But music was *our thing*," he says, and I roll my eyes.

"You never liked the bands I liked, you would never let me play my music in the car, you—"

Fumbling in his back pocket, Michael cuts me off—another habit of his I wasn't that nuts about—saying, "No, but listen." He pulls out his phone, scrolling through it, and I'm just about to turn away and walk to my car when there's a sudden cry from the Sur-N-Sav.

"NO BOYS!" a voice warbles across the parking lot.

I turn back to the store to see Mrs. Miller, my manager, standing on the sidewalk just in front of the sliding doors, hands on her hips. Her hair is probably supposed to be red, but it's faded to a sort of peachy hue, and thin enough that you can see her scalp through it.

"NO BOYS ON SHIFT!" she yells again, wagging a finger at me, the skin under her arm wobbling with judgment.

"I'm off the clock," I call back, then jerk my thumb at Michael. "And this isn't a boy. It's a sentient pair of skinny jeans with good hair."

"NO! BOYS!" Mrs. Miller hollers again, and seriously, Mrs. Miller's hang-up about her female employees having boys around them is both psychotic and ridiculous. I'm not sure why she thinks the freaking Sur-N-Sav is a hotbed of sexual activity, but the "no fraternizing with the opposite sex" rule is far and away her strictest.

"THERE IS ZERO EROTICISM HAPPENING HERE IN THE PARKING LOT!" I shout back, but by now, Michael has found what he was looking for.

9

"I wrote this for you," he says, touching the screen, and a tinny blast of music shoots out of his phone. The quality is crap, and I can't really make out any of the lyrics over the shriek of the electric guitar, but I'm pretty sure I hear my name several times, rhymed with both "crazy" and "hazy," and then Michael starts actually *singing along with it*, and please, god, let me die of sudden heat stroke, let a car take a turn and mow me down here in the parking lot of the Sur-N-Sav because between my ex warbling "Daisy's driving me crazy" and Mrs. Miller beginning to march across the asphalt toward us, I'm not sure this afternoon can get much worse.

And then I look up to see the black SUV parked at the edge of the lot, window rolled down . . .

With a telephoto lens pointed directly at me.

Chapter 2

I HUSTLE TO MY CAR NEAR THE BACK OF THE LOT, keeping my head down, my bag tucked close to my side. I can't hear the clicking of the camera over Michael's stupid song—he's trailing behind me still, the phone held out like an offering—but I imagine it anyway, my brain already racing ahead to what these pictures will look like, what the headline will say. Whatever it is, it will totally paint me as the bitch. In the past year since Ellie started dating Alex, I've learned that there's basically nothing that's not the girl's fault in tabloid stories. Two months ago, Alex and Ellie went to some ship christening in Scotland, and Alex frowned and winced through the whole thing, which led to all these stories about how my sister was making him miserable, and that her demands for an engagement ring were tearing them apart.

The truth? Alex had fractured his toe that morning tripping down some stairs. The pained look on his face had been *actual, literal pain*, not sadness because his evil girlfriend was bumming him out.

Yay, patriarchy, I guess.

That's what's so weird to me about Ellie buying into the whole royalty deal. It's *built* on crap like that. If she married Alex and they had a daughter and *then* a son? Guess who'd rule.

Yanking my car door open, I turn to face Michael. The song is ending now, and he pauses there, looking back down at his phone. I have a feeling he's about to start the song over, and that obviously cannot happen, so I put my hand over his. His head shoots up, dark eyes meeting mine, and, ugh, he's doing The Smile, which is almost as potent as The Hot Lean, which means I need to nip this in the bud right now.

"Is that your doing, too?" I ask, jerking my head toward the SUV, and he glances over. Michael is cute and all, but he's a terrible liar—I still remember the social studies test incident five years ago in middle school—so when he looks genuinely surprised and shakes his head, I believe him and sigh with relief.

He's still a douche who sold our prom pictures, but at least he's not actively calling the paparazzi.

"Look, Michael," I say now, painfully aware of the lens still pointed at us, at the sweat dripping down my back, at how my hair is sticking to my face, and how any makeup I put on this morning is a distant memory.

"We talked, okay?" I continue. "I get why you did it, and I hope the guitar is awesome and all you hoped it would be. But we're done. Like. Really, really done."

With that, I sling my bag into the car, slide into the driver's seat, and shut the door on him. He stands there, phone in hand, and I look at my ponytail holder on his wrist again, wondering if I should ask for it back.

No, that would just make this whole thing sadder, really, and given that Mrs. Miller has finally reached Michael, he's being punished enough. Her hair is trembling with righteous outrage, and as she shakes a finger at him, Michael—despite being a good head taller—actually cowers.

Which is fun to see.

I drive out of the parking lot, not bothering to look back in the rearview mirror.

The drive home doesn't take long since our neighborhood is only a few miles from the store. It isn't exactly the most scenic of routes, either. When my parents first moved to Perdido, it was actually kind of a cool place. I mean, as cool as a town in Florida that's nowhere near the ocean can be. It was quirky and eccentric, full of artists and writers and old houses that people had painted nutso colors. Lime green, turquoise, a shade I thought of as "electric violet," all slapped on these dollhouse-looking Victorian mansions and cozy bungalows.

But over the years, a lot of the cooler people moved out, and eventually beige started making its way back into Perdido. There's a country club now, too, complete with a golf course—something that made my dad threaten to move. But while Perdido might not be the idyllic little artist community it once was, it's still a nice place. Quiet, dull, and, as Mom was always pointing out, far enough away that it isn't really worth visiting. Today's photographer was the first one I've seen in months. There were better targets for the paps to go after.

Like, for instance, Ellie.

Beige had moved into Perdido, all right, but it still hasn't crept into our neighborhood. My house is actually one of the more subdued on the block, a cheerful yellow instead of magenta or indigo. Tucked back from the street, it's surrounded by banana trees and bougainvillea, the pink blossoms pretty against the sunshine-y paint. Wind chimes dangle from the porch, glass ones, wooden ones that sound like flutes, and the tacky shell-covered ones they sell in gift shops around here. Mom has a thing for wind chimes.

But it isn't the wind chimes that catch my eye as I pull into the driveway. It's the big SUV parked behind my mom's.

Suddenly, the photographer back at the Sur-N-Sav makes sense.

Chapter 3

I PARK MY CAR OFF TO THE SIDE OF THE SUV, AND
when I get out, I give a wave to the security guys. It's always the
same two when El and Alex come to the States, so I've gotten
used to them. "Hi, Malcolm!" I call. "David, how's it going?"

David, the younger of the two guys, lifts his bottle of water in acknowledgment while Malcolm just nods. As always,
they're in serious black suits, and I imagine that even with the
air-conditioning in the car going full blast, they're still dying.
The heat is no joke, but Alexander doesn't like bringing bodyguards into my parents' house, so it's the driveway for Malcolm
and David.

"Still disappointed you guys don't wear plaid suits," I tell
them as I pass by the car, and while Malcolm just keeps staring
at the house through his shades, David cracks a smile.

My keys rattle in my hand as I jog up the steps of the porch
to see the front door is open, but the glass door is closed. That
means I get a second to see my sister and her boyfriend sitting
on the couch, their posture perfect, before I come inside. They

look as gorgeous and polished as ever, Ellie with her ankles crossed demurely, Alexander sitting on my mom's floral couch like it's a throne.

He always sits like that—maybe he's practicing.

I think again about the guy taking pictures at the Sur-N-Sav and wonder if I need to mention that right off the bat. Ellie wasn't thrilled about the prom pics thing (which, I mean, hi, neither was I, and honestly I think *I'm* the one with cause to complain), and I'm not sure if I want to get into all that on top of dealing with this surprise visit from El and Alex.

Today's Michael thing probably won't even make the papers.

As soon as I walk into the house, El—who hasn't seen me since Christmas—takes one look at my head and says, "Oh, Daisy, your *hair*." Her voice, as always, takes me by surprise. Even though we have British parents, neither El nor I picked up the accent. Then Ellie went away to university in the UK and came back sounding like a character from *Downton Abbey*.

I lift a hand to tuck the bright red strands behind my ear, but then decide to heck with that, my hair is *amazing*.

Luckily, Alexander agrees (or at least pretends to) because he immediately says, "Personally, I approve, Daisy. Redheads, very popular in my family."

He tousles his own reddish-blond hair with a smile, and I'm reminded why everyone in the world is pretty much in love with him. Prince Alexander James Lachlan Baird, Duke of Rothesay, Earl of Carrick, next in line to become King of the Scots, is both cute *and* a surprisingly nice guy. Definitely nicer than El.

"It's her Little Mermaid hair," my mom says, coming in

from the kitchen with a full tray in her hands, complete with teapot and our nicest china cups. Before Ellie and Alexander happened, we didn't even own nice china. Or a teapot for that matter. We made tea in mugs with water from the electric kettle.

But I get it—once their oldest daughter started dating a prince, fancy china seemed like the least they could do.

Mom sets the tray on the table, but no one makes a move to actually pour any tea, probably because while Alexander—and now El—live in cold, misty Scotland, this is Florida in May, which means the idea of drinking hot beverages seems insane, if not masochistic.

"Wasn't it purple for a little while last year?" Ellie asks me now, and I raise my eyebrows at her.

"Did you really come all the way from bonny Scotland to interrogate me about my hair choices?"

Ellie's nostrils flare a bit and she laces her fingers together between her knees. "It just seems like there's always something new with you. That's all I'm saying."

I shrug. "I like trying different things."

This is one of the major differences between me and Ellie—she's been Princess Barbie since birth, pretty much. Me? I'm still . . . figuring things out. When Michael said music was "our thing" in the parking lot, he wasn't wrong, exactly. When I'd dated him, I'd been super into learning to play the guitar, almost as intense about that as I'd been about origami lessons the year before. Or the art classes I took freshman year. But honestly, how are you supposed to know what you like unless you *try* stuff?

Ellie says it's "flighty," but I think it's fun, and before she can get going on that train of thought, I change the subject back to her, where it always ends up anyway. "I didn't know y'all were coming."

Mom is sitting in her wingback chair, so I flop in Dad's recliner, and Ellie frowns a little.

My sister has always been one step away from having mice make dresses for her, but ever since she met Alexander, her Disney Princessness has been dialed up to eleven. While we both got Mom's light hair, El's was always shinier, more golden. Right now, it falls in soft waves to her shoulders, held back with a pair of sunglasses that probably cost more than my entire wardrobe. She's wearing jeans, as is Alexander, but even those look fancy on them, probably because they've paired them with expensive leather loafers. Alexander is wearing a white button-down with the sleeves rolled up, and El has on some kind of drapey navy blouse with little white polka dots all over it.

Basically, they look like they belong on a yacht, while I am wearing a T-shirt that says, "EVE WAS FRAMED."

"It was a surprise!" Ellie says brightly, and Alexander flashes me and Mom a smile.

This is the unsettling thing about Ellie and Alexander. They spend so much of their life being public people that sometimes they act that way in private, too, so it can make you feel like they're holding the world's smallest press conference in the living room.

"And a lovely one, too," my dad says, coming into the room. He's wearing a pair of khaki shorts that started their life as pants, a few stray strings hanging down to his bony knees. El's forehead creases a bit as she looks over his graying hair, which is pulled back into a ponytail, and the paint that's splattered all over his Pink Floyd T-shirt. Dad fancies himself an artist these days, although he's not very good at it. But he gave up music ages ago, and as Mom points out, it's good for him to have something that keeps him busy.

And for all that Ellie is clearly not impressed with Dad's appearance, he's kind of the reason she even met Alexander in the first place.

Here, let me give you the *Star Magazine* treatment.

"10 THINGS YOU NEVER KNEW ABOUT ELLIE WINTERS (OR, MORE ACCURATELY, HER FAMILY!)"

1) Ellie's dad, Liam, was famous for eleven months in 1992! According to Liam, that's the worst amount of time for a person to have fame—not long enough for anyone to remember you, but just long enough to ruin your life.

2) Liam was in a band called Velvet! It was every bit as embarrassing as the name implies, and full of more gelled hair and skinny suits than his daughter Daisy would like to talk about.

3) Velvet had exactly ONE HIT SONG, "Harbor Me," and while that title sounds pretty sweet, "harbor" is being used in a metaphorical sense, and the video was banned in seven countries. The less we say about it, the better.

4) Their second song only went to #22 ("Staying the Night," less gross than "Harbor Me" but with way too many references to sheets and skin for anyone's comfort), and the third never even cracked the top 100 ("Daisy Chain," surprisingly not offensive, but also not listenable).

5) By that point, Liam had a flat in London he couldn't afford, a fancy car he'd crashed twice, and a pretty significant drug problem. It was all very *Behind the Music!*

6) He moved back to his hometown, a tiny village in the Midlands, where he started working at his father's garden supply shop, only to meet a lovely journalist by the name of Bess Murdock, who was working for some hip London newspaper and came all the way out to little Glockenshire-on-the-Vale to interview Liam for a "Whatever Happened To?" piece.

7) Surprising absolutely no one who has seen a romantic comedy, the two fell in love and moved to Florida for a fresh start. Luckily for Liam, "Harbor Me"—or an instrumental version of it at least—got picked up for a car commercial, and since Liam was the sole songwriter on that track (a fact that fills his family with equal parts pride and mortification!) he became, as they say, "well off!"

8) It was this stroke of luck that allowed the Winterses to send their oldest daughter, Eleanor, off to the UK for university, and it was there that the blond girl with the shiny hair and teeth met the heir to the Scottish throne!

9) Ellie—as she's known to friends and family—and Prince Alexander have been dating for nearly two years now, making her the most famous person in her family, which is saying something since her dad was on the cover of *NME*, and her mom once made out with someone in Oasis!

10) Ellie's younger sister, Daisy, works at a grocery store and just got a killer dye job, clearly making her the *real* baller of the Winters family.

There. Now you're caught up.

"Are you staying long?" I ask. The last time they were here together was Christmas, and it had kind of been a disaster. Alexander had needed to sleep on our pullout sofa, which must have been a step down from whatever dynasty-making bed he had back in Scotland (even though he'd spent the entire time insisting that he was fine, and that the sofa bed was "surprisingly comfortable" and "such an interesting innovation"), and then my dad had given Ellie a plastic tiara as a joke, which embarrassed her so much that she spent most of that evening in her room.

Mom had been flustered about everything from setting the table to whether Alexander would be offended if we ordered pizza—our Christmas Eve tradition—and then more or less bullied Alexander's bodyguards into coming in to drink eggnog with us on Christmas Day, which made everyone so uncomfortable that in the end, we all sat there in total silence, Malcolm and David in their black suits, El and Alexander dressed like they were going to church, and me, Mom, and Dad all in our pajamas, Dad with a stray bit of tinsel tucked into his ponytail.

To be honest, after all that, I wasn't surprised Ellie and Alexander had decided on a "surprise" visit. The less time my parents had to stress and think up new ways to be weird, respectively, the better.

"Just through the weekend," Alexander answers, putting his hand on El's knee and squeezing briefly. They're usually so formal that a squeeze feels like the equivalent of them making out in front of me, and that is *so* not okay.

"We have to get back to Edinburgh by Tuesday," Ellie says, "but we wanted to talk to you first."

And then she smiles, covering Alexander's hand with her own, and for the first time, I notice the emerald-and-diamond ring on her hand.

Her *left* hand.

Mom gasps, but it's Dad's reaction that sums up what I'm thinking.

"Bugger me, Ellie's going to be a princess."